steering toward normal

REBECCA PETRUCK
AMULET BOOKS, NEW YORK

Cataloging-in-Publication Data has been applied for
and may be obtained from the Library of Congress.
ISBN: 978-1-4197-0732-2

Text copyright © 2014 Rebecca Petruck
Illustrations copyright © 2014 Sam Bosma
Photographs on pages 318, 322, 325
copyright © 2014 Laura Seljan
Book design by Sara Corbett

Printed and bound in U.S.A.
10 9 8 7 6 5 4 3 2 1

Amulet Books are available at special discounts when
purchased in quantity for premiums and promotions as
well as fundraising or educational use. Special editions
can also be created to specification. For details, contact
specialsales@abramsbooks.com or the address below.

ABRAMS
THE ART OF BOOKS SINCE 1949
115 West 18th Street
New York, NY 10011
www.abramsbooks.com

for CAROLINE KANE BUTTS

WITH LOVE ALWAYS

"A GREAT TEACHER, AND A NICE LADY."

FALL

DIGGY LAWSON STOOD IN THE

BARN AND PROMISED HIMSELF AGAIN THAT

he would not name this new calf. After three years competing steers at the Minnesota State Fair, he knew what to expect. Nothing could describe the long, final walk to the packer's truck, knowing that in only a few days his steer would be served at Hartley's Steak House.

He was an experienced cattleman now. No names, no tears. An eighth-grader shouldn't cry.

Diggy inspected his morning's work one more time. The stall was tidy, wood shavings evenly raked over the ground, water trough scrubbed shiny. The steer he had chosen would settle in to his new home fast and happily.

Diggy heard the distant whoosh of tires coming up the gravel road. He grabbed the rice root brush from its peg and shoved it into his back pocket as he walked to the driveway and watched July's truck crest the hill.

He patted his hair to be sure he hadn't broken the shell of goop that kept his cowlicks flat, then swiped sweat from his forehead. Mid-September weather was hit or miss in Minnesota, veering through summer, fall, and almost winter on a day-by-day basis. This Saturday was summer, but Diggy wore jeans and boots anyway. Anything less around a calf jittery after his first ride in a trailer would make July think he'd forgotten everything she'd ever taught him. She had chosen him to fill her shoes and become the next Grand Champion Market Beef, and there was no way he'd let her down.

Pop came out, his orange hair bright as a glow stick, and Diggy was glad he'd used the goop because it made his own hair darker. It didn't matter that July had seen him filthy before, covered in hay, dirt, and cow poop. He didn't like to look messy around her when he could help it. As her truck made the turn into the long driveway, he breathed deeply to chase away the stomach swirlies.

"Do I get to say hi to her, or do I have to make myself scarce?" Pop asked.

"Har, har," Diggy said, though Pop's tone was so straight on, Diggy wasn't sure if he was teasing or not. He squinted sideways at Pop.

Pop laughed and roughed up Diggy's hair. "What the—"

"Quit it," Diggy said. Luckily, nothing much had shifted. He pressed the shell back down.

"Is that hair gel or rubber cement?"

"Geezer. No one uses rubber cement anymore." Diggy snickered at his own joke. At thirty-five, Pop was probably the youngest "Pop" on the planet, but calling him old never got old.

"This geezer can still ground you."

"That would hurt you more than me."

Pop snorted. "I'm thinking you deserve a little something special for lunch today."

Diggy groaned. Pop was an expert prankster with a sub-specialty in food doctoring. July parked, and Diggy headed over to her truck, calling back to Pop, "As long as it's after July's gone."

Pop grinned, waved at July, and made himself scarce.

Diggy's gratitude doubled as he watched July climb out of the truck.

July Johnston.

Every time she was near, Diggy's heart became the sun.

July, like her five sisters before her, would be homecoming queen now that she was a senior. Her hair was long and dark and shiny, pulled back into the usual ponytail. Her face was clean, no makeup, and her brown eyes sparkled. She wore jeans, a T-shirt, and boots, and was pretty much perfect.

But it wasn't only that she was pretty. She was nice, too. Honest nice, not pretend nice like some of the popular girls. And she loved cows. Even though she didn't have to, she liked being there when Diggy had a new calf brought home for the first time.

Diggy had gone to his first 4-H meeting because of July. She had come to his class to talk about how cool 4-H was—all the different activities they supported, the community outreach, and the friendships with people from all over the county—but he had been hooked by her smile, her enthusiasm, and the sparkle in her eyes. He pretended to himself he would have gotten involved in raising steers on his own at some point, but he knew better than to believe it. As much as he had learned to love the animals, he competed for July.

"Hey there." She hugged him sideways, the way she usually did, this time so she could look at the fence and post they'd use for halter breaking. "Everything all set here?"

He nodded, reeling from her cut-grass smell and her bare arm over his shoulders and the little bit of sweat where her skin pressed against his.

"Of course it is," she said. She gave his shoulders a squeeze, and he let himself press that little bit closer to her. "You're an old pro." She smiled down at him and ruffled his hair.

Tried to ruffle it.

Her eyes widened.

Diggy jerked away. "Sorry, I, uh . . ." His face felt like a thousand fires. "My hair sticks up."

July grabbed his shoulders to make him stand still, then scratched his head like it was a steer's rump, breaking up the goop crust. "I like your head the way it is."

Diggy looked up into her smiling eyes, a good six inches above his, wishing he wasn't the youngest *and* shortest eighth-grader in his class and hoping all his hope that four years wasn't so big a difference.

He could have stood like that with July forever.

She patted his shoulder and turned to look up the drive. "Here he comes."

It took a few seconds for Diggy to hear the diesel engine over the thump of blood in his ears. Rick Lenz was coming with the calf.

Diggy joined July in waving Lenz in.

Lenz climbed out of the cab, walked back, and slid out the short ramp like it was one motion, proof of his having done it a thousand times. Their hellos to him were lost in the metallic clank of latches sprung and disgruntled moos, but Lenz heard Pop call out that there was fresh coffee inside. Barely a minute after Lenz's arrival, Diggy and July were alone again.

July shook her head. "Never get a word in edgewise with that guy."

Diggy laughed. Everyone knew Lenz talked more to his cows than to people. July's teasing helped Diggy relax a bit. His new calf was home.

Diggy had gone out to Mr. Lenz's last weekend to select the steer he'd compete from among the other spring-born calves, and he had felt an immediate bond with this one. But that was a week ago and in a different setting. Even though he knew all would go well with raising his chosen calf and had for the last three years, Diggy still got nervous when it came time to bring a steer home.

He walked around the back of the trailer and looked in, seeing mostly rump. The calf was in a simple rope halter tied through one of the openings in the trailer's side. It saved time with the breaking to let the steers fight the halter during the ride.

Diggy eased into the back as quietly as he could—pretty much impossible with boots and an aluminum trailer. The calf rolled back his eyes and bawled. Diggy scratched the calf's rump until he quieted, then pulled the brush from his back pocket and stroked it over the steer's hide.

Diggy couldn't help but admire what a fine calf he'd chosen. He had a long, straight top with a clean line through the throat and brisket. He was full but not too muscled, so he had room to grow in the year they'd be together, and his legs were sturdy, not too bent or too straight. What Diggy liked best was the way the calf watched him back. Calm and alert. The eyes and hair were almost equally black and absorbed light like it would help him grow. Only his nose glistened.

Diggy was so focused on his new calf, it took him a while to feel July looking in on them. He turned to her, scratching the calf's rump again. "He already looks like a champ. And did you see how quickly he calmed for me?" It was a sign of trust that meant they'd have a good bond.

The steer twitched his tail aside and pooped. On Diggy's boot.

"Crap," Diggy said, laughing. "You're a real joker, aren't you." It was Diggy's fault for having his feet in the line of fire— but the laugh burst like a bubble overhead, becoming a black cloud. He had promised himself he wouldn't name his steer!

He clattered out of the trailer, setting off fresh bawling, and dragged his boot in the grass.

July gave him the eye, clearly not happy with his behavior. "It's not like that's never happened before," she pointed out.

Diggy sighed. "I wasn't going to name him."

"Ah." The small sound was filled with echoes of Diggy's own regret. July knew exactly what it was like to care for an animal and have to let him go. She hugged him to her side. "I used to tell myself that, too, but every year . . . So, what's our sweet boy's name?"

"Joker."

July laughed. "Yeah, that's him, all right."

They looked in at the calf.

Joker looked back at them and winked.

Diggy chuckled despite himself. He knew the wink was really a blink, that he simply couldn't see Joker's other eye, but it didn't matter. Barely ten minutes was all it had taken for Diggy to break his promise to himself and fall in love again.

It was too late now. The name was stuck.

Diggy climbed back into the trailer and brushed Joker some more to apologize for stomping off the way he had. When Joker calmed enough that he might have been asleep, Diggy nudged the calf's rump to get him facing outward, then unknotted the rope from the trailer. He pulled until Joker took a step forward. Diggy immediately released the pressure, and

Joker took three more steps before stopping. Diggy repeated the pressure, easing up as soon as Joker moved again. Joker took several more steps and was quick to catch on to the lesson. A tug meant *walk*.

In no time they were in the barn, with Diggy offering Joker his reward, a bit of the alfalfa-grass hay he'd eat all fall and winter.

"You're a natural, Diggy," July said.

He liked the sound of her saying his name more than the praise itself. He knew that her words weren't true, though he had worked harder than he ever had at anything to make her think so. It wasn't lying, exactly, doing stuff to make her like him, but he wanted her to really, really like him, and now she thought he was a natural.

Diggy turned her attention from himself back to Joker.

They watched the calf and talked about his assets and their plan for the coming year. July had won Grand Champion last year, taken Reserve the year before, and had always earned at least blues before then. This year she had been elected 4-H president and was one of five National Beef Ambassadors—a big deal. She was going to be so busy with programs and traveling, she had decided not to compete at the State Fair. It was Diggy's duty to take up the purple ribbon of success that July was passing on to him.

He had to win Grand Champion at the State Fair for her sake.

After July left, Diggy stayed in the barn, petting and talking to Joker. The touch-and-talk method worked for a reason, but Diggy had been shy about rambling to the calf in front of July. He made up for it now, scratching Joker while he chattered about the calf's new home, the great food he'd get, how much fun they'd have training, and how much he'd like Pop, but warning him there would be early mornings and late nights.

The calf listened, head cocked like a dog's, and occasionally commented with a snuffle or a moo. Diggy felt they'd made a good start.

He sent a photo of the calf to his friends Jason and Crystal, as promised, and then Pop came out to the stall to look over the steer and deliver some lunch. Diggy took a bite of the tuna sandwich and only remembered his "geezer" comment when the tuna turned out to be spicy hot. He blinked the sting of jalapeño fumes from his eyes and took another bite.

"Okay?" Pop asked, a bit too casually.

Diggy nodded, afraid to speak. Fresh calves weren't fans of open flames.

Pop slapped Diggy on the back, laughing. "You're one stouthearted kid, Diggy Lawson." He pulled a plastic-wrapped sandwich from his pocket and offered it over.

"No, this is fine," Diggy choked out.

"I thought you'd say so." Pop set the sandwich down and patted Joker's rump. "He's a good one. You two are going to have a good year." He ruffled Diggy's hair and headed out of the barn.

Diggy smiled at Joker, then eyed the second sandwich. He slanted a glance toward Pop's retreating back.

"It's the same tuna, isn't it?" Diggy called out.

Pop whistled on his way to the house.

After dinner—an average, un-tampered-with dinner—Diggy went out to check on the calf again. The sun had taken its summerlike heat with it. A firm northeastern wind rattled fall-crisp leaves on branches that clacked and creaked. Diggy led Joker into the shivering night. A steer needed to get accustomed to all sorts of sounds so he wouldn't be easily spooked by the time he entered the show ring.

The chill air was a double bonus, because cold stimulated hair growth. Several kids he'd compete against at the fair kept their calves in cold rooms all the time, but Pop had absolutely refused, three years running, to air-condition a cow all summer long so his hair would grow thicker. Pop could be stubborn like that.

The improved weather was a sign. This *would* be a good year—*his* year to win Grand Champ.

The calf was not wild about leaving the cozy barn and bleated a protest, crowding into Diggy's side. Diggy hummed and patted and had Joker calm again—until a truck barreled down the gravel road and skidded to a stop at the end of their long driveway. Diggy looped Joker's lead onto the fence rail, just in case the calf thought about bolt-

11

ing, and talked quietly while scratching the steer's rump to soothe him.

The dust settled to reveal a man stumbling around the truck bed. He heaved a suitcase onto the ground, and it popped open like one of those 3-D party decorations. He lunged for the passenger door, jerking it so hard it squealed, then reached into the cab with two hands and hauled a boy out, tossing him onto the jumbled mound of spilled clothing. The door hung open. Momentum slammed it shut when the man gunned the truck and sped away. Gravel and dust spewed over the unmoving heap of clothes and boy.

Wind scrabbled through the grass. Clouds slashed at the moonlight.

Joker sidled into Diggy again but this time was soothed by a shaking hand.

Diggy really did not want to know what had been left on his doorstep.

DIGGY KNEW ABOUT DOORSTEPS.
WHEN HE WAS A MONTH OLD, HIS MOM HAD
bundled him into a laundry basket and left him on Pop's.

He felt a deep-gut rustle like the coming of a full-body shudder. This kid wasn't a baby, and he hadn't been bundled up and safely deposited anywhere. He had been tossed out of a pickup truck like trash and now huddled into his sprung suitcase as if he could burrow through it to somewhere else. Diggy couldn't leave anyone like that. No matter how much he wanted to.

He made sure Joker's lead was tight on the fence rail, then jogged close enough to the house to call out for Pop.

As he headed up the drive toward the abandoned kid, the boy moved. He knelt, swiped an arm over his face, then pushed things back into the suitcase, trying too soon to zip it all back up.

"Wayne?" Wayne Graf and Diggy had math and science together, that was it. There were nearly a hundred kids in their grade—it wasn't like they all hung out at each other's houses.

When Wayne looked up, the yard light tinted his face green. Diggy knew Wayne's hair was blond, that he was always pale pink, even in summer, and his eyes were a weird light blue. But the yard light washed those hints of color away. He stood trembling even though he was dressed for fall.

"Who was that?" Diggy asked.

Wayne stared at him like English was a foreign language.

Pop strode up to them. "You all right, son?" he asked Wayne.

"Don't call me that," Wayne bit out. He grabbed the suitcase, and, though he was a big kid—a lot bigger than Diggy, anyway—he stumbled under its weight. The suitcase fell and flipped open again. Wayne stood hunched over it.

Pop approached him the way he would a spooked animal, slowly and with quiet words. "It's late, and you must be tired." He pulled the suitcase closed, and Wayne neither resisted nor moved. "Why don't you come in and tell us what brought you here?"

Wayne looked up at Pop, his face intent. "Did you know my mom?"

Diggy stilled. The words themselves meant one thing, but it sounded like the question meant something else. Diggy suddenly felt like he couldn't get enough air.

"You know I did. Diggy and I saw you at her funeral," Pop said.

Diggy wanted to run. Wayne's mom had been Diggy's third-grade teacher. He and Pop had gone to her funeral only three weeks ago, the day after school started. But now Wayne was asking if Pop knew her.

"We looked for a marrow donor, but it was too late." Wayne added, "Her blood was type O."

"Come inside." Pop put a hand on Wayne's shoulder.

Wayne jerked away. "My dad's type A, and I'm B!" he shouted like an accusation. Diggy barely heard Wayne add, "He says *you're* my dad, and I have to live here now."

IT HAD NEVER SEEMED WEIRD TO

DIGGY THAT EVERYONE IN TOWN CALLED POP

"Pop" even though he was only thirty-five. Though he was mechanically inclined and had even become an engineer, he'd had a tough time learning a tractor's clutch when his family first moved to Minnesota and bought a farm. Mowing grass was a teenager's job, but it took on new meaning when there were twenty acres to cover. Rumors spread about Mark Lawson's bucking-bronco routine, and plenty of locals took a ride out to see for themselves that, yep, the clutch was winning the fight. They told Mark over and over he had to "pop" it. It was a joke at first, calling a fourteen-year-old kid "Pop," but after a while it had stuck.

When Diggy was old enough to understand the difference, he kind of liked that other people said "Pop" and meant one thing, while Diggy said "Pop" and meant another.

No one had ever doubted Diggy was Pop's kid. Diggy had the same bright orange hair, brown eyes, and large jaw, though on his thirteen-year-old face, the jaw was too big and square. Pop was over six feet, but he wasn't one of those long and skinny talls. He had broad shoulders and lots of muscle. The jaw fit him. Diggy couldn't wait for the growth spurt that would make all his own parts fit right. It was bad enough being the youngest boy in class—he hated being the shortest, too.

Wayne Graf was not only the oldest but also the biggest boy in class. Diggy hadn't messed with him because, for one, he never bothered Diggy, and two, he was a teacher's kid.

But now Wayne was standing in their driveway, and he looked tall and big, just like Pop.

Pop looked the way Diggy felt—cracked wide open. When Diggy reached an arm out for balance, he got Wayne instead. Wayne shook him off, Diggy shook his head, and the ground was back where it was supposed to be.

The suitcase popped open again.

The three of them peered at the knotted jumble of clothes.

After a while, Pop said, "Oh, right." He collected the clothes and carefully secured the suitcase. He began the long walk down the driveway. "We use the door around back."

Diggy did not like the idea of letting Wayne Graf into the house, especially not with a full suitcase. It felt wrong but somehow inevitable, too, so he waited for Wayne to move—no way would he turn his back on the guy. Until Joker bawled, and Diggy remembered he had stranded the calf at a fence post. Wayne flinched from the sound like a pack of wolves was on the loose.

"It's a baby cow, Wayne." Jeez. Mrs. Graf had lived in town, but a couple of her sisters were in the country. They might not have animals, but Wayne had to have seen, heard, and smelled plenty of cows before. Town kid.

Joker raised the volume on his complaining. Diggy did his best to rush the calf back to the barn without making him stubborn. He settled Joker into his stall, put out a bit of hay, and turned for the house, vaguely surprised to see that Wayne had walked up to it, even if he hadn't gone in yet. But then, where else could he go? The nearest buildings were a tilted-over farmhouse and a turkey hangar. Their neighbor, Kubat, was a mile over the rise, but Wayne would have to cut through the woods, and—at night, for a town kid?—that might as well be the dark side of the moon. Reaching anyone else the normal way, on roads, meant three miles of walking, and Wayne's dad was even farther.

Diggy's stomach clenched. The man who had dumped Wayne in the driveway was Wayne's *dad*.

Diggy may have been dumped by his own mom, but he'd been a baby—he didn't have any history with her. The idea of Pop changing his mind about Diggy and booting him out after all these years . . . Diggy could have puked, except that he wouldn't in front of Wayne.

Oddly, it was the thought of booting and puking that helped Diggy pull himself together. Pop had always been Diggy's dad and would never kick him out, even if he wanted to. Mr. Graf might have gone a little crazy tonight, but he'd be back tomorrow. Wayne was his *son*.

Diggy wouldn't let himself think about the "even if he wanted to" part, or the other part—of Wayne's being someone other than his dad's son—and, anyway, Pop hadn't actually said he'd known Mrs. Graf *that* way.

Diggy was almost calm when he walked into the house first, letting Wayne follow him in.

Inside, Wayne stood transfixed, staring wide-eyed at the walls.

The kitchen was fuchsia. Diggy hadn't really noticed that in a long time. He and Pop had had to pull out the refrigerator last year to replace a hose, and the wall behind it was a pretty dark rose color, exactly something his grandma would have picked out. But the rest of the paint on the other, exposed walls hadn't held up well. It had gone bright pink, like the color of someone's stomach from the inside. Summers when his grandparents came up from Texas, Grandma spent half her time nagging them to repaint the room. He and Pop had avoided the task by covering the walls with scraps of whatever—assembly instructions and posters from some of Diggy's model rockets, and advertising stuff Pop got at his agricultural-engineering conferences. It kind of worked but not really. Even with so much covering the walls, the color still engulfed the space.

"We keep meaning to paint it," Pop said.

There was no reason the small lie should have made Diggy's half-faked calm blow away like the wind had changed.

Two glasses stood upside down on a towel next to the sink. Pop filled them both to the top with milk, then set them on the kitchen table. "Go ahead and sit down." He got a third glass from a cabinet and filled it with water from the tap.

Diggy was aware of Pop's movements peripherally, but he kept his attention on Wayne, who stared back at him like he was supposed to do something. Diggy had no idea what Wayne expected, but he did know this was *his* house and Wayne wasn't getting any special treatment just because his dad was a jerk. Mrs. Graf had been his mom. Diggy would give almost anything to have someone like her as a mom. She was funny and nice and still his favorite teacher, and that had been all the way back in the third grade. Except that she was dead.

By the time Pop moved matters along, Diggy was the one feeling like a jerk.

Pop nudged Diggy off balance and led him to a chair, holding it out in a way that meant sit or be sat. Pop sat, too, and waited, watching Wayne, until Wayne finally took a seat on the other side of the table. He stared at his glass for a long time, then picked it up and drank the milk all in one go. Diggy couldn't help but be a little impressed.

After a while, Pop said again, "It's late. Give us a few minutes to clear some space, then you can get some rest."

The only "space" with a spare bed in it was the room where Diggy had moved all his model-rocket stuff after his grandparents' last visit, and Wayne would only be here one night. "What's wrong with the couch?"

Pop looked at Diggy like he was a wormy ear of corn.

"The couch is fine with me," Wayne said.

His jaw jutted out, and Diggy couldn't help it: he gasped at the familiar profile on this strange kid. Pushing away from the table so fast his chair almost tipped over, Diggy headed for the stairs, calling, "I'll get a blanket and stuff."

He heard Pop say the bed was more comfortable, and Diggy paused.

"I can go home tomorrow," Wayne said. "It's been rough, that's all, since Mom died."

Diggy had an idea that "rough" meant a lot more than it seemed, but he didn't stop any longer to think about it. He rushed up the rest of the stairs, ducked into the rocket room, and grabbed a blanket and pillow from the closet. At the top of the stairs again, he threw the blanket and pillow down, not caring that Pop would be ticked at him. He meant to hide out in his room but was waylaid by the sight of Wayne's profile in the doorway from the kitchen.

Wayne had a jaw just like Pop's. And Diggy's.

Wayne asked Pop again, "Did you know my mom?" This time Diggy understood what Wayne was really asking. *Is it true? Are you my father?*

Diggy didn't need to see Pop to know that he nodded yes.

At night, the house was noisy in that way old houses get when the temperature drops too fast. It creaked and cracked, sometimes because of a wind, sometimes because of nothing. Diggy listened to it for a long time.

He had thought Pop might come talk to him, but after settling Wayne in the living room, Pop had gone back to the kitchen and stayed there.

Diggy told himself to go to sleep. He told himself Wayne would go home tomorrow and by Monday at school it would be like nothing had happened. He told himself the two people in the rooms below him were only Pop and a classmate stuck for the night—but they might as well have been nuclear warheads, for all the sleep Diggy was likely to get.

He stared out his bedroom window at the star-framed outline of the tree he had practically lived in once he was big enough to climb it by himself.

It was a great tree, so wide at the base that his arms stretched out all the way couldn't reach even halfway around. The bark was thick and scratchy with lots of deep ridges for fingers to hook into. Six major branches arched out from the trunk and split so often, he could climb the tree every day for a month and never go the same way twice. It was old and tall and strong, so he could climb high enough to see over the roof of the house. If it was windy, he used to pretend he was in a rocket during liftoff, holding himself steady against gravity's pull.

Once upon a time, he'd hidden his mom's box in the tree.

It wasn't really her box. Diggy had bought it ages ago, a

red fireproof safe he'd saved up ten dollars to buy at Ole Jib's Hardware. Inside were the three things his mother had left with him in that laundry basket. He had wasted a summer hiding the box in the tree, checking on it, bringing it in when it was supposed to rain. He didn't know where it had ended up.

The tree had been like his best friend. Staring at the night-blackened branches, he couldn't remember the last time he'd climbed into them.

He opened the window and clambered onto the ledge.

The branch that could support Diggy's weight was about three feet away. Not far in footsteps but a lot farther when all there was beneath you was twenty feet of air. He had made the jump countless times—a long time ago. He was taller now, so that would help, but he was also heavier, and the branch might not be as strong as it once was. Diggy crouched on the sill, hands cupped under the window, and took the giant, twisting step he called his "leap of faith."

His bare feet easily made the branch, but his hands caught at twigs that broke. He slipped back, hands reaching, and finally snagged a branch that held. He pulled himself in and wheezed in the smells of cold bark, dry leaves, and dirt.

"Are you crazy?" Wayne whisper-shouted from beneath the tree.

Diggy had been thinking the same thing, so it galled him that Wayne would say it. "What are you doing out here?"

Diggy snapped. Quietly. He did not want Pop coming out. Pop was not likely to think Diggy's current position a wise one. And Pop was still in the kitchen. "How did you get out here past Pop in the first place?"

"You're barefoot in a tree in the middle of the night, and *I'm* the one who's supposed to explain stuff?"

"How can you see that?"

"It's not like I need night vision to see that you're in a tree, especially when you threw yourself out a window to get there."

"That I'm barefoot." The safety light was on the other side of the house. "How long have you been out here?" It had to have been a while, since his eyes had adjusted to the dark, but the temperature had dropped. It made more sense to stay inside. Diggy didn't linger on the fact that he wasn't inside, either.

Wayne might have shrugged. He didn't say anything, and Diggy wouldn't look down.

The cold blew in unsteadily. Branches heaved away from the sudden bursts of wind with such dismay, Diggy had to concentrate to make sure his eyes and hands actually coordinated as he shuffled toward the center of the tree. The barefoot thing was already becoming a problem. As he made his way down, the cold made every scrape of bark feel like cracked glass beneath his soles. He considered that this had not been one of his better impulses, though not far beneath that rational interpretation of events was a jittery thrill for the deep night, the rustling branches, and the clean, arctic scent of the air.

"Why jump into a tree?"

Wayne said it in that way that was less about getting a response and more about doubting the intelligence of the person in question. Which ticked off Diggy. The guy had shown up at Diggy's house, suggesting impossible things, and was, by the way, wandering around outside in the midnight dark, so . . . Pot. Kettle. Black. Diggy was not the one who needed to explain anything.

This was his home and his tree and his middle of the night. Wayne could muzzle it. Diggy was in the mood to make him.

He moved too fast and slid, scalding his heels, down the last deep vee and thudded against the trunk. From there, he flopped belly first onto a thick branch that dipped lower than the others, shimmying back until he could wrap his arms around it, then dangle and drop. He shook the sting from his feet.

"You must have the same IQ as that baby cow of yours."

Diggy tucked his head and shouldered Wayne into the side of the house.

Wayne got hold to push Diggy away and ended up forcing half his sweatshirt against his throat.

Diggy twisted and fell to one knee, grabbing Wayne's shirt. On the way down, Diggy managed to elbow Wayne in the gut before the guy landed on him.

Diggy bucked, slowing down Wayne's scramble to get back to his feet.

A knee connected with a hip bone. An elbow caught an ear.

They finally got apart and stood puffing at each other.

Diggy braced for the next round but was distracted by a swooping flash of light. Pop would be *ticked* if he caught them fighting out here.

"You want more?" Wayne said.

Diggy gave the guy credit for mustering some nerve, but his face already had that sheen of worry about what would hurt next. Wayne might be big, but he was one of the class brains. This was probably his first fight.

A flash again—headlights in the driveway—then a truck zoomed straight for them.

THE TRUCK STOPPED IN A HARD SKID.

THE BOYS DUCKED BEHIND THE TREE. WHEN

the dust cloud hit them, they held back coughs.

Nothing happened.

The safety light backlit the driver sitting hunched over the steering wheel, staring at the house. The shadows of cigarette smoke made the truck's cab look like a water tank.

Wayne turned away, slumping against the tree.

Diggy stared harder. Wayne's dad had come back now?

The front light flipped on, barely noticeable over the glare of the truck's headlamps. Diggy dashed to the corner of the house and peered around.

Pop came out, and Mr. Graf screeched open his door.

"He's going to wake Joker," Diggy muttered. Hadn't the man ever heard of WD-40?

"You've got my boy." Mr. Graf was way too loud for the silent night. "You can't keep my boy."

Disgruntled moos refuted the declaration.

Pop said something quietly, the way he'd spoken to Wayne earlier, as if to a spooked animal, only this one was riled up.

"I can't hear what he's saying," Wayne said.

Diggy thumped him to shut up, straining to hear.

"Ha. There ain't enough beer in the world to make me forget—"

Pop cut him off. His tone was sharp, though still low enough that his words weren't clear.

"Wayne! Get your butt out here!" Mr. Graf shouted.

Wayne wavered, like he meant to take a step but forgot how to move his legs.

Diggy grabbed his shoulder. When Wayne looked at him, Diggy shook his head. The kid had to go home, but not like this. This was the kind of thing they needed to let Pop take care of.

"Wayne!" The yell was thick with threat, and Mr. Graf stepped into Pop.

Pop held the line, not letting Mr. Graf pass. When he swung at Pop, Pop stepped out of the way and let Mr. Graf's momentum take himself down.

"I want my son back!" Mr. Graf howled. He was so loud, Kubat's dogs took to howling, too, and Joker's moos took on an edge of distress.

Pop said something, and Mr. Graf covered his face. His next words were only barely loud enough to hear. "I want my wife back."

As loud as the night had become, it suddenly felt really quiet, too. The dogs still barked, and the steer still mooed, but the man who'd started it all lay bunched on the ground like discarded clothes.

Was this what it had been like for Wayne since his mom died? His dad throwing him out, then screaming for him to come back?

Diggy got mad at Pop sometimes, and Pop definitely got mad at him, but it was never like this seesaw of rage and agony in front of him now. His heart stuttered with a combination of fear and sadness that left him feeling like the starter's pistol had only just fired but he was end-of-race worn out. This wasn't Diggy's normal. If it was Wayne's, Diggy didn't know how the guy could stand it.

Pop hooked Mr. Graf's arm, easily avoiding the hand Mr. Graf batted out, and hauled him to his feet. Mr. Graf stumbled toward the driver's side of the truck, but Pop grabbed him again and steered him toward Pop's own pickup. Once Mr. Graf was loaded into the passenger seat, Pop headed back to the house.

"Oh, crap," Diggy spurted, turning fast and smacking into Wayne. He shoved at Wayne to get him moving, but the guy was propped against the house, heavy as a bag of feed.

Then Diggy heard a telltale shudder in Wayne's breath, that sound like he was trying not to make any sound so no one would hear him cry.

This time Diggy murmured, "Crap."

He kind of patted Wayne's shoulder, feeling stupid, then stopped, feeling stupider. "We've got to get to the kitchen," Diggy explained quietly. "Pop's going to check on us."

Wayne sniffed hard and wiped his face.

They sped to the kitchen, then walked more normally into the hall. Pop had already gone upstairs to look for them and was on his way back down. He scanned Diggy's bare, dirty feet, then gave him the eye before searching Wayne's face.

"Your dad's here."

Wayne nodded.

"I'm taking him home. You know why?"

Wayne nodded again, not looking at anyone.

"He been like this for a while?" Pop asked.

Wayne shrugged. Pop took his shoulder and waited until Wayne looked up. "It got a lot worse when she died," he finally admitted.

"For both of you," Pop said.

Wayne's face crumpled suddenly, and he bit his lip hard, like the physical pain might hold back the other kind. But even Diggy could tell it didn't work.

Pop exhaled heavily. "He's scared without her and not all that clear about what he's doing. That doesn't mean he doesn't love you. He's lost." Pop's tone darkened. "But you don't have to lie in the road while he finds his way."

He held on to Wayne's shoulder until Wayne nodded he was okay, though no one believed it.

Pop gave them both a long look before heading out the door. Diggy couldn't help but think it was a look that was searching for something, and he tried not to think about what that something might be, especially not a resemblance.

He glanced at Wayne, then did a double take. He had taken off his coat. His sweatshirt was pink and had a large pink and white flower with the words *I'm a Minnesota state flower, too.*

"What?" Wayne said, sounding defensive enough to go at it again.

Diggy held up his hands. "I won't fight you with that shirt on. It'd be like hitting a girl."

Wayne glared at Diggy.

Diggy made a show of raising his fists. "Oh, all right. But take it off first. Then we can do some business." He hopped a bit on his toes, like a prize boxer. Even thumbed his nose.

Wayne's jaw was a hard-clenched square. "You're making fun of me."

"No, Wayne. Really." Diggy pointed at the shirt. "You're a state flower, too. There's probably a law about picking them."

"It's an orchid," Wayne snapped.

"So?"

"You don't pick orchids."

Diggy stopped his antics. "Are we fighting about picking flowers?"

Wayne stared at Diggy long enough for him to realize Wayne hadn't looked down to check what shirt he was wearing. He knew exactly what was on it, and something in Diggy's gut flopped like a fish on a riverbank.

Then Wayne bit his cheek. "It's a lady slipper orchid."

Diggy gratefully took his cue and laughed. "That's perfect. I couldn't have made up anything funnier."

Wayne grinned, too.

"I hope you haven't let anyone else see your PJs," Diggy added, then wished he could shove his foot into his mouth.

Wayne sighed. "This was my mom's go-to shirt. When she got home from school, she put this on, and it really seemed like it made her feel better, no matter how bad her day had been."

Diggy sighed back. "Crap."

"Yeah."

Quiet settled in enough to make room for other noises— the house's creakings, a scratching on the roof, the odd chirp of a confused bird.

Wayne kind of smiled. Not a great one. Someone else might have thought he was in pain. "I feel better."

"Weirdo."

"Come on, you've gotten into fights. Don't you feel better afterward?"

"Heck, no! There's Pop. And grounding. And some form of personal torture, like cleaning the bathroom, or sugary eggs for breakfast."

Wayne snorted. "He doesn't do that."

"Oh, yes, he does." Diggy nodded, rather proud of Pop's inventiveness. "Once he swapped the hot and cold water lines."

"He did not."

Diggy only nodded again.

Wayne's eyes got big. "That's, like, medieval."

"I spend a lot of time planning for April Fools' Day."

Wayne rubbed at his ear. Diggy rubbed at his hip, tested his knee.

"I don't think I can go back to sleep," Wayne admitted.

"You weren't asleep."

"Neither were you."

Diggy thought about asking what Wayne had been doing out there in the dark, but he didn't want to have to answer the same question.

"This time of night we should be able to find a really terrible movie. Like with plastic toys for monsters," Diggy said.

The idea tantalized him so much, he didn't pay attention to where he sat and ended up on the couch next to Wayne, both with their feet on the coffee table as Diggy zoomed through the usual channels.

"What did you do that made Pop switch the water lines?"

"We don't discuss the noodle incident, Wayne." Finally, he found a yeti.

They settled in to watch as the yeti, supposedly hungry, dug out a heart but didn't eat it or the body. The killing spree reached the epitome of D-movie perfection when the yeti tore off a rescue climber's leg and beat him with it. The boys were still cackling by the time Pop got home and suggested they get to bed.

DIGGY GOT MAYBE TWO HOURS OF

SLEEP BEFORE JOKER STARTED IN ON SOME

serious bawling and he had to drag himself out of bed. For some reason, Wayne waited for him in the kitchen, blond hair spiked in sleep-shaped angles and pale blue eyes wide with the shock of too-earliness.

"Why are you up?" Diggy asked.

Wayne shrugged. "I wasn't sleeping anyway."

It wasn't true or an answer, but the guy was going home today, and that was big, after everything that had happened last night.

Diggy walked outside into the early-morning cold, Wayne trailing him. The first thing they saw was Mr. Graf's truck in the driveway.

It sat like a rusted DANGER sign—old enough that the hazard probably wasn't all that hazardous anymore but daring you to investigate just in case. Wayne pretended it wasn't there, so Diggy walked on by, too, but the pickup might as well have been a yeti beating a guy with his own torn-off leg.

Joker was aggravated about having to wait for his breakfast, so Diggy piled hay, then filled the water trough while the steer ate.

"Pop seems okay," Wayne said.

"Why wouldn't he be?" Pop wasn't the one who had gotten drunk and turned crazy. Diggy winced and glanced at Wayne, not wanting him to guess what he'd been thinking. Mr. Graf was the kid's dad; Wayne had to live with him.

"I mean, like a good guy." Wayne took a Scotch comb from its peg and fiddled with it. Diggy was about to tell him to put it back, when Wayne added, "A good father."

It was like a steer had rodeoed, and his bucking hooves had caught Diggy in the chest. A part of his brain tried to make him believe Wayne was just talking, that his words didn't mean anything. But that animal part of his brain that warned him when a snake was poisonous or that he had just about climbed too high—that part screeched at him like every police cruiser, ambulance, and fire truck in the county had careened into their driveway.

Diggy clipped the lead to Joker's halter and hotfooted it out of there. He tried for what would become their normal route through the pasture, but steers responded as much to feelings as actual commands. Joker dug his hooves in, and Diggy was distracted enough that he *pulled*. He looked like a greenhorn, hanging from the lead in a forty-five-degree tilt. No one won in a tug-of-war with a six-hundred-pound animal, even if it was still a calf.

Wayne watched like he was at a show ring.

Diggy let go of Joker's lead and stomped away. The perverse cow followed him. Wayne trailed along perversely, too.

Diggy ignored them so he could seethe. He was an experienced cattleman. He had raised three steers. He could and had gone through the motions half in his sleep hundreds of times. Even his first day with his first-ever steer, Diggy hadn't acted so much like he was all hat and no cattle.

Worse, he couldn't pretend his discomposure had anything to do with the calf.

Mr. Graf was Wayne's dad. He'd been there when Wayne was born and changed his diapers and burped him and whatever else people did with babies. He'd probably taught him to ride a bike and helped with homework—well, maybe not, that would have been Mrs. Graf's territory. But still, Mr. Graf was Wayne's dad. Whether Wayne liked it or not.

The man had come to their house and *howled*.

Wayne didn't have any business thinking about Pop being a good father.

"He's going now," Wayne said. "That's what you wanted him to do, right?"

Diggy looked back, saw Joker's lead trailing in the grass, and snatched it up, lucky the steer hadn't stepped on it and tripped. The wrong kind of fall could be a very, very bad thing for an animal like Joker.

Heck, the wrong kind of fall could be a bad thing for anybody.

Diggy made himself concentrate on Joker. Not even here a

full day and already the calf had had to suffer several instances of bad treatment—stuck on the fence rail when Wayne arrived, awakened in the middle of the night by man and dogs barking, and pulled at like he was a goat and not a prize crossbred steer. July would be so disappointed if she saw Diggy now.

He led Joker into the pasture, trying to focus on its beauty, even though Wayne trailed behind. The rising sun made magnifying glasses of the morning's damp. The grass seemed taller because of it. A slope led down to the woods that Pop left thick between his and Kubat's land. The sun wouldn't light the trees until it was full up, so walking toward them was like walking to the night. The turn was borderland, the light growing brighter on one side, the woods keeping its secrets on the other. Then came the next turn, the one he never looked at until it was made. His favorite tree lit up like the Fourth of July. The colorful burst of autumn leaves was backlit by the sun, and walking changed the shape of the light shining through, so every footstep created a new set of fireworks. He walked toward the special tree, not blinking, not wanting to miss a thing.

"It's so pretty out here," Wayne said.

He had spoken softly, but it still annoyed the crap out of Diggy. "Why don't you go inside and wait for your dad to get here?"

"What are you so mad about?"

"Jeez, Wayne, what do you think?"

"You don't have to worry about my problems."

Diggy shot Wayne a dirty look. "Where's a yeti when you need one?"

Wayne marched ahead, then stopped.

"You know what he did when he got home?" Wayne said without turning around. "He passed out on the couch. He won't even remember he was out here. Will be freaked that the truck's gone. But it won't be his fault. He'll make excuses, apologize for the wrong things. Act like everything's fine now and *I'm* the jerk if I'm upset too long."

Wayne kicked hard at the grass. Then did it again.

"But you don't hate him," Diggy said.

"He's my dad. You know?"

Diggy nodded.

"But Pop—he was there for us last night. When we needed him."

All Diggy really heard was that "us" and "we" business, and knew he had to put a stop to it ASAP.

"My dad's a good guy," Diggy said. "He always stops to help people stuck in the road, even if he doesn't know them."

Maybe he'd used a little too much emphasis on the "my" part and the implication that Wayne's dad *wasn't* a good guy, but push Diggy, and he'd always push back.

He tugged Joker's lead, eased up when the steer started moving, and made a good walk back to the barn. He didn't pay any attention to whether or not Wayne followed them.

Diggy tied the lead so Joker's head was at middle height.

It would be weeks before they'd work their way up to show height. The calf didn't like the halter breaking—everybody had something they didn't like to deal with this morning—but at least he could soothe the steer with lavish attention and hair brushing.

Wayne wandered around the barn. He inspected the tractor that was currently outfitted with the grass-cutting attachment. Another month or two, and Diggy and Pop would unhitch it and attach the snowplow to the front.

"Did your mom really leave town on a tractor?" Wayne asked.

Diggy wished he could cut sentences out of his head the way he could cut them out of a book, then cut them in half and word by word and letter by letter until they were bits of nothing that drifted from the scissors' edges, gravity not even interested enough to pull them down.

Because, yes, his mom had left town on a tractor. And he had learned to smile about it like it was no big deal.

Everyone knew the story. How his mom had left him on Pop's doorstep. How she couldn't get her car started again, and, not having the keys to Pop's truck, ended up riding out of town on the field tractor. That's what people liked to talk about, a girl running away on a John Deere. Like it was cute.

Wayne's question—it wasn't like Diggy hadn't heard it a thousand times before and thought it a million times more than that. No one really left town on a tractor.

Unless she really, really, really wanted to get away.

From him.

"You and me," Diggy said, "we're not friends."

Wayne's jaw clenched in the echo of Pop's, firming Diggy's attitude.

Wayne walked over to Joker's stall, eyeing him as if he stank. "You enter it in contests and stuff, right?"

His disdainful tone prompted Joker to turn his rump Wayne's way. Diggy patted his approval.

"Joker's not an *it*. He's a *he*," Diggy said. "And no. We *compete* in the show ring. At the State Fair." He *hoped* they'd compete. "It's a big deal."

"You get a crown and roses? Wave to the crowd, crying you're so happy?"

"I get twelve thousand dollars."

Wayne blinked so fast, his eyelids could have flown away.

Diggy dragged over the blow-dryer and, scratching Joker near the tailhead, turned it on. The calf mooed, but his alarm at the commotion quickly waned. Diggy kept scratching Joker, pleased at how quickly the calf had settled. He needed to get used to the sound—before too long he'd get a daily wash and blow-dry—and Diggy needed the noise now to hide his unease that he had jinxed himself, talking like the State Fair was already his.

He wanted the win for a lot of reasons—for his steer, for Pop and himself, for July. He would not let this kid screw him up.

The blower wasn't quite loud enough to drown out Wayne when he repeated, "Twelve thousand?" Diggy went ahead and turned off the machine before Wayne asked, "Even if you don't win, you could make out pretty good just by placing, couldn't you?"

"It's not a horse show, where there are, like, ten different ribbons for fancy riding and stuff. With steers, it's the two purples for Grand Champion and Reserve. That's it. The rest are blues for good work and reds for showing up."

The steers sold at auction for $25,000 to sponsors who wanted to support 4-H, and advertise themselves. It wasn't like any steer was truly worth that amount—they weren't bulls, and Hartley's could only jack up the price of a Grand Champion steak so high. The person who showed Grand Champ cleared about $12,000—the other half of the auction money raised went straight into a 4-H scholarship fund—and the Reserve Champ got half that. The rest of the steers, even after having made it through their county fairs to get to State, would only sell for their $1,000 market value.

Like Diggy's had the last three years.

One thousand was a lot less than twelve, and a lot of it went to repaying the Farm Bureau loan he took out to buy and feed his steer. Not that Diggy cared much about the money. What he wanted—heart, gut, and soul—was the *win*, to be chosen over everybody else.

Last year, Diggy had made it to the final lineup with July,

when she took the win for their weight division. He had been really proud of *that* blue. But this year he was determined to get the purple of Grand Champ. He worked hard. Knew that he could earn it. By next year would deserve it.

"I could leave," Wayne said. "Go away somewhere else."

"And now would be good. An hour ago even better."

"I mean twelve-thousand-dollars away."

Diggy rolled his eyes. "Yeah. 'Cause thirteen is so old, you can do whatever you want."

"I'm fourteen."

Diggy glared. He knew Wayne was older than him. Because Diggy had been born so late in the year, everyone in their class was older than him. But did Wayne have to be so much bigger, too? It wasn't fair.

"You're not going anywhere but back to your house. And you're definitely not winning the State Fair. You don't even know what kind of calf Joker is."

"I know you plan to do it, so it can't be that hard."

Diggy lunged, but Wayne sidestepped, and Diggy ended up on his knees with a hand squished into cow poop.

"Do you ever think first?" Wayne asked.

Diggy lobbed a handful of poop at Wayne's head, but being on all fours messed with his aim. The clump smacked into Wayne's chest.

Wayne stared as it rolled down his jacket, caught briefly on the zipper tail, then plopped to the ground.

He turned wide, wide eyes to Diggy. "That was cow poop."

Diggy got back to his feet, dusting his pants with his clean hand and shaking poop off the other.

"You've got poop in your ear," Wayne said, pointing.

Diggy instinctively poked a finger into his ear. A finger crusted with poop.

Wayne grinned, and Diggy was ready to take another swing, until Wayne's expression suddenly shifted to sadness.

"Mom says people fight instead of think."

Diggy sighed for him. The guy was still using the present tense to talk about his mom. "What's so great about thinking?"

BACK AT THE HOUSE POP SERVED

BACON, EGGS, TOAST, QUARTERED ORANGES, and tall glasses of milk. The cut oranges were a tip-off—Pop usually stuck a whole one by his plate—but it was the place mats that put Diggy on full alert that Pop wanted to talk about something serious that Diggy probably wouldn't like.

He crumpled two strips of bacon into his mouth and gulped some milk. Pop wouldn't talk about the real thing he wanted to talk about until after they had eaten, and Diggy preferred to get things over with rather than stew.

He glanced out the kitchen window, but the view didn't include Mr. Graf's truck.

Diggy forked at his eggs. Pop had added cheese—tip-off number three. Diggy's knee bounced. He took a couple of bites of toast but needed more milk to get them down. Did Pop think dealing with Mr. Graf when they took Wayne back would be that bad?

Pop's coffee sat on the table, cupped between his hands. The mug, like the fork, was left in its place. Though he leaned back in his chair as if he was relaxed, his eyes squinted against nonexistent brightness, and his orange hair, usually combed first thing, already had its end-of-day muss.

Wayne didn't know the cues. He ate like it was breakfast. Maybe special for a Sunday, and like it was a lot better than anything he'd had in a while.

Which it probably was.

When Wayne finished eating, Pop eyed Diggy's plate. Diggy shook his head no, and Pop nodded.

He sat forward. The coffee mug slid back and forth from palm to palm a couple of times before Pop caught himself and set it aside. "We need to talk about what comes next."

The words might as well have been the snap of a twig in a dark wood. Wayne froze like he'd seen a yeti.

"I think Harold needs some time," Pop said. "He was out every night this week."

"You checked up on him?" Wayne asked.

"While you're my responsibility—"

Diggy cut him off. "Just because you might have—you know—with his mom doesn't make you his father." Diggy stumbled over the words, but he'd said them. They had needed saying.

"Maybe not," Pop conceded. "But Harold left Wayne with us, so we have to watch out for him. Even if that means we have to watch out for Harold, too."

It sounded like Pop . . . Diggy needed to puke up what little breakfast he had eaten. It was a greasy cannonball at the bottom of his stomach.

"You want me to stay?" Wayne whispered.

"I do."

Just like that. Pop had chosen Wayne just like that, like it was easy and no big deal.

He hadn't even talked with Diggy about it first.

"He's already got a father!" Diggy yelled.

"I know that," Pop argued. "I'm not suggesting anything else, but that father is not in his right mind just now." He turned to Wayne. "But he will be, with some time. Harold can do it. He was a little wild before Ann, but together they were good. He can do it for her, he can do it for you, and he will, because he loves you."

Diggy hyperfocused on the fact that Pop called Mrs. Graf "Ann." Mrs. Graf was Mrs. Graf, Diggy's old teacher. It was weird to think teachers had first names, and disorienting to think Pop had known Wayne's mom as Ann. Even if they had been circling around the idea of it all night, Diggy didn't like Pop calling Mrs. Graf "Ann."

He didn't like Pop telling Wayne to stay, either.

He didn't like what that seemed to mean. About Pop and Mrs. Graf and Wayne.

Mrs. Graf had married Mr. Graf, and if it hadn't turned out that great, it was just too bad for Wayne.

Diggy slouched deeply into his chair.

Mrs. Graf *had* married Mr. Graf. She was nice and smart. She wouldn't have married a total jerk. And even if she had, that jerk was Wayne's dad. He might be a wacko now, but Wayne had said things hadn't gotten bad until Mrs. Graf died.

That was the part Diggy couldn't get, though. Wayne's *mom* had died. Wasn't it supposed to be the dad's job to keep it together for the kid? Everything was all backward, and even though Diggy was there, he wasn't really part of any of it, except that he was. Wayne supposedly, maybe . . . was related to him. It didn't really feel like that meant anything, but that didn't mean it went away.

How was it possible that yesterday Diggy had sat at this table and had his breakfast and gotten ready for Joker to come home, and today he had . . . this?

"I think I should go back," Wayne mumbled.

"It's not your job to take care of him," Pop said. "You're just a kid whose mom has died."

That Pop's words so closely echoed Diggy's thoughts only made it worse. He didn't want Wayne here! But the thought of him going home was almost as bad.

"Diggy wouldn't leave *you*," Wayne said.

Pop didn't know what to say to that. He looked at Diggy, looked at Wayne, looked back at Diggy, and finally admitted, "No, he wouldn't."

The spurt of pride Diggy felt at having his loyalty acknowledged was almost immediately dampened by the face of Pop's defeat. Pop usually got his way because he was sensible about what he wanted and went about getting things with logic and kindness. Thinking so almost made Diggy feel like he should want what Pop wanted, too, but how could he? Pop couldn't rescue Wayne from his real life. No matter how great it might be for Wayne to suddenly have a new and improved dad, life didn't work that way. How could Diggy see the truth so clearly when Pop couldn't?

"I can't make you stay with us," Pop said, "but when I bring Harold back, will you talk with him here? So I know you'll be okay?"

Wayne's head stayed bowed while he nodded. When he did look up, the red in his eyes made the pale blue shockingly light. He stared at Pop almost like he wanted to stay, but he said, "We should call him first. To wake him up."

Diggy couldn't imagine the man would still be asleep so late in the day until he glanced at the clock and saw it wasn't even nine. It felt like years had passed, and Wayne hadn't even been here a full twenty-four hours.

Pop suggested they shower, as if he smelled something of their morning's activities, and said he'd call Harold before heading over there but that it might be better to give him another hour or two.

Even though Diggy was smellier, he let Wayne use the bathroom first. He sat in his room while he waited. Like last night, Pop didn't come up to talk with him, and Diggy stared out the window at his tree. He didn't want to think about what everything meant, especially about Pop.

Wayne would go home, and things would get back to normal, and they'd never have to talk about today again.

When Pop finally headed out, Diggy sat on the sofa and didn't complain when Wayne changed the channel every time a commercial came on.

Pop was gone a lot longer than he needed to be to drive to Mr. Graf's and back.

Diggy couldn't help but wonder what was going on over there. Was Pop trying to talk Mr. Graf into letting Pop keep Wayne? Even if only for a while? Pop had a choice this time, and he had chosen Wayne.

Did that mean he would have chosen Diggy, too, if the choice hadn't been made for him?

The worry haunted him the rare times he let himself think about it.

Diggy's mom had dumped him and taken off. Had Pop looked for her? Had he tried to make her parents take Diggy? Diggy didn't really think so—the Pop he knew wasn't like that. But that somehow only made it worse.

Pop did what needed doing. Like with Diggy. Pop had kept him, while some of Diggy's classmates lived with their moms, dads barely in the picture, if at all. He just wished he could make himself believe, deep down in that animal part of his brain, that he would be as close to Pop as he was now even if his mom had never left town.

As much as he hated this whole thing about Wayne, it kind of gave him hope. Which made him feel sick. Because Wayne didn't have Pop; he had Mr. Graf. And Mr. Graf was who he was, and maybe Pop didn't feel much like he had a choice after all. Which made Diggy's thoughts go back to the beginning, like they had ripped off one fingernail and moved on to the next.

By the time they heard the truck in the driveway, Diggy was more than ready to get it all over with. Even if it got bad, it'd be done.

When Pop and Mr. Graf came in through the front door, Wayne didn't move, though Diggy stood automatically and ended up fidgeting halfway in and out of the room.

Mr. Graf looked pretty beat up, but not in a fistfight kind of way—no bruises or anything. His hair was newly washed and combed, but that distinct bar smell of cigarettes and beer drifted from him. What hit Diggy all of a sudden was how Mr. Graf wasn't all that big. He was pretty tall, only about two inches shorter than Pop, but skinny in the shoulders and chest. His legs were actually beany. He had seemed so threatening—dumping Wayne in the driveway, raging at the house last night. It was like bringing Mr. Graf here was a mistake, like they had the wrong guy.

"Wayne? You all right?" Even Mr. Graf's voice was different. The menace was gone, and he wasn't hollering, but it was more than that. It drooped, like his jaw was too floppy to form words properly. His entire face, his whole body, slumped. He was pitiful.

Diggy wanted to kick Wayne for still sitting there, not even looking at his dad, but a glance at Wayne sobered Diggy up.

Wayne's face was like old snow. His shoulders were tensed so high up his neck, he'd practically plugged his ears.

"Wayne," Pop said, "we'll be right across the hall."

"I don't need a chaperone to talk to my own boy," Mr. Graf said.

Pop grunted, then looked at Wayne. "We won't hear anything from the dining room. Unless it gets loud."

"Listen here, Lawson," Mr. Graf began, but Pop cut him off.

"Harold. Remember why you're here."

Mr. Graf breathed hard through his nose a couple of times. "Yeah, yeah."

"I thought I'd clean my room," Diggy said. He'd be able to hear better from the top of the stairs, and that wasn't being nosy but responsible. Wayne was going home with this man.

"Uh-huh," Pop said, buying the story for what it was worth—nothing. "You're with me, kid."

"Diggy can stay." Wayne had finally looked around, though his attention was solely on Diggy.

Which was all it took for Diggy to not want to be anywhere near the conversation. "That's all right. I'll go with Pop."

"No. I want you to stay."

"We don't need anyone else in our business," Mr. Graf argued.

"Please," Wayne said to Diggy, as if his dad hadn't spoken.

Wayne had barely coughed up the word. It was the little bit of choking on it that sold Diggy, though at this point he'd really rather clean his room. He took the chair farthest away, over by the window.

Mr. Graf glared, then fidgeted, then got that hangdog look again. "I guess I deserve it."

Pop faded away toward the dining room. After a bit, Mr. Graf decided to go ahead and sit down, too, taking a seat next to Wayne on the couch and presenting Diggy with the fact that he'd chosen exactly the worst seat in the room. He faced them square on, like a judge, though neither looked at him. Wayne stared at the turned-off TV while Mr. Graf looked at his hands, at Wayne, and back at his hands. Diggy twisted away as much as he could, wanting the bookshelves to be as interesting as he pretended they were.

Mr. Graf cleared his throat. "I know I haven't been the best dad lately."

Right then, Diggy would have chewed off his own leg to escape. Because there was a *but* coming. He could hear it. The guy had kicked his kid out of his house, and there was a *but*.

"You know, my dad used to beat the crap out of me." Graf said it like it was funny now, like he'd learned that dads did what they had to do and he was a better man for it—no harm done.

Wayne didn't respond.

Diggy ground his teeth to keep from yelling. At Wayne or Graf—he wasn't sure which. At Wayne for not saying anything. At Graf for not saying what he should. *I'm sorry.* Stop. End of sentence. *I love you. I'll stop drinking and get myself together and do everything I can to let you know I love you and want you to come home.*

"I don't think I ever got it right with you." Graf scratched at his stubble. Pop might have waited for him to shower, but they'd skipped the shaving. "Except once, maybe. You were a colicky kid," he said, jovial-like, and slapped Wayne's shoulder too hard.

Wayne twitched with the impact but kept himself turned away.

Graf took his hand back. "Your"—he had to clear his throat—"your mom was up all hours trying to get you to sleep. She looked so bad one night, I made her go to bed, said I'd take care of you." He chortled, all fake-sounding. "You didn't want anything to do with me. Not that I blamed you. I'd have preferred Ann, too." He got that look, like it was then, not now. "You and that screaming. I don't know how she stood it all those nights. It got to where I about lost it, when I had my idea." He smiled. "My grandma used to say something about a teaspoon of bourbon curing most anything. All I had was beer, so I gave you some." He grinned at Wayne, excited by his story. "It did the trick. Ann was ticked when I told her, but that was your last night of crying—I'll tell you that."

Diggy gaped, awed by Graf's total lack of awareness that getting a baby drunk was not a proud-papa moment.

Apparently, Wayne was unmoved, too. Or he'd heard the story before.

After a while, Graf asked, "You got anything you want to say?"

Diggy would have jumped all over the opening, but Wayne remained silent.

"Listen, I'm trying here, okay?" The hangdog hadn't hung around long. Graf's tone was tinged with annoyance. "I don't know what you want me to say."

Wayne held his pose—boy watching TV—but it seemed hard now, like he was struggling to maintain the stance so he wouldn't ruin the shot.

Diggy could barely stand it.

"Look, I'm trying to apologize here—"

"Since when?" Diggy burst from his seat. "You haven't said one word that—"

"You keep out of our business!" Graf bellowed, on his feet, too. "This is between me and Wayne, and—"

Wayne stood, holding himself tall as he watched his dad. "I'm not coming back until you stop drinking."

Wayne might as well have set off a bomb in the room.

Diggy noticed Pop in the doorway, and that he seemed kind of unhappily glad, like he had expected this to happen. Was that why he had insisted Wayne talk to his dad here? Did Pop want Wayne to stay that badly?

"It's what Mom would want," Wayne said. "Until you get . . . better."

"You think your mom would want you to bail out on your family?" Graf shouted. "For some guy who couldn't keep his hands to—"

"That's enough, Harold," Pop said. Not loudly, but meaning it.

Graf clenched his fists tightly, breathing like a mad bull. "I'm supposed to roll over and give up my son because—" Graf suddenly deflated. "Because he asks me to?"

"It's because you won't give him up that you need to let him stay. Only for a while."

"You can't pretty this up, Lawson, just because you want to."

"You dumped me in their driveway!" Wayne raged. "I get to be mad, and I get to stay here as long as I want, and you get to deal with it, because *I* say so." He shook all over but still managed to add, "You threw me out like I was garbage."

The only sound in the room came from Wayne, and it wasn't that he was making any actual sound but more like the waves of what he felt were bouncing off the walls and making the room vibrate like a giant bell, and all anyone could do was let the echoes pass through them.

Wayne was staying.

Wayne was really staying.

Just as Pop moved forward as if to fix the situation, Graf mumbled, "I guess I don't deserve any better."

He peered at Wayne like Wayne was supposed to deny it. Which was more proof Graf was crazy.

"Okay. Well." His voice was rough, like teary rough. He cleared his throat and flopped an arm at the door. "I guess I'll go, then." But he didn't move.

Wayne's gaze was a dare.

Graf sighed. "Okay, then."

He headed to the doorway, dragging, clearly waiting to be stopped, and Diggy got a shiver down his spine. Had this scene played out before? Was this when Mrs. Graf would have called him back, and now Wayne was supposed to?

Minnesota would be hot in January before that happened.

When all there was left to do was walk out, Graf did.

Pop said, "A door that's shut too long gets hard to open. It's better to leave it cracked a couple of inches."

Wayne blinked at him. Heck, Diggy blinked at him, too.

"I think Harold did some barrel racing back in the day," Pop said. "Why don't you show him Diggy's steer, Wayne?"

Wayne's expression made it pretty clear what he thought of that idea, but he had just announced he was moving in whether anyone liked it or not, so maybe he didn't think he could ignore Pop. He followed his dad outside.

Diggy stood in the living room, feeling like he was in some weird time loop, like an infinity sign, and on one side he beat the crap out of a sofa cushion, and on the other he curled into a ball. Then he was back at the crossing point, not having moved, with Pop eyeing him.

"You all right?"

Diggy nodded, shrugged, and shook his head in one motion.

Pop ran his hand down his face. "Yeah."

After a while, Diggy couldn't stand it anymore. "You're letting him stay."

"We have to."

WE HAVE TO.

THE WORDS ECHOED OVER AND OVER IN

Diggy's head while he packed up his rockets to clear the bed-room for Wayne.

We have to.

Diggy's greatest, most secret fear was summed up in those words.

Pop would say it was different. The truth might really be different. But there it was.

We. Have. To.

No choice. Just an obligation a decent man couldn't ignore.

What else could Diggy think except that when he had been left on Pop's doorstep, Pop had picked him up and thought, *I have to.*

Sure, Pop loved him. Diggy knew that like he knew how to breathe. But Pop hadn't had a choice about it, and that made all the difference.

It was like a yeti had reached into Diggy's chest and torn out his heart and not even bothered to eat it.

So when Pop finally tried to talk with him, Diggy couldn't help but feel it was too late, even though he went ahead and asked, "Did you know?"

"No," Pop said, blinking in surprise. Then he sighed. "Diggy . . . no."

Diggy believed him, had already known the answer, really, but the real questions he had, he wasn't sure how to ask. *Did you love Mrs. Graf? What about my mom? How could both Wayne and me happen?*

Sure, Diggy and Wayne were almost a full year apart in age, but Pop had to have heard Mrs. Graf was pregnant. Had he never suspected, before he started dating Diggy's mom?

Diggy realized he hadn't asked the right question and didn't know how to rephrase it. *What did you know? When?*

Pop ran a hand down his face. "When Ann left me, I was . . . It hurt. She and Harold had been together forever, and she had even said she was just trying it out, taking some time off from him. But I thought . . . I don't know what I thought. We were having fun." He shook his head. "I heard she was pregnant and figured the baby *had* to be Harold's, that that was why she went back to him."

"Do you think she knew?" Diggy blurted, though he wasn't sure what it would mean if she had.

"I don't know. Ann was a wonderful, caring woman—no matter what, I know she did what she thought best for her baby."

Did Pop think Diggy's mom was a wonderful, caring woman, too? Did he think *she* had done what was best for her baby?

But those were questions Diggy *really* didn't know how to

ask, and it made him mad, though he wasn't sure if it was at Pop or himself.

So the next morning, after another mostly sleepless night, when Diggy didn't wake up right away and Pop tossed a bag of frozen peas onto his feet—a minor prank he had pulled many times—Diggy guessed he shouldn't have been surprised that this time the prank made him steam.

"You're just going to act like everything's normal?" Diggy shouted. "I have to ride the bus to school with WAYNE GRAF!"

Which wasn't the point but was the truth of everything all the same.

"What else can we do?" Pop sighed.

What else could Diggy do, either? He had to get out to the barn and take care of Joker. He had to shower. Choke down some food, with Wayne right across the table from him. Run for the bus, as always, when Mrs. Osborn honked for him.

"Wayne?" Mrs. Osborn said when they boarded the bus, shock popping her face wide open. "What in the— What has Harold done now?"

"Please, Aunt Em," Wayne said, his voice shakier than the bus. "We just need to get to school."

It seemed like Mrs. Osborn—Wayne's *Aunt Em*—would let Antarctica melt away before she moved the bus without hearing what had happened. But she was the bus driver, and Diggy's was only the first stop of her very long route.

"I'm calling Mom as soon as I get home," Mrs. Osborn said.

"I'll call Grandma after school—I promise."

Things went even further downhill when one of the girls, trying to be nice, asked Wayne if he was okay and why he had stayed out at Mrs. Osborn's. Stupid Wayne said he hadn't. After much conferring, the others figured out he must have been at Diggy's, and one of the guys sniggered, "Did you have a *sleepover* at Lawson's?"

Diggy hunched low in his seat and pretended to sleep.

———

Diggy had a couple of morning classes with Jason and Crystal, but it wasn't until lunch that they were able to corner him. Well, Crystal was able to corner him. Jason was a lot like his Uncle Rick, though where Lenz had his cows, Jason did most of his talking to sheep.

Jason and Crystal both competed sheep, though Crystal lived in town and had to keep hers out at Jason's farm. The three of them had always known one another, but it wasn't until that first 4-H meeting in fourth grade that they really became friends.

"So, Wayne Graf," Crystal said as soon as they all sat down with their lunch trays.

"How did you even hear about that?" Diggy wasn't unpopular, but he wasn't popular, either. Neither was Wayne. So the fact that a bit of gossip about Wayne riding the bus with him had spread around school so quickly was kind of baffling. It wasn't like anyone could know *why* Wayne had been on the bus. Diggy hoped not anyway.

"Darla told me. You know she likes you."

Diggy had meant to stay focused on the bus stuff, but . . . "She does?"

"You are such a boy."

"When did you get to be such a girl?"

"Birth."

Jason laughed.

Which made Diggy laugh, because Jason's laugh was kind of a suppressed snort from his years of trying to stay low-key around his sheep. Diggy knew animals reacted to human emotion, but Jason took it to a new level. Crystal shook her head at the two of them, then couldn't hold back her own grin.

"Tell us true," Crystal ordered, "or all you'll be hearing next is 'Diggy and Darla sitting in a tree,'" she sang. "That has a nice ring to it, doesn't it? Diggy and Darla. Darla and Diggy. I can go on like this the entire period," Crystal warned.

"I'd tell you, but who can get a word in?"

Jason grunted. Crystal thumped his arm. A normal conversation.

Then Crystal got serious and leaned across the table to give them more privacy. "But you're okay, right?"

Diggy sighed. He was really glad these two people were

his friends. They had already made him feel better than he had all weekend. But he had no idea how to explain this thing he hardly understood himself.

He cleared his throat. "Wayne's moving in with me and Pop for a while."

"But he's a town kid," Crystal said.

Diggy and Jason stared at her. That was her first reaction? Especially considering where she lived?

"I live in town," Crystal argued, "but I'm a country girl at heart. And you both know it."

"Why?" Jason asked.

"Because I love the animals and the land and the space and quiet and—" Crystal bit her lip. "You meant Diggy." She actually blushed.

Diggy didn't mind her answering the question—*he* certainly didn't want to. "His dad's a little messed up since Mrs. Graf died."

Jason nodded. "I've heard some stuff."

"You have?" Diggy asked, surprised. Though it wasn't surprising Jason hadn't passed on whatever he'd heard. He took that phrase "If you don't have anything nice to say . . ." seriously.

"But why you?" Crystal asked. "It's not like you're friends, and he's related to—what, half the county? Isn't your bus driver one of his aunts?"

"How did you know that?" Diggy said. He had been totally

caught off guard when Wayne called Mrs. Osborn "Aunt Em" on the bus. Even though he had seen Mrs. Osborn at Mrs. Graf's funeral and knew vaguely that they were related, he just hadn't thought it through all the way.

"Boys," Crystal said again, like that was an answer. "So? Why you?"

The problem with having 4-H friends who competed animals was that they noticed when something was out of place—a hoof, a hairline, a glaring absence of the whole truth.

"Wayne might be . . ." No, Diggy couldn't go that way. He couldn't use the word *brother,* or even *half brother.* "It turns out that . . . Pop might be Wayne's, uh, actual dad."

He had said it out loud.

Like it was real.

Everything before had been a denial, or at least an argument, but telling his friends was like accepting it was true no matter what he thought about it.

All of a sudden, the cafeteria seemed really quiet, like everyone was listening, even though the volume of chatter around them hadn't changed at all.

"His dad," Crystal repeated.

"Maybe."

"You're skipping your next class," she announced.

"Uh . . ." Diggy said.

"Lunch period's too short," Jason agreed.

"You're skipping class," Crystal explained, "and we're going to the activities room, and you're telling us everything." Crystal looked at Jason, who nodded, then back at Diggy.

He was reminded of her in the show ring, all determined and surprisingly pretty.

Usually she wore jeans and too-big shirts. If she didn't have a long ponytail, he'd hardly know she was a girl. But in the ring she was most definitely a girl—dressed like all the others with almost-tight jeans; a fitted, Western-style top that matched her blue eyes; rhinestones on her belt and on a clip holding back her blond hair. She was beautiful and confident, and he always cheered like crazy for her, even when they knew she wouldn't win. That wasn't the point.

They were friends.

"Okay," he said.

DIGGY FELT SO MUCH BETTER AFTER

TALKING WITH CRYSTAL AND JASON, HE HADN'T
thought about the riding-the-bus-home-with-Wayne business.
But it had been on other people's minds—both Mr. Graf and
Wayne's grandparents were waiting for the kid when school
let out.

All the other kids knew who they were, too, because as
soon as Wayne got outside, Graf started hollering at him to
get his butt into the car—so, drinking again—while Wayne's
grandpa yelled at Graf to stop yelling on school property, and
Wayne's grandma tried to bear-hug Wayne into their car. The
teachers tried to herd the students to the buses, but no one
made it easy, and quite a few of the parents watched with the
clear intention of not missing a thing.

Diggy honestly had no idea how he ended up in the middle
of everything, with Wayne clutching his arm like he was a life
preserver and with Wayne's grandma staring at him like he
was Jaws himself.

"You let him go this instant," Wayne's grandma said to
Diggy in her German accent, even though Wayne was the one
holding on to *him*.

Vogl. That was her name.

"Stay away from him!" Graf shouted at her, but Mr. Vogl had gotten hold of Graf, and he couldn't break free. Mr. Vogl might not be young, but he was still as strong as an ox and not drunk. Graf added, "He's my son."

"That you took to *Pop Lawson*," Mrs. Vogl said, like she meant a strip bar or, you know, hell. "He's *our* grandson. You bring him to *us*."

"You always hated me. Never good enough for your sweet, innocent little girl," Graf sneered. "But look what she did!"

Unbelievably, Wayne started pulling Diggy toward the buses, and Graf and the grandparents were mad enough at one another not to notice. It helped that the entire student body of 250 or so was there to witness the scene. Jason had gotten himself in front of Diggy and Wayne and helped make room for them.

Diggy didn't know where Wayne thought they were going, until, unbelievably, he tried to get on the bus. That Mrs. Osborn drove. His aunt.

"Oh, no, you don't," she said. "You march right on over to Mom and Dad. We've already got a family meeting planned to figure things out."

"Do you hear them?" Wayne shouted. "They're crazy! I'm not going—"

"Harold's the crazy one!" she told him. "That loser piece of— He doesn't want you, that's fine. But you're going with Mom and Dad."

"Jeez," Diggy said before he could stop himself.

"Don't you start," Mrs. Osborn snapped.

"Me? Do you even hear how mean you're being? You're talking about his dad. I mean, I want Wayne to go with you guys, too, but . . . jeez."

"Gee, thanks, Diggy," Wayne mumbled.

"You know what I mean," Diggy muttered.

Mrs. Osborn tried to speak more calmly. "We're adults. You're children. That means we have to decide what's best for you, and what your mom would have wanted." She turned her face away, then her shoulders started shaking. "Ann's not even gone three weeks."

It hit Diggy that Mrs. Osborn was Mrs. Graf's sister. He knew she was Wayne's aunt, and that meant she was Mrs. Graf's sister, but still, it was weird thinking of it that way. Mrs. Osborn's sister had died. And she was Wayne's aunt. And she drove the bus.

The sounds outside shifted. The yelling had stopped, but hundreds of feet shuffled closer to the bus while still making room for Mrs. Vogl to pass by them.

Graf staggered back to his truck, but that didn't make Diggy feel better at all.

"Aunt Em, please," Wayne said. "I just want to go home."

Mrs. Osborn turned around, not bothering to hide that she was crying. "So go with—"

"With Diggy. I want to go home with Diggy."

She studied Wayne's face. "That's what you really want?"

"Yes."

She slapped the door closed.

"Emilyn Rose Vogl, what do you think you're doing?" Mrs. Vogl shouted, her accent so thick, it almost sounded like she was speaking German. "Open this door!"

Emilyn Rose Vogl *Osborn* cranked the engine.

"Uh, Mrs. Osborn?" Diggy said, grabbing a seat back to keep from falling.

"I hope this is the right thing, Ann," she said as she took off.

Diggy looked out at the kids on his route who were not on the bus. Which was all of them. Because, despite their teachers' efforts, no one had gone to any of their buses, in order to watch the show.

He and Wayne rode off in an empty school bus.

"Uh, Mrs. Osborn?" he said again.

"They can take the activities bus." She gripped the steering wheel and stared down that road like it was a NASCAR race and every second counted.

And thank heavens she did.

Because when Graf swerved his pickup in front of her, she swerved the other way in time to get around him.

Diggy fell hard into Wayne. When Mrs. Osborn corrected again, the two of them were jolted in the opposite direction. Diggy's back felt split in half against a seat before he bounced off and sprawled facedown in the opposite seat, holding on before he rolled all the way to the floor.

"Are you two all right?" Mrs. Osborn asked. But she didn't stop.

Diggy turned over and sat up. Wayne pulled himself up from the aisle. He'd gotten a good smack to the side of his forehead—it was already bright pink but otherwise looked okay.

They stared at each other.

What the heck had just happened?

Diggy remembered Graf and raced to the back of the bus.

Graf's truck was in a ditch.

"Holy crap."

"He's fine," Mrs. Osborn said. "I saw him get out and walk around the truck."

Diggy thought Wayne would say something, but the guy only stared out a window. A side window.

"Don't you think we should go back?" Diggy asked.

"Wayne wants to go to your house, so I'm taking him to your house." Mrs. Osborn's smile reflected at them from the big rearview mirror. "The crazy people can be crazy on their own time."

Diggy decided Mrs. Osborn was the coolest bus driver ever.

Except, on the way home, Mrs. Osborn started talking. The ride should have been a lot shorter without having to make all the regular stops, but it felt longer and longer the more she had to say to Wayne.

About how he could stay with her if he didn't want to be with his grandparents. Or with another aunt who had offered to take him in. Or how he could move in with different members of the family until he decided where he felt most comfortable. How they all loved him, and would he please come to the family meeting tonight. How she would try to support him no matter what he decided, but he should really be with family who loved him.

Diggy wished he'd been left behind to wait for the activities bus, too.

Wayne had all those people who wanted him. So with all those choices, what the heck was he doing at Diggy's house?

MRS. OSBORN DIDN'T LET THEM

OUT AT THE END OF THE DRIVE. SHE PULLED

all the way up to the house, and Pop was already outside waiting for her.

Diggy went straight to the barn. He was sick of being in the middle of all of Wayne's crap.

Joker did a little hop, then bawled, like he was happy to see Diggy but was ticked it had taken him so long to get back. Being alone was a big adjustment for a calf. Weaning was tough, but usually other calves were around, and his mama was nearby even if he couldn't get to her. Diggy liked to think his steers' isolation gave him an edge against competitors who raised a lot of cattle. His animals had only him, so they bonded good and tight. But it made him feel bad to think that way, too—kind of merciless and hard-hearted. Raising a competitive steer took a lot of time, period. But Diggy always gave his steers as many hours as he could to make up for their being separated from the herd.

Diggy got the rice root brush from its peg and gave Joker a good brushing. There wasn't much dead hair to clean out yet, but it was never too early to begin training the hair to stand up straight. Calves were sensitive to their trainer's feelings, but just as often it went the other way for Diggy, and he was grateful for that today. He worked himself—and Joker—into a trancelike state, methodically brushing the calf's hair forward from the legs, rump, middle, neck, chest, and head. When he got to Joker's face, the calf was so zoned out, Diggy thought he could get away with a wash and blow-dry, but it was still early for that much noise and activity—it was enough that Joker was doing so well with the halter.

By the time Pop came out to talk with Diggy, Diggy had almost convinced himself they wouldn't have to talk at all. Pop's face cured him of that illusion and snapped him out of the zone so abruptly, Joker sidestepped until Diggy was pinned against the stall's slats. Pop got ahold of Joker's halter and whispered soothingly into his ear, but Diggy still had to do a fair amount of shoving to get himself free.

Before Pop could start a similar "calm down" routine on him, Diggy put the brush back and grabbed a hose to wash his hands. The water was the kind of cold that made it feel like his fingers might break off, but it was a relief, too. Like, if he could get the ache out through his fingers, it wouldn't get into his heart.

"I'm sorry about what happened today," Pop said.

Diggy wanted to duck his entire head under the water. Pop wasn't apologizing for the right thing.

"Is he still staying here?"

"Yes."

"Why?!" Diggy asked. "You should have seen them fighting over him. *Everybody* wants him back, so why do we have to keep him? It's not fair!"

"But it's right. Ann's family doesn't know how to be fair to Harold right now."

"So? Mr. Graf doesn't worry about anyone else's feelings, and it's not our business to balance the scales for anybody else anyway."

Pop frowned, but Diggy wouldn't let Pop make him feel bad.

"Harold is Wayne's father," Pop said.

Diggy snorted.

"Hey," Pop barked. "I'll listen to what you have to say, but you have to listen, too."

It was all so like what Wayne had said, about how his dad would apologize for the wrong things, then act like Wayne was the jerk if he stayed mad for too long.

"If Wayne goes with Ann's family, that'll be it for him and Harold. The Vogls certainly won't include Harold in anything and won't go out of their way to help Wayne see his dad."

"Like that's a bad thing," Diggy grumbled, earning a glare.

"You think it was easy for Wayne to say he wanted to come here? Did you think about *why* he said that?"

Because Wayne was just like his dad and didn't care about anyone else's feelings. Because he thought he was getting a shiny new dad.

"He might not have been able to explain why, but he knew in his heart that going with Ann's family meant giving up on his father, and he couldn't do that. Like it or not, we're neutral ground for Wayne, and with all that he's had to deal with these last few months, is it so impossible to think we can help him?"

Pop was putting a lot of thoughts into Wayne's head, not to mention wildly misinterpreting things, if he thought they were "neutral ground."

What was worse was that Pop was doing it; Pop was making Diggy feel like the jerk.

"You told Wayne it wasn't his job to take care of his dad."

"It's a father's job to care for his son." Pop rubbed a hand down his face. "Both of his sons. I don't know how to do that yet, but I know I have to try. And I could use your help."

Diggy felt like that ice-cold water had gotten to his heart.

He was supposed to help Pop with his new son? Pop might as well have turned into a yeti before his very eyes.

Wayne came in but hung back by the door. "Aunt Em is leaving. She wanted to talk to you again."

Pop put a hand on Diggy's shoulder. Diggy shrugged out from under it and went back to the hose. Pop had held Wayne's shoulder, too, the other night, when Graf had come back howling. Diggy wanted to run the hose over his entire body, but he could feel Wayne still there and knew that would make him look crazy.

Wayne cleared his throat, feet shuffling in the dirt. "I'm sorry about what happened today."

Wayne echoing exactly what Pop had said made it feel like they were ganging up on him. Like they had become a team when Diggy wasn't looking. Barely two days, and he was odd man out.

Diggy held the hose over his head after all.

THE ONLY BRIGHT SPOT FOR DIGGY

AFTER A TRULY CRAPPY DAY WAS THE MONTHLY
4-H meeting scheduled for that night. Which Pop said they might have to miss, because the Vogls wanted them at their family meeting.

Diggy protested, strongly, but it was thanks to Wayne that he got to go to 4-H at all. Wayne said he really didn't want to go to the family meeting because he'd have to look everyone in the face and tell them he didn't want to stay with any of them. He stuttered when he asked Pop to help him, and then he said it would probably be better if he and Diggy went to 4-H—for the distraction—while they waited for Pop to get back.

Pop bought it, though Diggy didn't know if he was grateful to Wayne or mad that the guy was able to talk Pop into doing something he clearly wasn't wild about doing. Mostly, Diggy was just glad that he'd get to see July.

He rushed to the church basement, hoping to catch July alone and . . . he didn't know what. Make sure she knew the truth? Check that she still liked him? Get a hug?

But Wayne was right behind him, and as soon as July saw Wayne, she hugged *him*.

Not the sideways hug Diggy got but a full-on, wraparound hug.

"Are you okay?" she asked Wayne, sparking Diggy's temper. *Wayne* was fine. *He* was getting his way *everywhere*.

"Wayne? What are you doing here?" Crystal said from the doorway, where she had stopped abruptly. Jason was stuck behind her, carrying a little Cloverbud under each arm, the children giggling at being handled like sheep.

Crystal looked at Diggy, and he knew she was trying to gauge how to react—if Diggy had invited Wayne or was okay with him being there. It had to be obvious that he wasn't.

July had her hands out to Crystal like she could calm the cattle before they stampeded, but the heifer had seen the snake and took off.

Crystal went over to Wayne. "I'm sorry your mom died and your dad's . . . you know"—she spoke quietly, and her voice trembled, but she went on—"but you don't get to take over Diggy's life to make yourself feel better."

Diggy stared wide-eyed at his best friend. It was nice to have someone on his side, especially when he could tell it was hard for her, but he couldn't believe she had said what she had said. Even July was shocked into silence for a few moments.

Jason set down the little kids, who immediately grabbed his hands, sensing that something was wrong.

July pulled Crystal aside. "4-H welcomes everyone, and considering what—"

"I pledge my head to clearer thinking," Crystal recited from the 4-H pledge, "and my *heart* to greater *loyalty*. I'm loyal to Diggy."

Wayne was as white as a Charolais steer, staring at Diggy as if this was his fault, too. And Diggy felt bad enough that he let him.

The thing was, what Crystal had said was *true*. It was unnerving to have the past few days summed up in one sentence that was so true, it hurt. But Diggy couldn't focus on the last part. All he kept hearing was, *I'm sorry your mom died and your dad's . . .*

Hearing Wayne's life summed up like that made Diggy feel small. He was really mad, because it did feel like Wayne was trying to take over Diggy's life to make himself feel better. But Diggy couldn't help thinking about how he felt when people joked about his mom leaving town on a tractor and he had to smile like it was no big deal.

Wayne's mom was dead. His dad was losing it.

Pop had said, *We have to. What else can we do?*

Diggy thought he had seen what else they could do— Wayne had too much family not to have options. But just the way Crystal had said out loud that one true thing no one else had seemed to notice, let alone admit, Diggy suddenly felt another true thing *he* hadn't wanted to admit.

Wayne was trying to save himself.

The world kept breaking up around him, and the only

person so far who had really tried to help him find some solid ground was Pop.

Everyone else had been too busy with their own corners of the world—Graf dousing his grief with liquor, the Vogl family fighting their grief with anger, Diggy wanting to keep his happy, safe corner to himself. That didn't feel wrong, exactly, but he could picture Mrs. Graf so easily, how she'd see him at the farmer's market and brush his hair off his forehead, then laugh and muss it up again. He'd never bump into her like that again. She was such a good person, and she wasn't out there in the world anymore. *I'm sorry your mom is dead* just didn't cut it.

So before Crystal felt like she had to say more, he told her it was okay and went to their usual seats. She was shaking, but Diggy didn't know what to do to make her calm down or to let her know how much he'd appreciated her defense. Jason patted her shoulder, and the corners of her mouth turned up— not quite a smile but close enough.

Wayne didn't have a usual seat, but Diggy didn't have it in him to find him one.

July pointed Wayne to a seat and got the meeting started. They recited the Pledge of Allegiance and the 4-H pledge before roll call. The Cloverbuds, the kindergartners to second-graders, reliably acted like roll call was the coolest part of the meeting, shouting "Here!" *and* raising their hands. After the secretary and treasurer gave their reports, the Cloverbud leader took the little kids to the back to work on some craft activity or to learn more about 4-H.

Most of this meeting was about reminding people of deadlines for reenrollment, getting their fair records in for judging, and laying out various deadlines leading up to the next fairs; checking the status of projects in the works, like planning for the road cleanup, awards banquet, and family dinner; and hearing any new business.

Diggy didn't really hear much, because he kept thinking about what would happen when everyone broke off into their three loosely related groups—basically the livestock competitors, the plant and environment kids, and the arts and family science group. Wayne would come to their table. Because he thought he could get a steer and earn a trip to State and compete and win $12,000 and get back some kind of control over his life. Ha.

To make matters worse, when Wayne did come to their table, July followed. Crystal and Jason had positioned themselves on either side of Diggy, and with the small-animal competitors clumped together, that left Wayne and July looking like a team facing off against Diggy, Crystal, and Jason. Diggy had ended up on the wrong side of the July Johnston equation.

"Wayne said he wants to get a steer," she said.

Crystal took a breath to share her thoughts on the topic, but July got in hers first.

"I'm not sure it's a good idea."

This time Wayne opened his mouth to say something, but July beat him to it.

She explained that during the year Wayne and his steer were together, the calf would come to feel like a friend, even more so than a pet cat or dog. But a steer, any steer, was only ever market beef. It would be slaughtered after the fair. Considering Wayne's recent loss, and the timing of that loss—the anniversary would nearly coincide with the next State Fair—July suggested Wayne might try a breeding heifer or something completely different. There were categories for rabbits, lambs, ducks, chickens, or pigeons, stock dog trials, even rooster crowing contests.

She signaled to some of the others at the table, and a couple of the rabbit and chicken kids talked about what they did, what the work was like, and how the competition was judged. Jason even said a few words about raising sheep, and, rather than feel betrayed, Diggy was weirdly glad. 4-H was full of nice people— he and his friends among them. He might not want Wayne there, but he also didn't want Wayne to think badly of 4-H.

Diggy also wanted to be grateful that July was discouraging Wayne from entering, but her words only made his bad day even worse. Words like "market beef" and "slaughter" tended to have that effect on him.

"It probably doesn't matter," Wayne mumbled. "I mean, how much does a steer cost?"

July explained about the Farm Bureau loans. The majority of competitors were from farms that already raised cattle and simply chose a steer from among their stock. Other students bought a steer outright or took a special loan from the Farm Bureau, like Diggy had all but the first year. Pop liked for Diggy to know the steer was truly his, and Diggy liked that the loans were how July bought her steers, too.

"But the money isn't why I want you to reconsider raising a steer," July concluded.

Wayne said he'd think about it, but Crystal shook her head, clearly not believing him.

July sighed. "Wayne, I'm sorry, but I won't feel good about helping you unless I feel like you've really thought through everything. I, um, understand you're out with Diggy for a while, so if it's okay with him, why don't you spend a couple weeks observing his routine? Then we can talk."

She glanced apologetically at Diggy for putting him on the spot, but he felt the first stirrings of hope. Wayne was a town kid. Working with steers was dirty, time-consuming, and required actual physical labor. Wayne looked like he'd hardly even been outside, let alone worked at anything more than taking out the trash.

July might not have meant it quite the way Diggy was taking it, but he had a feeling she had just saved him a ton of aggravation. All he had to do was put up with the guy for a few weeks, and if Diggy had any kind of luck at all, Wayne would move home by then and forget he'd ever thought about raising a steer.

FOR THE NEXT FEW WEEKS, DIGGY
INSTITUTED HIS CAMPAIGN TO SCARE WAYNE

away from steer raising by doing what he always did every morning and night. Walk Joker. Brush him down. Give him a wash and rinse. Blow-dry. Feed and water. Shovel poop. Repeat. He had thought it would only take three or four mornings of waking up before dawn to convince Wayne he'd rather sleep, but he came back every day. The weirdo seemed more spooked by doing all the same stuff at night than he did about waking up early, so Diggy tried changing out a few bulbs in the barn to make it a little darker and creepier, but after stubbing his toes a couple of times, scraping his knuckles, and taking a good whack to the head, he opted to stick with decent light and trust the manual-labor part to work its off-putting magic.

He made Wayne sweep and rake the barn floor, scrub the water trough, and, of course, shovel poop and feed it into the anaerobic digester Pop had rigged to generate electricity from the methane gas. Cow power.

Diggy had to give the guy credit—Wayne had a heck of a poker face about how he felt about his assigned jobs—but Diggy felt pretty confident he was wearing Wayne down. The kid got so pale, his eyes were practically black and blue, and several mornings he didn't make it out to the barn until ten or fifteen minutes after Diggy. Apparently, his grades were taking a hit, too, and that was big for a teacher's kid who always made honor roll.

All in all, Diggy felt that things were going okay.

Until Pop got another call. This one from the jail, and Diggy's hopes of Wayne's imminent departure nosedived. Turned out Graf had broken some stuff at Otto's bar, and the police had kept him overnight until he sobered up. Otto wasn't pressing charges, but the officers on duty had gotten called away for something, and Graf needed a ride home. The fact that Pop was the only person he could think to ask pretty much said it all.

Pop tried, but Wayne didn't want to talk about it.

And the next morning, when Diggy led Joker back to his stall and put out the alfalfa-grass hay, Wayne said, "I called July."

"What?"

"July Johnston. From 4-H."

"I know who she is."

"She said she'd take me out this weekend to look at steers."

Diggy couldn't believe it. Not only was Wayne going through with getting a steer, he had called *July*. "Seriously, Wayne, what have I ever done to you?"

"It's not about you."

"You move into *my* house, and we all act like it's no big

85

deal. You want a steer so you can beat *me* at the State Fair, and now this," Diggy fumed. "July is *my* friend."

"You should be glad," Wayne said through gritted teeth. "When I get that prize money, I'll leave. You won't have to put up with me anymore."

"You are so stupid. No one's going to let you leave. And you definitely won't win the fair. I will."

Wayne stomped away. "I'm getting a steer."

Diggy threw a brush after him, huffed, then went to pick up the brush and hang it on its peg. Joker chewed his hay and stared at Diggy.

"I know," Diggy burst out. Wayne had made up his mind a month ago. Diggy had never had a shot at changing it. All he'd done was train the competition.

Saturday morning, when Wayne tried to follow Diggy out to the barn, Diggy blocked the kitchen doorway.

Wayne looked like he might insist, hard, but then sneered. "Fine. It won't matter soon anyway."

Wayne's going back to bed should have been the beginning of a good morning alone with Joker. Instead, the calf wouldn't settle. He kept looking around, like someone was missing. Their walk around the pasture was all stop-and-go.

Diggy had three years of knowing that steers sensed human emotions. He didn't like thinking that Joker's being all pigheaded and contrary was an echo of Diggy's confusion or that the steer missed Wayne.

Diggy was not worried. Wayne could get ten steers and still not have a shot at Grand Champ. He could spend every day of every week with July and still not know her as well as Diggy did. He could live with them for the rest of his life and still not be Diggy's brother.

The word tripped him up again. Diggy hadn't really let himself think about Wayne's relationship to him. Why should he? They didn't have a relationship. Pop would make Graf finally get his act together, and Wayne would go home. Diggy couldn't wait for Wayne to go home.

At the turn, Joker ignored Diggy and charged forward, jerking his head to try to pull free. Diggy curved the lead across his forearm and drove his elbow into the calf's neck, strong-arming him to go where he was told to go. Joker did not like it and bucked hard enough that Diggy had to let go. Joker was only half his finishing weight, but that was more than six hundred pounds. If the meathead wanted to rodeo, he'd rodeo.

The outburst was over in all of ten seconds. Then the steer hurried back to Diggy's side, shuddering, head low and wanting reassurance.

Diggy patted him. "It's not you," he said. Because it really wasn't.

The rest of the morning, Diggy stayed in the barn and rambled nonsense to Joker, brushing and brushing and brushing him to make up for getting him so upset earlier. The work—and being solo after so many weeks with Wayne's quiet but still-there presence—helped to clear out his head.

He liked all the things he had to do. Sometimes he felt like if he watched just a little bit harder, he would actually see Joker grow.

At about six hundred and thirty pounds, the steer was exactly where he should be for October. A little more than a pound a day through winter, and Joker would hit eight hundred pounds by April 1, right on target. The food and growing schedule was the easy part, simple math. Hair growth, agility, and temperament were the true markers of a calf that would show well in front of a judge.

Diggy tied Joker's lead at nearly show height. The calf dropped his usual load of poop to make the point that he still was not a fan of this whole halter breaking thing, but he stood calmly, dealing with it.

"Who's a good boy?" Diggy teased with baby talk, laughing and thumping Joker's rump. If cows could raise eyebrows, Joker would be best in class. What he thought of Diggy's teasing was pretty clear. He had even saved a little poop, just in case. Diggy laughed again, shoveled the pile away, and gave Joker a quick once-over with the blower to free any dirt or dust from the hair. Then he let the hose run until the water was extra cold and rinsed the hair forward from the rear to the neck, doing about ten minutes a side. Like cold air, cold water stimulated the hair follicles.

After he squeegeed the excess water off, Diggy used the rice root brush, again working from the rear forward, to train the hair up. He spent extra time around the legs, splitting the hair forward on the front half and backward on the back half.

He worked the same pattern with the blower at a forty-five-degree angle. He made sure Joker was completely dry under his belly and the insides of his legs and brisket. At the legs, Diggy held the blower right at the bone so the leg hair would bloom straight up.

The routine took about an hour, twice a day, and didn't include the time Diggy spent simply brushing and talking with Joker. Soon, he'd introduce the show stick and start practicing setups. Before long, four- and five-hour days with the steer would be the norm.

Mid-morning, Pop brought out a grilled cheese sandwich. He asked if Diggy wanted to talk and let it go when he shook his head. By the time July arrived, Diggy felt much calmer.

Except that she didn't walk to the barn.

Wayne came out the kitchen door, and July went and hugged him.

Not a sideways hug, but another of those full-on, wraparound hugs. "Hey there, Wayne," she said in that voice Diggy had only ever heard her use when she talked to the youngest calves. "I heard about your dad again."

She held on to him, and Wayne not only let her, he hugged back. A long, long time.

Diggy overheated. The sun was bright, like the weather had changed its mind about fall. He slung his vest onto a fence post.

Sure, Graf's latest episode was embarrassing—the man had a knack for making his business everybody's business—but Wayne was taking advantage.

When July finally leaned away from Wayne, she didn't let go. "Are you all right?"

Wayne wouldn't look at her. Diggy wanted to smack him—for hugging her or ignoring her, it didn't matter.

She squeezed him again. "You're in a good place."

Wayne nodded a little, and July finally let him go. "Mom sent food."

Diggy's mood perked up at the prospect of Mrs. Johnston's cooking but quickly sagged again. She had cooked for Wayne.

"I'll need all of you," July said, leading the way to her truck. Three casserole dishes and a Tupperware container of what looked like poppy-seed bars lined the bench seat. July handed them over. "She was upset."

"Please thank her, and tell her not to worry," Pop said. "We're doing fine."

July snorted, looking pointedly at Pop. "Mom would worry even if you really *were* fine."

The casserole dish Diggy held warmed his hands, but July warmed his heart. He hated that she was out here because of Wayne, but she was one of those rare people who said what was what and faced what needed facing. Like asking Wayne if he was all right and really meaning it and not buying Pop's assurance that they were fine. She made it seem easy, but Diggy knew from experience how tough it was to be straight with himself, let alone other people.

They settled things on the kitchen counter, then July put her arm around Diggy's shoulders, hugging him to her side the way she always did. She looked out the window toward the barn. "How's Joker doing? I've been looking forward to seeing him." She hugged him tighter and rested her cheek on top of his head. "You, too," she whispered. "You doing okay?"

She turned to look him in the eye. Diggy had to swallow a couple of times. He didn't want her to worry, but it felt really good to know that she did.

"You're coming with us, right?" July added.

Diggy nodded, not quite up for talking yet.

July patted his shoulder and turned to Wayne. "You'll want to change."

Wayne had dressed in normal day clothes, like for school. Both Diggy and July wore their steer-tending usuals—water-resistant pants and steel-toed boots. It was kind of stupid that

Wayne's having to change his clothes made Diggy feel better. Wayne might be able to join the club, but he wasn't a real member yet.

Normally, Diggy made a stink every time he was relegated to the middle seat because he was shorter than someone. Today was different. The middle seat was now prime real estate, right next to July.

She spent the whole ride talking about steers. She mentioned how lucky Wayne was to follow in Diggy's footsteps, because he was all set up with a proper fence, shed, water trough, feed boxes, hay racks, and the post for halter breaking.

July encouraged Wayne to touch and talk to all the calves and to not be afraid. Animals were sensitive to human fear and wouldn't bond if they felt it. She hoped Wayne would meet a calf that almost immediately slowed at his touch, a sign of trust that meant they'd have a good bond.

Diggy knew how important the touch-and-talk method was, too—he could always tell in the show ring how much time a kid had or hadn't spent talking to his steer. But July seemed to be putting more emphasis on Wayne's bonding with the steer than on choosing a winner. That was fine by Diggy.

She also talked about frame, size, muscling, structural correctness, style, disposition, balance, weight per day of age, hip height measurements, etc. Diggy was absolutely positive that it all was over Wayne's head; he may have let Wayne trail him, but he hadn't made a point of teaching him stuff. July had had her first steer when she was nine—she knew cattle the way some guys knew cars. But Wayne listened like he was truly interested.

Most of the calves were already weaned and grazed in the pasture, but a few stood in individual chicken-wire enclosures. They watched the new arrivals with dark, shiny eyes, hopeful that their mamas with their body-warmed milk were coming back. All of them were uniformly black but unique in poky-boned, gangly ways. Legs were too long or too short, spines arced too high or too low or were invisible under hair that tufted like dandelion snowballs or was glued down with spit, mud, and sweat. Not one looked like he would grow into the stout, rounded barrel of cow that would enter the show ring. They were bumpy and clumsy, and Diggy loved them all at first sight.

He let one suck his first two fingers. The tongue was rough, and the calf sucked hard enough to pop Diggy's knuckles. He grinned. This calf might not be smart, but it was determined. Wayne watched like he was grossed out, even though he had spent weeks around Joker.

"These are all crossbreds," July told Wayne. "Crossbreds are popular because they're usually top winners at competitions. They're a combination of the best traits of different breeds."

She pulled lightly at the hair and skin under a calf's neck.

"This one has a little extra leather here. You want a calf that looks cleaner through the throat and brisket."

She went to another and patted his rear. "This one is a bit round here. Calves with bunchy muscles generally grow short-rumped and show seams and creases in their rear quarters. Some people think the more muscle, the better, but too much too early doesn't leave room for your calf to grow."

July pointed to a calf watching from the side of the pasture. "I like that one."

Diggy saw why. He had a long, straight top, sturdy legs, and looked full, not too skinny or too big. July might have seemed to put more of a priority on Wayne's having a good bond with his steer, but she had picked him a winner, too.

July stood close to Wayne, helping him get used to touching the calves still being weaned. When he seemed fairly comfortable with them, she led him to the calf she liked. Watching the three of them together made Diggy's heart hurt. They were like a matched set. Perfect and shiny and meant to win at the State Fair.

While he stood to the side, hands sticky with cow spit and boots wet with poop.

WINTER

THE CALVES GOT ALONG GREAT.

JOKER ACTED LIKE HE'D BEEN WAITING FOR

Wayne's calf all along, and Wayne's calf, after the long drive home alone, seemed glad that he wasn't solo after all.

More and more, Diggy holed up in his room. He had commandeered a table from the hallway and set up his rockets and supplies in a corner of his bedroom. A series of model diagrams covered his 4-H certificates and blue ribbons for showing his steers and showmanship—they reminded him too much of what he wanted and how far from it he still was.

The room was crowded, and pretty soon his desk was useless for doing homework, covered instead with catalogs, rocket-body tubes of different sizes, balsa and plywood fin stock, plastic nose-cone sets, adapters, engine mounting tubes, parachutes and streamers, shock cord, recovery wadding, launch lugs, decals to decorate rocket bodies, steel rods of different lengths and thicknesses, and launch pads of varying durability. He had cleared out a desk drawer to more carefully store the launch controllers, wicking, and igniters. Most precious were the model-rocket motors. Diggy had found a little box for the cylinders with their black-powder ejection charges so they wouldn't get lost in the jumble, crushed, or accidentally ignited. Pop would not be happy if a motor ignited. He was pretty strict about things like fires inside the house.

Not that Diggy cared much about what Pop thought these days.

He had cleared the top of his bookshelf to line up the rockets he and Pop had built. A few were from kits—a Sprint, a Screamin' Demon, and an Egglofter—but most were scratch-built. Pop didn't like paying for something he could figure out how to build himself. He and Diggy used to spend a ton of hours tinkering with different designs, but that felt like eons ago.

Diggy was all about altitude. His level-one rockets had all flown more than eighteen hundred feet. Although level-two rockets usually didn't go as high, he had several, because Pop wouldn't let Diggy near a level three until he had mastered the twos. When Diggy had had to move all his rocket stuff to make room for Wayne, he decided he had mastered level twos and began researching the Navaho rocket to build as a level-three, two-stage design. He didn't need Pop's approval.

But the November slush that spattered the windows dulled Diggy's creative power too much to sketch plans for the level three. Instead, he was painting the second color coat of his level-two scale model of the Saturn V rocket when Pop came in.

Pop studied the white body tubes. "How are the thicknesses? You stack them all together yet?"

Diggy shrugged. Paint thickness was one of the criteria

judged in model-rocket contests, because a rocket was more aerodynamic if the paint was mostly uniform when the pieces of the body tubes were put together. But he didn't care about it much for this model. The Saturn V was cool, but they'd built it for a C motor. Diggy's plans for the two-stage were for D- and E-class motors. Only eighteen-and-olders were allowed to buy them, and Pop hadn't caved yet, despite much begging and bargaining. Diggy would figure out how to get it on his own.

"You've been in here a lot lately," Pop said.

Where else did he have left to be? Wayne was in Diggy's old rocket room, or in the living room doing homework in front of the TV, or in the kitchen eating stuff, and Pop's latest project had taken over the dining room. Most of his engineering work was on a computer, but sometimes when he did work for international nonprofits, he had to figure out what could be done with existing equipment—usually many years old and half-broken—and cheap alternatives, so he'd collect what he could, take it all apart, and spread it out to see what he could make from the pieces.

"We haven't talked much lately," Pop added.

Because Pop was so busy talking with Wayne. The kid had lived with them for almost two months, had his own steer, and called Pop "Pop." He was supposed to have moved back to his own house by now, but instead he hung around Pop like a noose. Diggy suspected that if he timed it, Wayne would have more hours in with Pop than with his own calf, and that was not fair to the calf.

"It's been an adjustment, but we're still a team. And we're doing something really good by helping out Wayne."

"He's supposedly your son, not a charity case."

"Ann was a good woman. She deserved to live a lot more life than she got. We honor her memory by taking care of Wayne until Harold gets it together. He's finally going to Alcoholics Anonymous meetings, so that's a start."

Diggy didn't want to hear all this. He knew it already, and, sure, life pretty much sucked for Wayne, but he was in Diggy's house—life pretty much sucked for Diggy, too.

When Diggy mumbled, "What about my mom? Was she a good woman?" Diggy was as caught off guard as Pop.

Diggy remembered when he was younger, during that summer when he messed around with that red fireproof safe that held the few things his mom had left behind, that he had asked about his mom then, too. Pop had answered as many questions as he could, but the truth was that he hadn't known Diggy's mom all that well, and Diggy got to feeling weird about asking, like it meant he didn't love Pop. Now, though, he could see how his little-kid logic didn't make any sense.

Pop blinked away his surprise. "She was smart, and so funny." He laughed a little. "She remembered all sorts of odd facts and paired them up with whatever we were doing or talking about in ways that didn't seem to make sense at first but would hit you all of a sudden. She had the greatest laugh."

"And she left me on a doorstep."

Pop sighed. "She was sad. I didn't see it at first because she laughed so much, and when I did . . . Well, it seemed like women were making a habit of leaving me."

Diggy stared at Pop. This was new information. *She* had left *him*? And, "She was sad?"

"She didn't have a good relationship with her family." Pop winced, but he needn't have. Diggy had guessed that truth a long time ago by her parents' complete lack of interest in him. "I think after graduation everyone had expected her to move away, including her."

But she hadn't, not at first. Not until she had met Pop. Not until she had had Diggy.

Diggy couldn't help but notice that though Pop had said a lot, he hadn't said she was a good woman.

Even though he knew the answer, he asked, "How much longer is Wayne staying?"

"We can talk more about your mom, Diggy. I understand why you'd be thinking about her now." Diggy just looked at him until Pop sighed again. "As long as he needs to." Pop patted Diggy's shoulder, then just before he left added, "This could be an opportunity for you, if you let it. You boys have the steers in common now. I'm sure you could find other things.

You might become friends if you tried a little."

After he left, Diggy wondered if Pop had had a similar conversation with Wayne. Had Pop told Wayne this could be an opportunity to help out Diggy because he didn't have a mom, either? That they could become *friends*?

The idea ticked him off so much, his determination to build a level-three rocket, no matter what Pop thought about it, was reignited. Diggy shoved aside his Saturn V stuff, not caring about wet paint, and started looking for parts. He pretended his urgency wasn't at all because his mom hadn't been cured of her sadness when she had him.

When Pop called up that he was heading to Ole Jib's Hardware, and did he want to come, Diggy declined. He had had enough of Pop for one day, partly because he wasn't sure what to think about Pop realizing Diggy's mom was sad but letting her leave anyway. But the offer did get him to notice that the sleet had stopped and it was full dark.

He ducked into the barn and let Joker loose to putter in the field. Cold and dark were essential elements of good hair growth.

The sky was like a half-erased chalkboard, black smeared with white. The cold was so sharp, it was like everything had been stopped in its place—even sound. No birds, no insects, no tractors in the distance. No wind, not even a creaking in the tree. Joker's presence barely made a dent in the quiet.

Until Wayne came out to let his own calf loose. Diggy jumped like a spooked cow. He had been sure Wayne had gone with Pop to the hardware store.

"Hey," Wayne said.

"Hey," Diggy replied. Conversation over, he headed back to the house. As much as he hated it, he had a crapload of homework to do.

Since Wayne had his stuff spread out in the living room, Diggy took his backpack into the kitchen. He was looking for an excuse to stop conjugating Spanish verbs when the phone rang, but Wayne beat him to it.

Wayne was answering the phone at Diggy's house.

Sometimes Diggy just wanted to thump his head on the table. Repeatedly.

When Wayne came into the kitchen, Diggy ignored him, per the usual, but the guy didn't get a glass of milk or whatever—he stood in the doorway until Diggy finally looked up. "What?"

"I didn't think Pop went out anymore."

"You mean like how he's not out now at Ole Jib's?" Weirdo. "Who was on the phone?"

"A guy calling about meeting at Otto's later. He said if Pop changed his mind, it looked like they'd have a decent group for a pool tournament."

"So?" Wayne acted like the message was a big deal, but it sounded to Diggy like it didn't even matter—Pop had turned down the invite.

"*Does* Pop go out? He doesn't even go anywhere for work."

"He just works from home, Wayne. Jeez. He has friends and stuff."

"Does he go out with women?"

Diggy shrugged, but suddenly he got why Wayne seemed spooked. Diggy wasn't comfortable thinking about Pop and women, either, especially after the talk they had just had. Some nights when Pop went out, he came home pretty early. Other nights he was very, very late. He went out so rarely, it didn't seem fair to think anything bad about it. But Diggy did wonder. He wondered what Pop had been like when he knew Diggy's mom. What it was about Pop that Diggy's mom had liked for a few nights—and maybe hated by the time she left Diggy on the doorstep.

"How'd he meet your mom?" Wayne asked.

Now the guy was spooking Diggy. It was almost like he had read Diggy's thoughts. "How should I know?"

"Well, why don't you? Where is she?"

"Not here." Which explained everything, as far as Diggy was concerned.

"But she's not—" Wayne looked out the window. "But she's still alive, so you could look for her."

No, he couldn't. Because if he looked for her, she could never *choose* to come back—he'd have decided for her that she should. Not that he ever thought about it in the first place.

"*Have* you looked for her?"

"What do you care?" Diggy had had enough of Wayne and enough of the entire conversation. "She was my mom and she left. I've got homework to do."

"She still *is* your mom—that's the whole point."

Exactly. She still was his mom, and she still was somewhere else. *That* was the whole point for Diggy, and he certainly didn't need Wayne thinking he knew anything about it.

He was wishing for anything to stop Wayne from saying whatever he was about to say next, when he heard something.

Diggy sat up straight, one ear cocked toward the kitchen door. "Did you hear that?"

"I don't care if Pop hears us talking about—"

"Shh." Diggy listened, then heard it again. A moo—no, more like a cry but brief. No, cut off—that was it. He stumbled to the kitchen window and cupped his hands to cut the reflection. He couldn't see the steers. It was too dark, and the sound had been far away.

"Is there really something, or are you just—"

"Something's wrong with the steers."

Diggy half fell out the back door, then finally got his feet organized beneath him and started running. He reached for the gate and caught barbed wire. "Crap."

Wayne got the gate open, but Diggy charged through first. Then he heard it.

Three sharp barks.

"Get!" he hollered into the dark. He ran faster, spurred

by a snarl, a thud, a short yelp. One of the steers had gotten a kick in.

Diggy could see them now, darker black forms outlined against the tree line. He ran faster than he ever had in his life and was still too far away.

The dog leapt. He got hold of a calf, near the shoulder point, under the neck.

The steer screamed. He tried to kick at the dog with his front legs but couldn't reach, and the dog wasn't coming loose.

Diggy slammed into the two of them. His momentum tore the dog away, and both tumbled across the ground. Diggy was at the dog's back, so when the animal snapped its teeth and tried to scratch itself free, it couldn't quite reach. Diggy felt the roll ending and pushed the dog away. The dog righted itself fast and turned back, barking.

"Get!" Diggy shouted, stumbling to his feet.

A rock whizzed past his ear. "Get out of here!" Wayne yelled, too. He threw another rock, advancing on the dog. "Go on!"

The dog growled, but Diggy and Wayne kept advancing, then Wayne scored with his next throw.

The dog yelped, then ran away.

The boys waited. They strained to see into the darkness.

"I don't think he's coming back," Diggy said.

Wayne punched Diggy's arm. "That was the stupidest thing I've ever seen!" he yelled. "What if he'd been rabid? He could have torn you to pieces."

Diggy knew it. His head felt funny, like it might float away from him, and he thumped to a seat on the ground.

"Did he bite you?" Wayne said, still yelling.

Diggy thought about his body. His back and legs and arms hurt from the rough roll. "I think I'm okay," he said.

The calf bawled.

"Check on him," Diggy said.

Wayne shook his head at Diggy but went to check on the steer.

Diggy stood carefully. Achy but not too bad.

"It's too dark to see," Wayne said. "His neck's sticky, though."

"Let's get them to the barn."

Diggy went to the other calf. The smell and feel of the unhurt steer was entirely familiar. Joker had been spared.

They didn't have leads, but the steers were well trained and spooked enough to be easily led—they wanted to go back to the safety of the barn.

Once there, Diggy turned on one of the clip-on lights. It was way too bright—everybody flinched, including the steers.

Diggy blinked until the brightness didn't hurt, then checked out Wayne's steer. There was blood. His hide was punctured in a perfectly shaped dog bite. "I'll go call Pop."

He ran to the house and prepared to punch numbers into the phone, then realized he didn't know the number at Ole Jib's. Diggy cursed Pop's stubbornness about cell phones. He thought for a second and dialed a number. It rang twice, and then Mr. Johnston said, "Yup."

"A dog attacked Wayne's steer."

"Diggy?"

"Yes, sir. Is July there?"

"Hang on."

Diggy noticed his hands. He checked the phone. He'd gotten blood on the numbers.

"Where's Pop?" July asked.

"Ole Jib's." He wished Pop were home, too.

"Hang up," she said. "I'll call the vet and drive over. Are you all right?"

"Yes." He hung up as instructed.

He grabbed a couple of towels and wrapped them around his hands as he went back outside. "July's coming. She's getting the vet."

Wayne looked at the towels bundling Diggy's hands. "You didn't know it wasn't your steer."

Diggy's hands hurt, and now he was ticked off. "You think I would have stood there and watched if I had known it was yours?"

Wayne kept his eyes focused on his calf. "I appreciate it, is all."

Diggy shuffled his feet. "Yeah, well. No big deal."

"Yes, it is."

"You would have done the same."

"I don't know." The steer bawled again. Wayne scratched its rump. "I was scared," he mumbled. "I didn't know what was happening."

"You found the rocks pretty fast. And in the dark."

Wayne nodded.

"You can't throw for crap," Diggy added, "but you found them okay."

Wayne squinted at him. "Yeah. I was aiming for you."

Diggy spurted a laugh through his nose. "Good one." He eyed Wayne's steer. "Now you can finally name him."

Wayne cocked an eyebrow.

"Fang. 'Cause those are like vampire marks on his neck."

Wayne considered the name. He shrugged. "Works for me."

A truck skidded into the drive. July left the door open in her rush to get out. "You're both okay?"

She wore a white parka that looked like a marshmallow and blue pajama pants dotted with winged cows and clouds. Her feet clopped in big rubber boots.

"Nice outfit," Diggy said.

She frowned at him. "So, you're fine." She looked at Wayne.

"Me, too," he said.

She examined the calf briefly, then grabbed a brush off a nail and started working Fang's hide down the back, away from his wound. "It'll help him calm down," she explained.

And, Diggy thought, help her calm down, too. Her hands

were a little shaky. She had really been afraid for them. He couldn't keep from smiling.

"What?" she said.

He blushed but still smiled. "Your braid's falling out."

Her hand went to her hair. She shrugged and went back to brushing and scratching.

They told her what had happened, the details pretty confused, with Wayne adding and Diggy correcting and back and forth until another truck pulled into the drive. Fast. Pop jumped out.

"You boys okay?" He ran to join them.

"How'd you hear?" Diggy asked.

"Mr. Johnston." He grabbed Diggy's shoulders and spun him around to look him up and down. "What happened to your hands?"

July made a sound. "Why didn't you tell me?" she exclaimed, and she rushed to his side, too.

Diggy had kind of forgotten his injuries. Or maybe he had let Joker's body block July's view of his hands. They looked stupid wrapped in kitchen towels, and he didn't want her to think he was a wimp.

Pop unwrapped the towels and carefully cupped Diggy's hands in his palms. "Son," he said softly. "That steer going to be okay for a while?" he asked July.

"I'll stay with him until the vet comes. They should both

sit down." Her eyes were wet. "I'm sorry I didn't send them into the house right away."

"You did good, girl. Thanks for coming so fast."

She nodded but didn't look convinced.

Diggy wanted to say something, but Pop got him moving toward the house. Inside, Pop ran warm water at the sink. Diggy winced pretty good when the soap and water first hit, but no way was he going to cry with July right outside. She could see him through the window if she wanted. Pop hugged Diggy's head against his chest, and Diggy let him.

While the water ran, Pop looked back at Wayne, who had taken a seat at the kitchen table. "You okay?"

Wayne nodded.

Pop waited.

"Really," Wayne said. He showed his hands and that he could move everything the way it was supposed to move.

Pop nodded. "So, what happened?"

Wayne told the story again.

Diggy didn't interrupt this time. He was too tired. Another truck came up the drive. "The vet should have gotten here before you—it's an emergency."

"He's coming from the other side of town," Pop reminded him.

Diggy turned off the water and headed for the door.

Pop stopped him. "July can handle it." He draped fresh towels over Diggy's hands and directed him to a chair. He studied them again. "A pretty deep scratch on the side here and a puncture in your palm. Doesn't look like teeth marks, though. I don't think they're bad enough for stitches."

Diggy looked, too. Most of the injuries were shallow scrapes, like you got when you fell on asphalt and caught yourself with your hands. Except for where he'd grabbed the barbed wire, the scrapes were mostly on the backs of his hands. The one deep cut was along the outside, under his pinky. The dog must have gotten a claw in after all.

"Must have been one of Kubat's," Diggy said. The dogs were wild but not mean. At least, Diggy hadn't thought they were.

"I'll call him tomorrow," Pop said. "He can pay the vet's bill."

Diggy yawned. He blinked fast to wake up again. He wanted to hear what the vet had to say.

Pop mussed Diggy's hair. "Stay awake a little longer, kid. I want to cover those hands with some gauze."

He went upstairs to get the first-aid kit.

"Go out and see how Fang's doing," Diggy said to Wayne.

"The vet will come in when he's done, won't he?"

Diggy squinted. "You don't have to stay with me."

"I know," Wayne said. And stayed anyway.

Diggy sighed.

Pop came back, applied some antiseptic, and wrapped Diggy's hands loosely with gauze.

Diggy studied his mummy hands. "How do I pee?"

"You're on your own with that one, kid." Pop grinned.

"Don't look at me," Wayne protested.

"Thanks a lot." Diggy stood. "Now, can we please go see what's happening?"

They went outside. The vet stitched three of the bigger holes in Fang's neck, probably caused when Diggy's momentum ripped the dog away. The other wounds would heal on their own, the vet said, and he gave them an ointment to apply several times a day to keep infection from setting in. After he left, Diggy finally realized what he was looking at.

"He shaved the hair!"

July winced. "It will have plenty of time to grow back."

Diggy glanced at Wayne. Back at Fang. "Will he be scarred?"

"A little." July nodded, also glancing at Wayne. She put an arm around his shoulders. "It's low on the neck, so the judge won't be as likely to notice it. We'll be really creative with the clipping, too. Your steer will show fine."

"I hadn't even thought about that," Wayne said.

Diggy believed him. But Wayne was thinking about it now, and he wasn't thinking very positive thoughts. It sucked that this had happened to Fang. But Diggy was glad that it hadn't happened to Joker. Really glad. Really, really glad.

Later, Diggy was exhausted but wide awake, and he busied his restless mind with how to say he was sorry about Fang.

The next day Diggy tricked Wayne with the mousetrap-in-an-egg-carton prank—no easy feat, considering how stiff and sore his hands were. When Wayne opened the carton to get some eggs, the plastic bottle cap loaded with flour popped out on cue, covering the front of his shirt with white powder. He jumped about a mile, then laughed and made Diggy show him how to rig the mousetrap again. They tried to get Pop to open the carton, but he knew better than to take the bait. When Wayne asked him how to do another trick, Diggy showed Wayne how to blow a hard-boiled egg out of its shell by peeling a dime-sized hole on one end and the bottom from the other. They had to blow hard to get the eggs out, and quite a few of them ended up on the floor, but, as they explained to Pop, that's what water was for. They practiced until the whole dozen was "peeled."

CRYSTAL COULDN'T GET OVER THE
FACT THAT A DOG HAD ATTACKED A COW, BUT

Jason said that it had happened to one of his Uncle Rick's calves before, too. Even a mean dog wasn't stupid enough to mess with a mama, but when the calves were being weaned, they were vulnerable.

Diggy's injuries scored him an extension on a paper and a complete pass on a take-home Spanish test. He suspected his teacher was simply using the excuse of his "brave act" to spare herself his terrible translations, but a pity pass was better than a C he had to sweat over.

When they got a dusting of snow, Diggy's mood improved again. The colder the weather, the better Joker's hair growth.

There wasn't enough powder to shovel, but Pop figured it was time to get the plow attachment hooked up to the tractor. Diggy had already broken open his scabs twice doing stuff with Joker, so Wayne had to help, since Pop said no kid of his was getting septicemia because said kid was stubborn as a goat. Diggy figured Pop just liked saying "septicemia," because who the heck knew what that was? Of course, it turned out that Wayne did—one of his aunts was a nurse. When Wayne and Pop got the giggles at Diggy's expense, pondering what would happen if he got blood poisoning from dog germs or cow germs and maybe turned into a zombie, Diggy figured now was as good a time as any to take a crack at that paper he'd put off—and maybe set up the juice-carton prank for Wayne.

He cracked another scab putting the water balloon into the juice carton he'd cut the bottom out of, but he decided it was worth it when he heard the tractor start up and saw Pop teaching Wayne how to drive it.

Diggy loved driving that tractor. The story about his mom didn't bother him when he was the one driving. It was *driving*. And he was an absolute master of the clutch.

Wayne bounced around out there and laughed so hard, Diggy could hear him over the motor and from inside the house.

It set Diggy's teeth on edge.

Pop shouldn't encourage the guy like that. Driving was something dads taught their sons, and Wayne was already getting too cozy with Pop. It wasn't right.

Wayne's dad had been in AA for almost a whole month now, and he made a point of calling a couple of times a week. He had even driven out as soon as he heard about the dog attack, to make sure Wayne was okay. The man was trying.

Wayne should have been thinking about moving back home. Instead, he was out there joyriding with Pop.

The fool was still laughing when he came inside, went for orange juice, and had a water bomb land on his feet. "I saw this on YouTube!" Wayne said. "That Russian guy is so funny."

Diggy went to his room to finish his paper.

⁕

Thanksgiving Day, Pop started cooking by setting up a wind barrier for the turkey fryer. The rest of the meal would consist of frozen corn, boxed stuffing, carrots microwaved soft, rolls from those cans that popped when you twisted them, and a pumpkin pie from the store. None of that took any time. Heck, even Diggy helped cook that stuff. The turkey was the reason for the season and made Diggy proud to be an American. Americans could figure out how to deep-fat fry *anything*.

When Pop asked Wayne if he wanted to invite his dad to dinner, Diggy was relieved and not. He wanted Wayne to remember he was going home someday soon, but he wasn't sure he wanted Graf around all day, either.

Pop didn't pressure Wayne about it. But then he got another call from the Vogls—the third one this week—trying one last time to convince Wayne to go to their house for the holiday. This time Wayne told them he couldn't because his dad was coming to dinner.

Graf was over earlier than he needed to be, his hair still wet from a shower and his cheeks so raw from a shave they glowed. He tried too hard at first, but soon Pop got him standing at the turkey fryer, watching the oil temperature and injecting marinade. Having something to do helped him relax.

Same went for Wayne. The calves weren't used to so much

outdoor activity that didn't include them, and they kept wandering over to see what was what. The boys could have tied
the steers or closed them in the barn, but it was more fun to
let them stroll about in the leavings of a barely there snow
and chase them away when they got to where they shouldn't
be. Diggy didn't exactly worry about Kubat's dogs anymore—
Kubat had promised to keep them tied up or in the barn if
he wasn't outside with them—but he also didn't let the steers
wander too close to the woods, either.

After a while, the day settled into a weird kind of normal.
They got the big table cleared off and the food heated up. Pop
twisted off the turkey legs and gave them to Wayne and Diggy,
then cut big chunks out of the bird's sides for himself and Graf.

Diggy and Wayne told the story of the dog attack again, a
much-improved version with greater heroics and more laughs.
The cuts hardly bothered Diggy at all anymore except when
he tried to do things like use his fork, and he was not particularly coordinated with the other hand.

"He's probably got rabies," Wayne explained.

"Har, har." Diggy ate his food with his fingers. Until he
squished some stuffing into a ball. Pop gave him the eye, and
he grudgingly picked up his fork again.

It never took as long to eat dinner as it did to put it together,
but no one rushed away from the table. Everyone was stuffed,
but that didn't stop anyone from picking at the offerings until
all the dishes were about empty and the bird nearly skeletal.

"Did we eat a whole turkey?" Wayne asked.

"It wasn't that big," Diggy said.

"It can't be too big and still fit in the fryer," Pop added.

"Still," Wayne said.

Pop chuckled. "Guess that means it's time to get the pie warming in the oven."

He went into the kitchen, and the weird normalcy wavered. Graf cleared his throat. "Thanks for inviting me."

Wayne nodded, but he didn't really look at his dad.

"I got my thirty-day coin this week. From AA."

"That's good," Wayne said.

Pop got the pie into the oven, then hung back in the doorway. Diggy wished he could hang back, too, but was stuck at the table. Graf was just so . . . sincere. It was painful to see.

"I realized . . ." He cleared his throat again. "I wasn't sure you had anything from your mom here."

Wayne was surprised enough to look at his dad this time. He shook his head.

"I've been going through some stuff." Graf caught himself and explained quickly, "Not getting rid of anything."

Wayne nodded, clearly not sure what he was supposed to say or do.

Graf pulled a photo out of his shirt pocket. He looked at it and had to breathe deeply. Then he set it on the table and slid it toward Wayne. "This is one of my favorites."

It was a photo like they took at Sears, but instead of being all posed, Mrs. Graf had her arm hugged around Wayne's neck, the both of them smiling cross-eyed at the camera.

Wayne looked at it, then abruptly cracked. He started crying and doing that funny-breathing thing, stubbing his chair on the floor, trying too fast and too hard to get away from the table, until finally he stumbled from the room and up the stairs.

Graf and Diggy stared at each other, wide-eyed. Graf pushed his chair back, too, but Pop stopped him with a hand to his shoulder. "He needs to let it out."

Graf looked like he might argue the point, but only a few seconds passed before he pulled his chair back to the table. He rested his forehead against his clasped hands.

"You're doing good, Harold," Pop said.

"The day I need you, of all people, to tell me that . . ." There should have been more to the sentence, but Graf added instead, "Jeez, I want a drink."

Pop said the oil in the turkey fryer should have cooled down enough by now to be emptied, and he asked Graf to help maneuver the pot so they could clean up.

Diggy stacked dishes but was soon distracted by the photo.

Mrs. Graf looked so healthy and Wayne so young, though the picture was probably only two years old. They looked like family. It was more than the similar coloring in the light hair and eyes. The funny faces and tilt of their heads and just the way they looked at the camera proclaimed, *Family!*

Diggy and Pop rarely remembered a camera for anything

other than the show ring. Diggy had more pics of his steers then he did of himself and Pop. He couldn't help but wonder if that might be different if his mom were around.

The photo glared up from the table, colors bold, faces bright.

It was a perfect example of why Diggy didn't let himself think about his mom anymore. Even if he found her, he would never, ever have with her what shone between Wayne and his mom.

When he heard a car engine, Diggy almost wasn't surprised Graf was leaving without saying good-bye, when there was a photo like that and everything it meant in the house. He finished stacking dishes, but then from outside he heard raised voices and went to the window. Graf hadn't left. Wayne's grandparents, Mrs. Osborn, and a few kids had arrived instead, and Graf was not happy about it.

Diggy called upstairs, "Wayne, you might want to get down here," then went outside to help Pop.

"You can't keep us from our grandson," Mrs. Vogl was saying to Graf.

"Why not? You'd have kept him from me if you got your hands on him," Graf said.

Pop tried to calm things down by explaining, for what sounded like the second or third time, that Wayne wasn't feeling well. Mrs. Osborn tried to calm her mom down, too, but one of the kids was little and maybe scared and kept trying to get her to pick him up. Wayne's other two cousins pretended they didn't hear anything and weren't even there.

When Wayne came outside, Mrs. Vogl's eyes got round just before her face went red. "He's been crying!" she exclaimed. "What did you do to make him cry?" she accused Graf.

"It's not that, Grandma," Wayne tried to explain, but Mrs. Vogl had her sights set on Graf. Not that he was taking any of it.

"Maybe he's sad because it's Thanksgiving and his mom's gone," Graf said. "You ever think of that, huh, before you start accusing me?"

"Don't you talk to me like that. My daughter is gone, and you did nothing to deserve her."

"Mom, we aren't helping anything by—" Mrs. Osborn tried.

"Anything we do will help. Ann's *liebchen* with strangers on the first holiday since she's dead." Mrs. Vogl's English had gotten so thick with her German accent, it took Diggy a second to figure out what she'd said.

"He's with *me*," Graf argued.

"*Puh.*"

"Why don't we all go inside?" Pop offered. "There's pie in the oven. We can take a breath and—"

"You!" Mrs. Vogl shouted. "You don't speak! My daughter was a good girl, then you come along."

"Stop!" Wayne yelled. "Just, everyone. Stop. Please."

"I'm sorry, Wayne," Mrs. Osborn said while Mrs. Vogl sputtered in German. "I thought if I came, too, it would keep her from getting so upset." She picked up the little one, though it seemed as much for herself as the child. "It's hard, you know. Thanksgiving."

"I know." Wayne sighed.

Mrs. Vogl had started to cry, and Mr. Vogl led her to the minivan. Wayne ran over to hug them and tell them he loved them, but he didn't let his grandma keep ahold of him too long. After saying some stuff to his cousins, he hugged Mrs. Osborn and waved everyone good-bye.

They were pretty well down the road before Graf said to Wayne, "Stuck up for Lawson, didn't you, when she went after him? Didn't see you saying anything when she was at me."

"Dad—"

"No. Hey, I'm carrying around this chip like it means something," Graf said, pulling out the red coin from Alcoholics Anonymous.

Wayne didn't say anything.

Pop was the one who said, "It does mean something, Harold."

Graf stared at Wayne. "I see how it is. You've got a new life where you don't have to think about me or your mom."

"Harold—"

"Back off, Lawson."

"It's not like that," Wayne said.

"Yeah? I don't see you packing your bags. You going to pack your bags, Wayne?"

Graf didn't leave much room for Wayne to reply, but he didn't need to—Wayne's only movement was to hunch his head down in that way he had, like he could plug his ears with his shoulders.

"You want to stay here? Fine! Maybe it's what Ann would have wanted. It's not like anyone thinks I make a good dad anyway." He stomped off to his truck.

Diggy waited for Pop to do something, but all Pop did was run a hand down his face. "He needs to cool down. But I should see if he's got a sponsor in AA yet." Pop held Wayne's shoulder. "You going to be okay?"

Wayne shrugged.

"Setbacks are a normal part of recovery, and Ann's mom isn't helping. He didn't mean what he said."

"That makes it worse, doesn't it?" Wayne said.

Diggy had to agree with him. Pop's making excuses for Graf was not okay, especially when Pop was wrong. Diggy was pretty sure Graf had meant exactly what he said, because it was pretty much stuff Diggy had thought, too.

NO ONE WAS SURPRISED TO HEAR

THAT GRAF SHOWED UP AT OTTO'S BAR THAT

night, already drunk, and broke a window when he found the place closed for Thanksgiving.

The police had to pick up Graf, and Pop had to do some fast talking to keep Otto from pressing charges this time—he was losing patience for the "grieving husband" and banned Graf from returning to his bar. Which was kind of the point of the whole Alcoholics Anonymous thing anyway.

Diggy wasn't sure why Pop bothered. Graf was doing just about everything he could to screw up his life and make sure he never got Wayne back. Wayne hardly seemed to care.

He went through the same routine Diggy did every day, minus the friends. Wayne used to hang out with a couple of guys who were always on honor roll like him, but lately he seemed to have dropped them. He spent his lunches in the library and went straight to the buses after school.

To make things worse, Crystal and Jason were being weird. Crystal was, anyway. She came back from Thanksgiving dressing more like a girl and acting as if everything Diggy said was so funny and smart, especially when Jason was around. Diggy had kind of always thought she liked Jason, so the way she acted made him feel bad, like he was stealing his best friend's girlfriend, even though he wasn't.

Diggy had way too much to do to deal with her weirdness. Pre-Christmas at school was always a ton of presentations and papers due and getting ready for finals. Not to mention all the usual 4-H community-service stuff, caroling at nursing homes, and the family potluck. So when Crystal cornered him after school and asked him on a date, he didn't have the patience to be nice.

"What is going on with you?"

"Gee, thanks, Diggy," Crystal said. "A girl asks you out, and you yell at her?"

"You're not a girl. I mean, a girl who'd ask me out. You don't even like me."

"Of course I do! We've been friends since fourth grade."

"You know what I mean." Sheesh. It was bad enough he had to talk to her like this at all—she didn't have to pretend she didn't know what he meant.

She twisted the end of her ponytail, which she had *curled*, and she had some kind of shimmery, powdery stuff on her eyelids. Finally she huffed out a breath. "Darla asked Jason to a winter-dance thing at her church."

"I thought you said Darla liked me."

Crystal rolled her eyes. "That was months ago, and it's not like you did anything about it."

Because he'd found out about it at the same time Wayne

arrived. The guy had lived with them for months now.

Crystal twisted her ponytail tighter. "Anyway, Jason said yes."

"Of course he did. He wouldn't want to hurt her feelings." Diggy had spent plenty of time with Jason around his sheep. The animals fell all over themselves to get close to him, and when he sheared them, they never struggled—they practically fell asleep in his arms. Jason was like the sheep whisperer or something. But part of it was that he was so nice. Animals *and* people tended to be calmer when he was around.

"So what do I do?" Crystal asked.

"You don't go out with me, that's for sure."

She glared at him.

"I don't know! Just ask him out. He'll say yes."

"I don't want him to say yes to be nice! I want him to say yes because he likes me!"

"Everyone likes being picked!" Diggy couldn't believe he was stuck in the middle of this stuff and wished for maybe the first time ever that he had gone with Wayne to the library instead of trying to hang out with his friends for a few minutes before getting on the bus. Where the heck was Jason anyway?

Plus, now Crystal was looking at him funny. "Are you okay, Diggy? I mean, I didn't think you'd get so upset."

"Me? You're the one being all girl and stuff."

"If you ever want to talk about things with Wayne and—" Her eyes got big, and her cheeks reddened. "Uh, hi, Wayne."

Wayne grabbed Diggy's arm. "Come with me."

"We're already late for the bus."

"We'll take the activities bus."

"No way. That thing stops everywhere." It would take for-ever to get home, and they had Joker and Fang to think about.

"This is important," Wayne said.

"Maybe he doesn't want to, Wayne," Crystal said.

Diggy appreciated how she always tried to stand up for him, but he kind of wanted to get away from her. So when Wayne said they needed to go to the library, Diggy waved at Crystal and followed his accidental rescuer. Girls were crazy.

Sure, he had kind of known she liked Jason, but things were different now. Now she cared if Jason liked her back. Dressing like a girl, acting like a girl . . . that was only the beginning. What if she and Jason did start to go out? They'd be a couple, and he'd be—what? The guy they had to get rid of so they could be alone? He didn't want to be that guy, but he didn't want to lose his friends, either.

Why didn't she like *him*, anyway? He might not like her like that—his heart was July's—but still. Crystal could have liked him a little bit. Why did she choose Jason instead of him?

With his head swirling, Diggy barely heard Wayne's mumbling about how he'd been looking through old school newspapers and wished he hadn't lied to Mrs. Schafer, the librarian, about it being for a school project, because she fig-ured out what he was really doing, and he never would have found them without her and had wasted all that time looking in the wrong place.

He led Diggy to a back corner, then held out a book, holding it as if it was of the thinnest glass.

It was a yearbook. An old one, even though it looked brand-new.

The way Wayne was acting, Diggy was almost afraid to take it. He sat at the table and flipped through the pages. He wanted to laugh at the horrible hairstyles, but Wayne's behavior kept him quiet. It was hard, though. The clothes were so funny.

Diggy froze.

He looked up at Wayne.

Wayne pushed four more yearbooks closer. "The library has copies of every year."

Diggy stared at the dates marked in large block numbers on the spines.

He sorted through the freshmen *D*s, then stopped at the sophomores. There she was. Sarah Douglas. His mom.

She was blond with light eyes. Though it was a color photo, it was hard to tell if they were blue or green. She was pretty, straight white teeth showing through a carefully constructed smile. She wore her hair simply, in long curls down her back, and had on a plain white blouse. The other students were dated by hairstyle and dress, but she stood out, looking as normal now as anyone else Diggy knew.

He went back to the very beginning and methodically

turned every page, studying the candid shots, until he found her again, at the top of a pyramid. She was a cheerleader. The smallest on the squad, standing tall on the other girls' shoulders, her arms in a V over her head. Diggy laughed faintly. He'd gotten his size from her. He'd been around steers long enough to know about genetics and breeding—his hopes of a big growth spurt faded.

He scanned more pages and found a shot of her in the cafeteria with some girlfriends. Each dangled a French fry from her lips and crowded together to smile for the camera.

He thumbed pages again, and then he saw Mrs. Graf. She held a trophy, surrounded by other members of the volleyball team. She was sweaty, like all the girls, and her ponytail was half undone. She looked so *alive*.

Diggy breathed deeply.

Wayne had picked up a yearbook and stared down at a page. "This was the way Pop knew our moms. This was them before us."

Diggy found Pop in the junior *L*s, looking much like he still did; then he found his mom again. Flipping back and forth, back and forth, he almost made himself dizzy trying to imagine them together, even only for long enough to make him.

He settled on a photo of his mom in the yearbook office, walls filled with pictures of her friends, as she studiously sorted even more photos spread out across a table. She seemed like she had a plan. Like she was looking for something in particular. Like she knew what she wanted and would find it at any moment.

Diggy studied the books stacked between him and Wayne. Wayne had found her other years. "I bet Pop has copies at home," Diggy said.

"I hope so," Wayne replied. "Mrs. Schafer will know it's me if these go missing."

Diggy flipped some more, thinking suddenly of Gs. When he found Graf, it was like there had been some mistake. Graf was a scrawny teen and looked a little afraid, like the photographer had caught him off guard, even though it was one of those posed school portraits.

They had all known one another—Pop, Diggy's mom, Mrs. Graf, and Wayne's dad. They had all been in the same school when they were young, and who knew what they had been like then? The photos were like pictures taken of other people from another town, from another life. But they weren't. They were photos of people he knew.

But they weren't.

As well as he knew Pop, Diggy didn't know *this* Pop, the one in the pictures.

"We can find her," Wayne said.

"What?"

Wayne flipped slowly between two pages. On one, Mrs. Graf kicked leaves at the camera. On the other, Diggy's cheerleading mom did a high kick.

"We can find her," Wayne repeated. "Your mom."

Diggy blinked at him.

Then he pushed all the books to the floor.

"What's wrong with you?" Wayne protested. "You'll mess them up!"

"You all right over there?" Mrs. Schafer called from her desk.

"You will not look for my mom," Diggy said.

"*We* will," Wayne said. "Just think. If she came back—"

"She hasn't come back!" Diggy hissed. "I am exactly—literally, *exactly*—where she left me. Have been for thirteen years."

"But she doesn't know how much we—"

"Hey, what's going on?" They heard the librarian coming closer.

"How much we what?" Diggy whispered. "There's no *we*."

Diggy picked up the books and was shoving them at the empty space on the shelf when Mrs. Schafer arrived. "You two okay?"

Diggy could barely nod. He was sure he looked the way he felt, that he could blow any second.

Wayne sat at the table, a lump, not even staring at the wall, just . . . staring.

"If either of you would like to talk," Mrs. Schafer said quietly, "I knew your moms. Ann, of course, but, Diggy, I had some classes with your mom, too."

Diggy couldn't stand it. "I've got to get the activities bus."

He ran out of there like a wolf was on his tail.

The bus wasn't anywhere near arriving, but Diggy opted to wait outside. The weather suited his mood. The wind had kicked up. Clouds buzzed across the sun, casting fast-moving stretches of shadow that could pass for swarms of locusts. Every now and then a sudden blaze of light broke through as if making a desperate last grab at fall. Winter had poked around for a while but now was tearing its way in.

The steers would be spooked, and Diggy wouldn't be there for them for another hour plus. He told himself it was good for them—the weather was nothing compared to the show ring. The entire fair was *loud*. The constant noise in the cattle barn, the herds of people walking through all day, the bustle of two hundred competitors prepping as many animals—blowers, clippers, and sprays in perpetual use. And that was before they got to the show ring. The coliseum was like an echo chamber, with every sound magnified to nearly unintelligible. Calves not trained to be used to the distractions tended to rodeo. Heck, even calves with experienced exhibitors sometimes rodeoed. *Loud* had a different meaning in the coliseum.

He could use that loudness now.

Diggy was ticked and got more ticked the more he thought of Wayne and those stupid yearbooks.

He should have known. Wayne had asked Diggy about his mom that time. And after Graf brought over that picture of Wayne and his mom, Wayne had been weirder than usual. Still.

What made the kid think it was okay to get in the middle of Diggy's life? Was Wayne so crazy he really believed they could find Diggy's mom and be together like some picture-perfect family? If that was even a little bit possible, Pop would have made it happen years ago. But he hadn't, and it wasn't. You don't ask a woman who left you on a doorstep and drove off on a tractor to be your mom.

When the bus finally arrived, Diggy sat as far from Wayne as possible and counted the minutes until he could be with Joker again. The steer always calmed him down, and Diggy needed all the help he could get today.

Wayne let Diggy go to the barn on his own, for which Diggy was grateful—for about five seconds, until he realized the guy was probably searching the house for Pop's old yearbooks.

Joker and Fang bawled at him as soon as he walked in the door. "I know, I know. It's freaky out there." The moon was already out and bright, so all that flashing light from the clouds passing over so fast was even creepier than in the daytime.

Diggy scratched the steers' rumps in greeting and brushed them while telling them about his bad day. Joker listened for a while, then pooped, which Diggy took as agreement that his day had, in fact, been crappy. The steer kept looking at the barn door to make sure the wind and crazy light stayed outside where it belonged, but he was otherwise stoic.

Fang, however, crowded Diggy so much that, at one point,

he pinched Diggy between the two steers. Diggy had to thump him hard to get him to back off.

Tied up, he bawled so much, Diggy left Joker to tend to Fang. "You can't be a baby in the ring, buddy." Diggy combed and coached, "You're still little, so it's okay, but you're going to have to toughen up."

Like he was one to talk. A few yearbooks, and look what happened. A part of him was mad that Wayne was going to get his hands on Pop's yearbooks. They should be Diggy's. He should have thought of them first. Pop should have offered them first. Diggy had barely anything from his mom, just those three things in that box he used to hide in the tree, a box he didn't even know where to find anymore. Had Pop never thought that Diggy would be curious? Or had Diggy been so good at not being curious?

To distract himself, he measured Fang's hip height. The calf *was* little, probably a good twenty-five pounds behind Joker. Not the end of the world, but Wayne would have to work to get the calf's weight up a bit. Joker was right on schedule to hit eight hundred pounds by April.

Diggy finally had both calves pretty well settled when Wayne slammed in. "I found them."

DURING THE WEEK LEADING UP TO

CHRISTMAS BREAK, DIGGY SPENT ALL THE
time he could stand in the freezing barn. It helped distract
him from the yearbooks. He didn't want them; Wayne could
do whatever he wanted.

Diggy stepped up Joker's setup training, using the show
stick to press just above the front of the hooves and move the
foot back or to pull on the dewclaw and move the foot forward. In the show ring, when the steers lined up side by side,
Joker's feet would be set at all four corners under him, bearing
his weight evenly. At that view, the judge looked at the front
and rear. For the side view, when the cattle lined up head to
tail, the feet were set staggered to give the judge a sense of
depth and thickness. Diggy also used the stick to correct the
topline, sometimes putting pressure on the navel or flank to
raise the top and other times pressing on the rump or loin to
bring it down.

Proper setups were only a few of the thousand things he'd
have to do and remember on show day. He had to know which
hand to use to hold the halter, where to hold the halter, when
to switch hands, when to use the show stick, when to use the
Scotch comb, which way to put the comb in his pocket so he

wouldn't injure anyone with it. Diggy had done it all before, but this year was different. He planned to win.

Each day, Joker put up with Diggy's instruction a lot longer than any of his other steers had. But when Joker was done, he was done. He turned his back on Diggy and kept turning when Diggy tried to get back to the calf's head. When Diggy finally put the show stick away, Joker permitted himself to be washed, blown out, and brushed.

There was more homework than ever. Final exams were both boring and horrible. Home was quiet—a loud quiet.

By winter break, Diggy was ready for a break. His first morning of freedom, he wanted to sleep in but woke well before dawn. It was like he hadn't had time to think before, and now all the thoughts that had been lurking scuttled back and forth between his ears.

He tried to go back to sleep and tossed and turned for what felt like an hour, though the clock showed only two minutes had passed. He grabbed his steer-tending bundle of clothes and tiptoed downstairs.

At the back door, he pulled on the fleece-lined flannel shirt, sweatshirt, and down-filled coat. He held his breath and stepped outside.

If it was possible to step into a block of ice, it would feel like this. The cold was a shock that temporarily froze him in place. He concentrated on his breaths. His body made the adjustment from warm house to frozen outside.

A picture popped into his head, that photo of Wayne and his mom. Ever since Thanksgiving, out of nowhere, he'd see their faces again. Then his brain tricked him, replacing Wayne's face with his. Why did Wayne want to find Diggy's mom when he had had one of the best moms in town?

Joker mooed. Diggy pretended it was the steer asking, "You coming or what?"

Diggy went through the routine of feeding and walking and brushing Joker. He worked without turning on any lights, relying instead on the glow from the tall safety light across the yard. His muscles loosened despite the cold. He attempted to form rings out of the clouds of his breath. Joker watched and chewed cud. Diggy laughed. Joker could always be counted on to play the straight man.

Except that he couldn't. Joker would be sold. For steak.

Diggy was startled every time he remembered where Joker would end up. Though he had gone through it before, that walk to the packer's truck was hard every time. It was simply self-preservation to go for days without really thinking about the steer's ultimate role.

Diggy watched the ghostly swirls of his breath.

It was barely dawn when Pop found him in the barn.

Pop greeted Joker first, giving his rump a good scratch. "You're up early."

Diggy was so used to talking to Joker himself, it took him a moment to realize that Pop wasn't addressing the steer.

Diggy shrugged.

Pop waited.

The dawn light, shaded orange, added enough color to Pop's hair that it should have looked silly. It didn't. As far back as Diggy could remember, Pop had looked as he did now: orange hair, square jaw, tall, strong, face scuffed by weather. One day he would be old. It was as impossible to imagine as Pop at thirteen, like him.

His head fizzed. If he were alone, he would have put his head between his knees. But Pop had already walked to Diggy's side.

He held the back of his hand to Diggy's forehead. "You feeling okay?"

Diggy pulled away. Feeling foreheads was the kind of thing moms did, but Pop had been stuck doing it all this time.

Because Diggy's mom had never come back.

And Wayne wanted to find her.

"I wanted to talk to you about something," Pop said.

Diggy's heartbeat jumped about ten seconds ahead of itself.

"We may not have done much the last few Christmases, but we've marked it in our way. I thought we should ask Wayne what he'd be comfortable with this first year without his mom, but I don't want to be unfair to you."

Diggy hoped his face was blank, because he could feel Pop watching him. Give up Christmas? Was that what Pop was asking?

When Diggy was little, Pop had put up a tree each year and stocked it with presents from Santa. The tenth Christmas, Diggy had changed things. At the tree lot, he saw all those cut trees lined up, the green so dark and strong it was nearly black. Their scent was as sharp as the winter air itself. He thought of where they had come from, and it was a postcard of perfectly formed pines poking up from a white hillside. Then it was like a gray slurry washed over the image, and he was left with piles of dry brown trees no one had bought, needles pooled underneath in wasted protest.

Though Pop had suggested a fake tree, Diggy wasn't interested anymore. Instead, he and Pop had driven into the city Christmas morning, found an open restaurant for lunch, and went to a matinee. There were still a few presents to exchange, but mostly they tried to make each other laugh with them. Diggy's longtime favorite was the T-shirt that read *I support recycling. I wore this yesterday.*

"I thought we might take flowers to her grave," Pop said.

Grave was one of those words that blacked out everything around it.

"And we've got to figure out what to do about Harold," Pop said. He hugged an arm around Diggy. "We'll still do Christmas."

It was weird how Pop could make Diggy feel bad but then make him feel better at the same time, just by being there and trying to think ahead about stuff like this.

Then Diggy pulled away. Pop was trying to think ahead about stuff like this for *Wayne*. Meanwhile, Wayne had those yearbooks with pictures of *Diggy's* mom. Yearbooks that had been in the house Diggy's entire life.

Pop squinted at him. "We *can* talk."

Wayne stamped into the barn. "I swear it gets colder out here than it does in town." He rubbed his gloved hands over his cheeks, then flapped his arms around.

"You'll spook the steers," Diggy grunted.

Pop turned from Diggy and let his attention focus on Wayne.

Wayne frowned, suspicious. "What were you talking about?"

"Christmas," Pop replied.

Wayne grabbed a brush and started working it through Fang's hair. The calf shuffled his feet and snorted.

Pop soothed the animal, though Wayne continued to brush too forcefully.

"How do you feel about calling your dad?"

Wayne froze, though Diggy wondered if it was the prospect of calling Graf or because he had gotten used to thinking of Pop as his dad. "He hasn't called much lately."

"I think he's embarrassed," Pop said. "But he told me he's been working the steps and will have a new thirty-day chip from AA soon."

Wayne slanted a glance at Diggy, but Diggy didn't have

any energy for him. His brain had gotten hung up on Mrs. Graf's grave, her under there in the frozen ground. It had been four months since she died. How could that seem so short and so long at the same time?

Pop sighed. "Your grandparents have been calling."

"They have?"

"I wanted you to have time to think about what you want to do before you speak with them."

"We used to go there on Christmas Eve." Wayne brushed in short, quick strokes. "I don't think they'll let Dad come without Mom."

"Is there something you did with your mom and dad that we can do together?" Pop asked.

Wayne was bent too close to the steer, like he was trying to see every hair he worked over. He hadn't pulled his hat on straight. Part of it was folded under in back, and sleep-twisted blond hair poked out, looking like the end of a calf's tail.

"Me and Mom went to church," Wayne said. "Really late on Christmas Eve. We liked all the candles." His voice barely covered the sound of the brush whisking across the calf's back. "Then we'd go out by the old bridge and search for Santa."

Wayne darted a glance at Diggy, but Diggy remained silent. His body popped all over with goose bumps.

"Dad stayed home, said we were crazy, but I knew it was to put out the presents from Santa so he could joke how we'd just missed him. Mom had blankets and hot chocolate. We sat on the hood and watched the sky until we got too cold."

If Diggy had been asked to guess how Mrs. Graf cele-brated Christmas, he would not have guessed what Wayne had described. But now that he knew, it seemed obvious. It was exactly the kind of thing Mrs. Graf would have done. She was the only teacher from elementary school Diggy remembered in any real detail.

Diggy knew what it felt like when he thought about his own mom. He multiplied that by ten and pictured a combine not only cutting and stripping corn but also chopping the tough stalks into inch-long pieces, leaving nothing behind but a vast stretch of crusty, jagged, sand-colored trash. It was vio-lent and painful, and if Wayne felt like that every day, Diggy didn't know how he could stand it.

Maybe Wayne couldn't. He stood over his calf, brush on his back, not moving, not seeming to breathe. Diggy remem-bered a TV doctor talking about a disease that made people vibrate so intensely, they seemed frozen in place. Wayne was like that now, vibrating to a standstill.

Pop put a hand on Wayne's shoulder, and the shaking became more visible. Wayne swiped a forearm across his face and resumed brushing.

Diggy grabbed a handful of hay and let Fang lip it off his palm. He didn't like it, but maybe all Wayne's talk about find-ing Diggy's mom was Wayne's way of easing his own pain. Which Diggy was still not okay with, but . . .

"I don't know about the church stuff," Diggy said, "but the bridge sounds good." It sounded more than good. It sounded so Mom-like and so Mrs. Graf–like that Diggy suddenly looked forward to sitting out in the cold searching the skies for a nonexistent fat man. He thumped Wayne's shoulder.

Wayne flinched. Words tumbled around in his mouth. "I don't think I want to this year."

Pop patted his shoulder and released him. "That's okay, son. Let us know."

Pop left. Diggy unhooked Joker's brush again and set to work on the steer's hair. Joker didn't seem to appreciate the extra attention, but that didn't slow down Diggy.

He hated it when Pop called Wayne "son." He didn't say it a lot, and most of the time Diggy convinced himself that when Pop *did* say it, it was in a general way, like he used it with the bagger boy at the grocery store. Still, Diggy didn't like it.

It was enough that Wayne lived with them. He had his own room, he got an allowance from Pop, he had his steer. Wayne should be grateful, not stingy about sharing Christmas.

How different would a Mom-Christmas be? Pop always did something to make the day special, and he listened to how Diggy wanted to spend the holiday. Diggy had nothing to complain about, but a Mom-Christmas, even if they did the same thing Pop and Diggy always did, would be different. Moms probably noticed different things and thought in different ways. Wayne knew something about that; he had already had thirteen Mom-Christmases. Diggy hadn't had a single one. He'd had grandparent-Christmases but no mom, and he was pretty sure there was a difference.

"Maybe you should go to your dad's for Christmas," Diggy said. If the kid didn't want to share his Mom-Christmas, Diggy didn't have to share his.

Wayne sighed. "I was thinking that."

"You were?" Diggy hadn't even really thought it yet.

"I haven't been back since Dad . . ." Wayne trailed off. "All her things."

He sniffed, and Diggy pretended it was the cold making the kid's nose drip.

Wayne hadn't been back to his *house*. Diggy hadn't really thought about it that way, but all Wayne's stuff, all his mom's stuff, the house he'd lived in with her his entire life—one day he was there, and the next, he wasn't. The guy had to feel like he was in a parallel universe sometimes.

"But after what happened at Thanksgiving, I'm kind of afraid to." Wayne whispered the last part. Then he added even more quietly, "And I'm afraid to go and have her not be there."

Diggy hated that that was exactly what would happen. Wayne would go home, and his mom would not be there.

The boys fussed over the calves. Joker and Fang snuggled into the boys' sides, as close to a hug as a steer could get. Steers were so smart. People liked to think they had the lock on emotions and understanding, but Diggy's calves usually worked with his mood. When he was mad, they were pissy. When he was sad, they were calm and affectionate. His steers were more like pets than some people's dogs. He could hardly stand to think about the end of next summer.

Or Mrs. Graf. It hit him all over again that she wasn't out there in the world somewhere, waiting for him to bump into her at the grocery store so she could tell him to put back the candy bars and get some fruit already.

"There's an old telescope in the attic," Diggy announced. "We would have a pretty clear view from your window to watch for reindeer."

Wayne's Adam's apple bobbed.

Diggy looked away. He squinted back again. "You know there's no Santa, right?"

Wayne thumped Diggy's arm. Diggy thumped him back.

CHRISTMAS WENT OFF PRETTY WELL.

AFTER SOME COACHING FROM POP, WAYNE DID

go to the Vogls for Christmas Eve and seemed really glad to have seen all his cousins. Diggy wasn't even jealous of all the loot he brought home—most of it was clothes anyway.

Graf came out on Christmas Day, and they all rode into the city for dinner and a movie. Graf seemed so grateful to be included, it made Diggy uncomfortable and kind of sad. He hadn't really thought about what it was like for Graf being alone in his house all the time, even if it was of his own doing. But after Wayne had said that about not having been home in so long, Diggy kept picturing the house waiting for Mrs. Graf to come back, sort of puffed up from holding its breath. It was crazy thinking, but he couldn't help it.

The rest of Christmas break, Diggy kept Joker outside as much as possible so his hair would get nice and thick. The snow acted like a megaphone—every time Kubat's dogs barked at something, the steers heard it—but Joker and even Fang seemed to have gotten over the biting incident, which was very encouraging. If they were still skittish about dogs, they'd be terrified when they got to the fair.

Diggy went to Jason's to snowmobile a couple of times—

Crystal went to Florida every year for Christmas to visit grand-parents—but snow and ice kept most people home when they could help it. So Diggy got a lot of work done on his level-three rocket design. He hadn't decided if he was going to enter it into the 4-H contest at the fair or not. Like everyone else, he usually entered a couple of non-livestock things, but this year he felt he should stay focused on winning Grand Champion. When Pop came up to help with the rocket, Diggy had confessed to the level-three design. Pop took it okay, partly because Diggy didn't mention the design was for D- and E-class engines. He wanted Pop to see that he knew what he was doing first. Wayne got interested in the rockets, too, so Diggy showed him some stuff.

And set up the air-horn prank. When Wayne sat on Dig-gy's desk chair, sounding the air horn Diggy had rigged, Diggy fell out of his own chair from laughing so hard. Pop rushed in like a fire alarm had gone off. Diggy wasn't really surprised later when he and Wayne tried to twist open some soda bot-tles and got squirted with the old pinholes-in-the-side-of-the-plastic trick. He *was* surprised when he tried to squirt some ketchup onto his burger and it oozed out of the sides instead, where Pop had sliced the bottle's neck after gluing closed the hole in the top. Pop must have really had a heart attack when that air horn went off, for him to double down on his return prank like that.

All in all, Diggy was feeling pretty good by the time school started again. Until he saw Crystal wearing a *dress*. He avoided her in the hallways, even though it meant getting to classes early. But at lunch she sat down before she got any food and huffed, "It's only a dress, Diggy. Jeez."

"It's *why* you're wearing it that I don't want to have to talk about. You have girl friends." Not to mention, it was kind of creepy that she knew him so well, she'd guessed why he had dodged her all morning.

"Who says I want to talk to you?"

"Great."

"Though you could use the practice if you want to date a girl someday."

Diggy thunked his head on the table.

"See?" Crystal said, like he had proved her point and ignoring the fact that *she* had proved *his*. "It was something you said, anyway, that made me—"

"Don't blame me!"

"—realize Jason doesn't think of me as a girl, and I need to make changes if I want to fix that."

Why hadn't Diggy gone to the library for lunch? Or outside? Sure, it was twenty degrees with wind chill, but he had a coat. "He doesn't even like Darla that much."

"He told you that?" she asked hopefully.

"No." Jeez. "Boys don't talk like girls."

She rolled her eyes. "Just tell me why you think he doesn't like Darla that way."

Because Jason didn't get stupid around Darla the way Diggy did around July, but Diggy would roll around in a giant pile of cow poop before he told Crystal that. "Just tell him you want to go out, and he'll go."

Crystal studied him for a bit. "Remember how you said he'd like being picked?"

"Quit using my own words against me," Diggy mumbled.

"Girls like to be picked, too."

Diggy blinked in surprise. Rationally, he knew that everyone, boys and girls, liked to be picked, but in his experience girls had all the choosing power. Until now, he hadn't realized he believed that. He had never thought of himself as having any real choosing power. But what if he did?

Suddenly the cafeteria and everyone in it looked funny—the same but totally different—like he had flipped into a parallel universe.

Fortunately, Jason sat down and snapped Diggy out of it.

"I thought you were having lunch with Darla," Crystal said.

Jason shrugged. "Her friends keep talking about some actor who broke up with some other actor."

They weren't anymore. One glance at the girls' table and Diggy could tell they were talking about Jason, and they weren't saying nice things.

Diggy waggled his eyebrows meaningfully at Crystal. It looked like her problem had been solved. Darla would dump Jason, and then Crystal could make her move.

Being the friend he was, he actually said out loud to her, "You look nice today."

Crystal immediately turned red. "Shut up, Diggy."

What? She wanted Jason to notice her, didn't she? He was helping!

Jason glanced back and forth between them. "What's wrong?"

"Nothing," Crystal said. "I'm going to the library."

Diggy gaped at her as she left. She was wearing a dress. Jason had left Darla to sit with them at lunch. Diggy had pointed out that she looked pretty so Jason would notice. It was like a triple play, but Crystal had refused to run the bases. "Girls."

Jason grunted his agreement.

THAT AFTERNOON, WAYNE CAME SO
CLOSE TO MISSING THE FIRST BUS HOME, DIGGY

thought Mrs. Osborn might take off anyway to teach him a lesson. But Wayne made it.

And threw himself into the seat next to Diggy.

"What?" Diggy asked.

"Not here." Wayne jiggled a knee.

Diggy kicked Wayne's foot out from under him. "Tell me now."

"I don't think you'll want to talk about it on the bus."

"I'm pretty sure I don't want to talk about it at all."

"Your grandparents are only the next county over," Wayne whispered.

Diggy's grandparents were in Texas. They had gladly given up Minnesota winters when Grandpa's job offered him a promotion in the Lone Star State and when Grandma was convinced Pop knew enough about taking care of a kid to not drop him, lose him, or cause him to spontaneously combust. They typically visited for a month in June.

But then Diggy realized Wayne didn't mean Pop's parents.

A surge built in Diggy's chest. He spoke calmly so as not

to spook the kid until he found out how far Wayne had gone. "How do you know where her parents are?"

"Your grandparents," Wayne repeated. "The secretary in the principal's office knows everyone."

Now everyone would know Wayne had been asking about Diggy's mom's parents. And they'd think it was because Diggy wanted to know.

"Why are you mad?" Wayne asked in an aggravated tone.

Diggy tried Pop's tactic and ran a hand down his face. It didn't work.

"This town talks, Wayne. I *told* you not to look for her."

"Who cares who knows? Your mom's out there somewhere."

"She can stay out there!" Diggy yelled.

Heads turned in their direction, and Mrs. Osborn frowned at them via the bus's huge rearview mirror.

Both Diggy and Wayne hunched lower in their seats.

"You don't know what it's like," Wayne said. "You can have a mom. I can't. Not ever again."

"I don't need a mom. I have Pop," Diggy explained, slowly.

"That's not how it works."

"When your mom leaves you on a doorstep and runs out of town—on a tractor," he emphasized, "that's exactly how it works."

Diggy got up and shoved past Wayne so he could get away from this kid who seemed to go out of his way to not get it. Normally, Mrs. Osborn would have said something about staying seated, but maybe she knew it was let Diggy move or deal with a fight on the bus. Diggy slung his backpack onto another seat and dropped down beside it.

Wayne was crazy. Just crazy. Diggy didn't know what else to think about the kid.

Mostly, he was tired of having to think about him at all.

He had *told* Wayne, but Wayne kept doing whatever he wanted, no matter what Diggy said. It wasn't fair.

By the time the bus pulled up to their drive, Diggy was ready to rodeo and knew he couldn't go anywhere near the steers yet. He clomped through the snow all the way to the tree line and in.

Diggy kicked through foot-high snow crusted with a sheen of ice, the crunch and crackle an echo of his own disjointed thoughts, the drag on his feet like his ankles had been cuffed by two-leg hobbles.

He almost wasn't surprised when he walked out of the woods and saw Pop coming toward him, not looking happy.

"So, what's going on with you two?"

"Did you talk to him?" Diggy asked.

"I'm talking to you."

Which wasn't fair, either. Wayne had started it.

"You seemed to be doing okay after Christmas."

"What did you think? That one Christmas together would make us brothers?"

"You *are* brothers."

"*Half* brothers," Diggy corrected, then burst out, "You act like it's supposed to be easy!"

"It's not easy for any of us," Pop said. "We all have to work at it."

"Tell Wayne that."

Pop rubbed his hand down his face. "You know what month it is?"

"January," Diggy huffed. He had a feeling he would not like where this conversation was going.

"January. Four months."

Pop waited long enough for Diggy to figure out what that meant. Four months. Mrs. Graf had died in September.

"He's the one being a meathead," Diggy grumbled.

"He gets some leeway."

Didn't Diggy get some leeway for finding out his father had another son no one knew about for fourteen years who suddenly moved into their house? When did Wayne's free pass to walk all over Diggy run out?

"I'm not asking you to fix things," Pop said. "I just want to be sure you've got the whole picture in mind."

Like Pop did? Ha. He had Wayne's picture in mind, not Diggy's. But that made Diggy think of Wayne's picture, where he and his mom made funny faces at the camera.

"Why do I have to be the reasonable one?" Diggy muttered.

"Because you are." Pop hooked his arm around Diggy's

neck and mussed his hair. Then he laughed. "And because you like hot showers."

Diggy wanted to be cheered up by Pop's teasing, but mostly it felt like he was getting a red ribbon for showing up while Wayne got the purple rosette. Diggy shouldered away and trudged off to take care of Joker on his own.

Diggy decided he was glad to give Wayne leeway—planned to give him so much of it they wouldn't see each other for weeks— but the very next morning, the stupid kid was waiting for him in the kitchen.

"We should call them."

Diggy clenched his teeth.

"Why hasn't Pop called them? Shouldn't he know where she is, for your sake?" Wayne persisted.

Did Pop already know? Diggy wondered. He couldn't help but think about the yearbooks—why hadn't Pop ever given them to Diggy?

"*Does* he know where she is?" Wayne asked.

"Of course not." Diggy did *not* like the feeling of Wayne practically pulling thoughts from his head. If Pop knew . . . It didn't matter. Diggy didn't want to know where she was anyway.

"Why not? You need to know—"

"I don't need to know anything!" Diggy yelled. "There's history, remember? Abandonment? Tractor? And her parents know where I am, just like she does."

Wayne shook his head. "Pop must have done something. Maybe he's not that great after all."

Diggy shoved Wayne hard enough that the chair the kid was sitting in tilted. Wayne stood and shoved back. Diggy hit the counter. He dug a shoulder into Wayne's chest and drove him across the room. He started to lose his balance, but then Pop got ahold of them and pulled them apart.

"He started it!" Diggy yelled.

"I never get a chance to!"

"Enough!" Pop roared.

Both boys immediately slumped into sulks.

Pop hauled them to the door. "You've got enough clothes on that you won't hurt each other much, but if you're going to fight, do it outside."

They didn't have time to brace for the cold before they were out in it, the door slammed behind them.

"Is he kidding?" Wayne asked.

Diggy slouched toward the barn.

"See? What kind of father encourages his kids to fight?"

"It's reverse psychology. Who wants to fight when you have permission to?"

"What it is, is crappy parenting."

Diggy was at Wayne, a fist thrown, before he'd had time to plan where to land it. The blow slid across Wayne's weather-resistant coat and twisted Diggy almost fully around, so he had to crash to a knee to keep from a full-body dump in the snow. Angled toward the road, he saw a truck's dark profile tilted in the ditch not far from their driveway. He had only a glimpse before Wayne tackled him.

Diggy shouted at him to stop, fending off Wayne's stiff-armed punches. "There's a truck in the ditch."

Wayne froze, knees pinned tightly around Diggy's sides, then twisted to look. Diggy bucked his hips, tumbling Wayne off. Diggy scrambled backward and onto his feet but got his palms up fast. The safety light shone just far enough out into the predawn darkness to suggest the truck was Graf's.

Wayne dove in for another go.

Diggy sidestepped. "Wayne. I think it's your dad."

Wayne pushed up from his hands and knees. This time when he looked out, he saw the truck and went pale.

He charged up the driveway.

Diggy shouted for Pop, then went after Wayne, worrying about the last time Graf had gotten himself into a ditch chasing the school bus.

The truck was at a full forty-five-degree tilt, and snow was mounted on the roof's back edge like a pair of Texas longhorns. The windows were cloudy, either frosted from the outside or fogged from the inside. Either way, the truck had to have been there awhile.

At the ditch, Wayne stopped. Diggy caught up and studied

the ground for a few seconds, then sidestepped at an angle down to the driver's door.

But Wayne didn't follow. "He's dead."

"No, he isn't," Diggy said automatically. Then he gaped at the clouded window. What if Graf *was* dead in there? Frozen, maybe, or from hitting his head.

Wayne half slid into the ditch. They stared at the truck.

"Pop will get here in a minute," Diggy said.

"This is probably something I need to do." Wayne took hold of the door handle, breathed in deeply, and opened the door.

Graf was slumped forward, arms hugging the steering wheel, snoring.

Diggy got a noseful of smoke and beer.

"So much for Alcoholics Anonymous, huh?" Wayne said. "That's another thirty-day coin out the window."

Diggy felt the blood pulse in his cheeks. Graf was supposed to be staying sober so he could take Wayne home.

The alcoholic in question turned his head, his cheek smearing drool on the steering wheel. "Thirty-four," he slurred.

Huh?

Wayne slammed the door shut.

"Is he still drunk?" Diggy asked.

Graf fumbled inside, loudly, then the door flopped open. "You home now?" He got a leg out but missed the ground and fell to all fours. "What the . . . ?"

"You're in the ditch," Wayne snarled. He dug his toes in to make the climb out.

"We can't leave him here, Wayne." Diggy sighed. The man was still drunk. He shouldn't drive and couldn't get the truck out anyway. Wasn't dressed properly for the cold. If he wandered . . . Diggy didn't want to think about what could happen.

Wayne slipped a couple of times but used his hands to get enough purchase to make it to the top. Then he kept going.

"Wayne!" Diggy yelled. The kid was crazy if he thought he was leaving Diggy to deal with Graf. "Wayne!"

Too far away, Wayne turned back around. "Just leave him."

"You know we can't. Help me pull him up—" The truck lurched forward a foot, and Diggy jumped back about ten.

Graf leaned on the open door, pulling himself up. Back on his feet, he gawked at the truck. "Am I in the ditch?"

Wayne's sigh was so explosive, Diggy heard it despite the distance. Wayne finally headed back.

"Come on, Mr. Graf." Diggy shut the door. A heavy arm thudded across his shoulders, and he stumbled. He pushed the arm over his head and ducked back, letting Graf tip forward against the ditch's slope. Wayne reached down, Graf reached up, and Diggy was stuck shoving the rear. But they got him out.

Graf slung an arm around Wayne. "I miss you."

Wayne staggered under the weight, so Diggy caught Graf

on the other side. He and Wayne guided his dad in as straight a line as they could.

Diggy concentrated on keeping their three sets of feet from tangling up. The smells distracted him. Graf was smoky and beer-stained, but the BO was worse. The guy really needed to do some laundry. At least one load. For all their sakes.

He didn't do much to carry his own weight. Diggy was about to say something, when Graf moaned, "Only thirty-four."

"What's he talking about?" Diggy asked.

Suddenly, Graf was a lot heavier. Diggy huffed and said, "Front door," but Wayne had staggered out from under his dad's arm, leaving Diggy half crushed.

"Come on, Wayne," Diggy protested.

"It was her birthday yesterday!" Wayne shouted at him. "I was so busy with your crap, I didn't even . . ." His face looked on the verge of collapsing in on itself. He whispered, "She was thirty-four when she . . ."

Diggy shifted Graf's weight. He sighed. "Push the doorbell, Wayne, okay?"

Wayne swiped at his face and pressed the ringer, taking hold of his dad's arm again.

Pop opened the front door, his questioning "What the . . ." very quickly replaced by a growl of a frown. He took over for the boys, muscling Graf to the living room, and barked, "I thought you were going to the meetings."

"You don't get to bawl me out, Lawson," Graf blustered. "You're the one took my son."

"You dumped him with me. If you want him back, you gotta keep working the steps."

"The steps," Graf cried, flopping onto the couch. "AA can't do nothing about Ann missing her thirty-fifth birthday."

Pop ran a hand down his face, but there wasn't any energy in it, like the information wore him out as much as it drove Graf to drink.

Diggy felt the same, but it was because he kept hearing, *You dumped him with me.* He knew Pop was mad and probably didn't mean it that way, but Diggy had been "dumped" once, too. He had always tried to convince himself Pop didn't think of it that way, and he knew Pop loved him, but it still made Diggy skittish to hear the words. He glanced at Wayne, but Wayne's pale, blank face could have been wiped bare by his mom's birthday or his dad's fall off the wagon as much as by Pop's comment, if he'd even registered it.

Pop straightened suddenly and looked back at where Diggy and Wayne stood in the doorway. "You boys all right?"

Diggy shrugged.

"What happened?" Pop asked.

Diggy waited, but Wayne stared at the bookshelves rather than at Pop or his dad. Finally, Diggy said, "His truck's in the ditch."

Pop pulled in a long breath, then let it out as his fingers unclenched. "We might as well haul it out while Harold . . ." He trailed off. Graf sat with his head tilted against the sofa back and snored.

Wayne crashed outside, slamming the front door behind him.

Pop went for his coat, and Diggy followed. They didn't speak. Diggy climbed into the pickup's cab while Pop rummaged in the toolbox always in the truck bed. Pop got in and passed Diggy the tow strap to untangle.

Wayne reached his dad's truck before they did. Pop idled while Diggy jumped out; then Pop went on into the road and backed the truck into line with Graf's. Diggy had already hooked one end of the tow strap to the mount under Graf's bumper. When Pop idled again, Diggy hooked the other end of the strap to their trailer hitch. He signaled, and Pop eased forward until the tow strap went taut. Diggy stepped far out of the way, checking that Wayne followed; then Pop inched forward. Minutes later, Graf's truck was back on the road.

Diggy unhooked the tow strap, then looked over at Pop, eyebrows up. Pop nodded. Diggy tried not to look too excited as he hopped into the driver's seat of Graf's truck. As he'd expected, the keys were in the ignition.

"What are you doing?" Wayne said, sliding into the cab.

"I know how to drive."

"Like it's driving to pull in and park."

"You're not fooling anyone," Diggy said, putting the truck in drive. "I called it." He inched forward.

"It's my dad's truck."

"Shh," Diggy said, making the turn. "I need to concentrate."

"To go down a driveway?"

Diggy ignored him. He drove the tractor all the time to mow or plow snow, but Pop hardly ever let him drive the truck. Diggy savored the occasion, no matter the circumstances.

"How could I forget her birthday?" Wayne whispered.

There was nothing to say to that.

Diggy pulled up alongside Pop's truck, where Pop stood drumming his fingers on the hood.

"What am I supposed to say to him?" Wayne asked.

Diggy glanced out at Pop again. "I think he's worried, not angry—not at you, anyway."

Wayne blinked at him, then shook his head. "Not Pop. My dad," he said. "I don't know what I'm supposed to do."

It was Diggy's turn to blink. Wayne had a "Pop" and a "Dad" and talked about them in the same breath. *Weird* hardly covered it.

Pop opened the driver's side door and leaned against it, making the effort to smile. "Good driving?"

"Good," Diggy said.

"Wayne, you drive any?"

"About as much as this," Wayne said.

Pop nodded. "I thought you each might want to take a turn around the block."

"Yes!" Diggy said immediately, and would have had the door shut as fast, too, if Pop weren't leaning on it.

"But what about . . ." Wayne trailed off.

"He'll keep." Pop slammed the door, and Diggy suspected the driving lesson was as much about getting some cool-down time as it was about teaching them anything. Driving around the block was significant. A country block was a square with sides a mile long. Diggy had only ever driven some in the fields, mostly in the driveway, and now he was getting four miles. He bounced in his seat, then pretended it was part of the business of Wayne moving over and Pop climbing in.

"He's still going to be there when we get back," Wayne mumbled.

Pop sighed. "Sometimes you've got to take the moments you can."

When Wayne pulled into the drive and parked, Diggy leapt out and pretended to kiss the snowy ground.

"I wasn't that bad," Wayne grumbled.

"You drove at wherever you looked," Diggy argued. "We're lucky *we* didn't end up in the ditch."

As soon as the words popped out, Diggy wanted to shove his foot into his mouth. Wayne probably would have helped, except he was staring at the house like it was the mouth of hell.

Pop squeezed Wayne's shoulder. "I can take care of this."

Wayne hovered. A calf mooed, and Wayne nodded. He headed toward the cows.

Diggy didn't like the idea of Pop going in there alone, but Pop shooed him off.

Wayne had turned on the radio by the time Diggy got to the calves. Though it was part of the routine to get the animals used to noise, Diggy worried about being able to hear if Pop called out from the house. He turned it off.

Wayne froze for a second, then hunched more tightly over the Scotch comb he worked through the hair on Fang's hind legs. The calf's head was tied high, and Diggy matched it when he tied Joker. The calves needed to get used to the posture they'd hold in the show ring.

With both Diggy and Wayne's attention only half in the barn, the cows shuffled and fidgeted. When they got even more fidgety, Diggy checked the door and saw that they weren't alone anymore—Pop hung back, while Graf edged forward.

"Wayne," Diggy hissed over Joker's back.

Wayne didn't move for so long that Diggy almost believed the guy didn't know his dad was there—but not quite. After a few more seconds, Wayne patted his calf's rump, then looked over at his dad.

Graf's hangdog look hung lower than ever. Diggy was afraid the man might start crying—he looked that pitiful.

Graf cleared his throat and walked on over to them. "He's filling out good."

Wayne may have left the door cracked open for his father to redeem himself back when he first moved in and Pop encouraged him to, but Diggy was pretty sure that door was closed now.

Graf cleared his throat again. "You still feeding him that alfalfa hay?"

Wayne shrugged.

The silence got to where Diggy was embarrassed, so he filled it with talk about how they would get the steers transitioned to feed in April, the flakes of hay they went through each day, and the linseed oil he mixed in to promote hair growth.

"Good, good," Graf said, like he hadn't really been listening. He scrubbed his hair, then muttered to Wayne, "I owe you an amend."

Wayne snorted. "Yeah, like the steps are working out for you."

He might as well have smacked his dad; his words had the same effect.

"I've got a sponsor," Graf said.

"Don't come out here anymore."

"It was a slip, but I can—"

"Don't come out here anymore." Wayne turned to his calf and brushed long, smooth strokes along its back.

Graf flopped his hands a couple of times, but no words came. He even looked at Pop, like he wanted help, but Pop only shook his head—not mean or anything, but as if to say now was not the time.

Diggy guessed that Pop was right. Wayne had his shoulders up in that way like he could block his ears with them.

Graf watched Wayne for a while, then walked on out. Pop spoke quietly with him on their way to the man's truck.

Diggy turned back to Wayne. "You were kind of hard on him, weren't you?"

It was a long time before Wayne answered. "Your mom leaving you like she did was bad, but you've always had Pop."

Diggy didn't need any time to get Wayne's meaning: Diggy had gotten the better end of the deal.

AFTER THE THING WITH HIS DAD,
WAYNE DIDN'T MENTION DIGGY'S MOM'S PARENTS
again, and January rolled into February with the routine of steers, school, steers, homework, and steers. Normal.

Until Valentine's Day, when Crystal got asked out by one of the guys from 4-H, and she said yes. Chad didn't go to their school, but Crystal started spending some of her lunch periods with her girlfriends, leaning in to one another to whisper things, then laughing loudly. It was surreal. Even though she hung out with him and Jason most days, it still felt like one day she was one of the guys, and the next she was a *girl* girl.

Jason didn't say anything about it, and he was the one who had to be with her every day, since her sheep was at his place, so Diggy didn't bring it up, either. But by the next 4-H meeting, Diggy's excitement to see July was dimmed by worrying about how Crystal would act when she was actually with her boyfriend. He felt stupid for thinking about it at all, but if she was different in school, it seemed likely she'd be even more different at 4-H.

After Pop dropped them off, Diggy headed for the church basement and found Jason in their usual spot, while Crystal watched her boyfriend demonstrate his latest robot.

Jason kept looking over at them. Diggy didn't really want

to have this conversation, but he also felt he'd be a bad friend if he didn't ask. "Why didn't you ever ask her out? She wanted you to."

"She did?"

Diggy blinked at him. Even before Crystal had made Diggy talk about it, he had pretty much guessed that she liked Jason. Jason spent more time with her than Diggy did, so it had seemed obvious that he would have guessed, too. Though Diggy hadn't realized Darla liked him until it was too late, either, so he supposed he wasn't one to judge.

"Huh," Jason added.

When Crystal finally sat down with them, her boyfriend followed. They all said hi and stuff, but the usual talk about rate of gain and feed was replaced by junk-drawer robots and the display Chad's team was planning for the fair. Only high school teams competed, but Chad and a group of kids hosted exhibits in the 4-H building to demonstrate how the robots worked.

It wasn't until Jason asked Chad a question about the supplies 4-H considered junk-drawer stuff that Diggy relaxed enough to realize he had missed his chance to talk to July before the meeting started—and to see that Wayne hadn't.

———

The weather turned into the kind of ice-age freeze that kept Diggy in the house when he was home. He puttered around with his Navaho model rocket. The level-three design wasn't all that different from others he had built. The trick was in fitting the two stages together, aligning the two sets of fins, and setting the engines in the body tube correctly so the ejection charge from the first would ignite the second. It wasn't difficult; it only required patience and time. Pop could have let Diggy have a go at a level three ages ago.

Every now and then Wayne came in to see what he was doing, so Diggy made him hold together pieces while glue dried. The next time Wayne came in, he was carrying something in his hands.

"You're a fast learner," Diggy said and laughed, figuring the guy didn't want to get stuck waiting for glue to dry again.

"I thought you'd want this back."

Wayne set the red metal box on the bed.

Diggy looked over, dusting balsa-wood shavings from his fingers, and froze. It was his mom's box. The small fireproof safe he'd bought all those years ago to protect the three things he had from his mother.

"Where did you find it?"

"In my closet."

Diggy glared. "How did you know it was mine?" It was a locked box. There was no reason to think it was his unless it had been opened.

"Do you know what's in there?" Wayne asked.

Diggy didn't have to respond. Wayne already knew the answer.

"I guessed it was yours," Wayne said. "I suppose Pop

could have locked it up to hide the stuff from you, but that didn't seem like something he'd do."

Diggy grabbed the box and felt the lid give too much. "Did you break it? You shouldn't have messed with it."

"It was an old, locked box that obviously hadn't been touched in years. You would have looked, too. Besides, it was rusty. It practically opened itself when I picked it up."

Diggy yanked on a drawer too stuffed with rocket supplies. When he tried to jam the box in, the lid broke from its hinges and slid off.

"You want to find her, too," Wayne said.

"I was a little kid," Diggy argued. "I might have wondered about her for a while, but I don't anymore."

Or he hadn't until Wayne kept trying to make him.

"Is that all you have?" Wayne asked.

Diggy nodded. A cap. So small, he marveled that it had ever fit his head. The card from the hospital crib that read *Douglas, Lawson*. His mom must have given the nurse both her last name *and* Pop's. By the time the third item was put on Diggy, the plastic name band from the hospital, his mom's last name had become his first. Even when he was little, the small pile had fit into one palm. "I think she tucked them in with me so Pop would know who I was." Though Diggy had seen baby pictures; the tuft of orange hair said it all.

Since he had nothing else, those three things had been everything. But, really, they were nothing.

Wayne put his hands in his pockets. "I thought you'd want them back. That's all."

Diggy fit the lid on again as well as he could. He cleared a spot for the box on the shelf in his closet and pushed clothes around until it was gone.

"She could have left you with her parents," Wayne said.

Diggy squinted at him.

"She chose Pop for you. She can't be all bad."

Diggy had never once thought of that, of her having chosen to leave him with Pop for Diggy's sake. He suspected that might be giving her more credit than she deserved, but part of him didn't care.

When Wayne left, Diggy knew he wouldn't be able to concentrate on the model anymore, so he figured he might as well head downstairs and do his homework. Wayne was already propped on the couch. Diggy dropped sideways into the armchair and pulled books around him.

Had his mom wanted to make a point? Or had she thought Pop would give him to her parents in the end? Or had she wanted Pop to have him?

By the time he was old enough to understand about grandparents and that he was supposed to have two sets of them, he had lived without his mom's parents for so long, it was weird to think about them being around. He didn't even know what they looked like.

Not that it mattered. His mom had left town on a tractor.

He tossed aside his math homework and pulled out his charts of feed percentages and weight gain per time period. It never took long to get lost in that math.

"You're going to flunk eighth grade," Wayne said.

Diggy calculated how much feed Joker would need after April 1 rolled around.

"That means no 4-H," Wayne added.

Diggy looked up. He hadn't thought of that. No 4-H meant no county fair and definitely no State Fair. "I won't really flunk."

"How will you not?" Wayne gestured at the unfinished homework.

Diggy slammed his notebook closed. "Do you work at ruining my day, or does it come naturally to you?" He picked up his huge, boring social studies book. Why couldn't the teacher have asked true-or-false questions? He hated all these answer-with-sentences things.

Wayne tapped his pencil on his notebook, over and over and over, until Diggy looked up again. "Stop it."

"We have the same homework," Wayne pointed out.

"So?"

Wayne waited.

Diggy thought. They only had math and science together, but the same teachers taught the other classes. They probably gave the same homework for all seven classes. His and Wayne's notebooks were probably filled with the same notes.

They probably answered the same questions every week. His eyes widened. Wayne was a teacher's kid. For him to even hint what he was hinting was mind-boggling. More important, Diggy was usually the one with the plan. He should have thought of this ages ago. "I'll do math and science."

"No way," Wayne protested. "I don't like English or social studies any more than you."

"You get all A's."

"That doesn't mean I like it."

"And how are you at Spanish?"

"Crappy."

Wayne sighed. "If we each do every other question, then check the other's work when we copy it, we should improve our odds of getting most of the answers right."

Diggy didn't like having to check over the work. But it would be better than actually doing it. Plus, he really had been doing particularly crappy in school lately. "I'll take even numbers."

"I've already done half the math homework. You do the rest, and I'll start odds on science."

They worked for a while. Pop ducked in, left, then came back with glasses of milk and a bowl of baby carrots. "Brain food."

Diggy and Wayne exchanged pages to copy the other's work, but copying didn't take much brain space, and after a while Diggy caught himself tapping his eraser against his notebook. He tried to focus on the task, but soon the pencil was tapping again.

Wayne looked up.

Diggy cleared his throat, straightening a little in his chair. "Has your dad called or anything?"

Wayne looked back at his work. "I told him not to, remember?"

Was the heater always so loud? Its hum was broken by periodic ticks.

Wayne pushed his books back, leaving a messy pile. "Done. I'm going to the barn."

Diggy planned to follow, but he ended up sitting a bit, the eraser tapping.

SPRING

AFTER DINNER, DIGGY DRAGGED
WAYNE OUT TO THE BARN AGAIN.

"I was coming out anyway. We always do," Wayne said, tugging his arm away.

Diggy checked to be sure Pop hadn't followed them, though he rarely did.

"What's with the secret-agent business?" Wayne said.

"The Ides of March are upon us," Diggy intoned.

"You don't even know what that is."

"I watch TV."

"Right," Wayne said. "So? Ides?"

Diggy faked a wildly exaggerated sigh. "It's March, Wayne. You know what that means?"

"That it's March."

"And soon it will be April." He nodded meaningfully, waggling his eyebrows.

"Are you having a seizure?"

This time Diggy didn't have to fake the big, fat sigh. "April, Wayne. April *one*. As in April *first*. April Fools' Day? We've got to plan."

Wayne laughed. "No way. You two are bad enough year-round. I'm not getting in the middle of anything."

"Wayne, Wayne, Wayne." Diggy shook his head sadly. "So young. So innocent."

Wayne crossed his arms.

"You're in the red zone, buddy. You can take the hits, or you can fire back."

"Pop dipped your toothbrush in salt!"

"And that's a level-one prank. Do you want to do nothing while Pop preps a level ten?"

"Ten? What was switching the hot and cold water lines?"

"An eight," Diggy replied.

"You guys are crazy."

"Planning is key." Diggy's eyes gleamed. "With two of us, we can go big."

"Oh, crap," Wayne groaned. "What have you got planned?"

Diggy cleared his throat. "Nothing yet. That's where you come in."

"No," Wayne said again. "I'm staying out of this."

"You're kidding yourself if you think you can. Pop will prank you—I guarantee it. He'll do it so you won't feel left out."

"And I'm supposed to be the idea man? You're the one with all the experience."

"Exactly," Diggy explained. "I've pulled enough pranks that Pop knows my style. We'll surprise him this year. You're an unknown factor in the equation."

"I'm not that unknown," Wayne mumbled. "I've been here six months."

That took Diggy aback. Had it been six months? Some days, it felt like Wayne had been there forever. Six months was a long time.

The calves bawled at getting no attention, so the boys went through the routine, blowing dust out of the hair, rinsing the steers down with cold water, then blowing them dry again, training the hair to bloom nicely. The drone of noise prevented secretive conversation but was good for thinking.

Diggy mentally put together a decent list of low-level gags for the big day. Ideas for the prime prank, however, continued to range from subpar to positively crappy. So he was ecstatic when he turned off the blower and Wayne announced, "I have an idea."

Saturday, when July skidded into their drive, Diggy's heart rodeoed. He ran out to greet her, wishing Wayne didn't follow, but skidded to a stop himself when he saw her face. She slammed the door, hard, and marched to them.

"I know you wouldn't do this," she snapped. "But I want to hear it straight from you."

Diggy didn't think he'd ever seen July mad. He blinked like a deer in headlights.

"That's good, Diggy," July said. "I want you to be surprised. I want you not to know what I'm talking about at all."

"I don't," he assured her, wide-eyed at her tone. "What's going on?"

"Apparently, two boys, driving a truck like Pop's, were seen hightailing it from Goodhue County."

"Goodhue?"

"You remember the Goodhue chapters," July said sarcastically. "Lots of great exhibitors, good steers. Do well at the fair each year."

"Yeah, but—"

"Seems a couple kids' steers were shaved."

"We'd never do something like that!" Diggy protested.

"Wayne?" July asked.

"I didn't even know Goodhue was a county." He frowned.

"But?" July glared.

"Nothing like that!" Wayne looked at Diggy. "Doesn't one of your pamphlets say something about shaving the hair for better hair growth?"

Diggy shook his head. "Not in March. It will be getting warm soon." If an exhibitor buzzed a steer at the start of winter, the hair was said to grow back thicker, but July had never done it, so Diggy never had, either.

July continued to give them the eyeball.

Diggy felt like his heart was under her boot heel, and she was grinding it into the ground. "We would never, ever hurt a calf—you know that. Or cheat. How could you think so?"

She relented. "I couldn't. But the description was pretty specific and sounded exactly like you two. The police called Pop."

"They did?" Diggy squeaked.

July threw an arm over his shoulder, grabbed Wayne, and headed to the barn. "So, how are your calves doing?"

"They're not really calves anymore," Wayne pointed out. At seven months and nearing eight hundred pounds, the steers looked more and more like the show animals they would become.

She smiled. "Oh, they'll still be your calves when they're fourteen months and twelve hundred and fifty pounds." She asked Diggy, "You got your grain mix ordered?"

As of April 1, the calves would start on finishing rations, filling out for the fair. Diggy talked percentages of protein, grain, and mineral supplements with July, but for possibly the first time ever, Diggy didn't do everything he could to keep her around longer than she wanted to stay. His ears rang with the words, *The police called Pop.*

Diggy didn't even watch July drive away like he usually did. He was too busy crashing into the house, Wayne trailing behind. "Pop!"

"In here," Pop said from the dining room. "Is there a fire?"

Diggy flung himself through the door. "What? No."

"Then let's try for a more reasonable entrance and tone of voice next time, all right?"

Diggy scowled. "The cops called?"

Pop huffed out a long breath. "I forget how small this town can be."

"Why didn't you tell us?"

"Because it wasn't you, and it was ridiculous for them to think so in the first place." Pop held together with one hand a half-assembled motor part to something while he sorted through pieces spread out on the table.

While he regained his breath and his mental balance, Diggy pocketed a wad of elastic shock cord meant for his model rockets that had somehow found its way downstairs. Pop hadn't asked them about the steers getting shaved because he didn't need to. He trusted them. "Thanks, Pop."

Pop frowned. "How did you hear about it at all?"

"July came out," Wayne said.

"She was ticked." Diggy grinned.

"I suppose it makes sense she'd have heard about it," Pop admitted. He groaned and let the pieces he held together fall apart. "I'm done. Dinner in front of the TV tonight? I'm actually in the mood for one of your brain melters."

That's what Pop called the low-budget sci-fi movies Diggy liked to watch.

The three of them chowed on two frozen pizzas in front of a movie about giant lizards running around and eating people at *night*, unlike any other cold-blooded animal that would be more active during the day. Such a basic, huge mess-up was only a taste of yet better screwiness to come. Even Wayne got into the act when the people who were soon to be reptile dinner lost the generator that powered the compound but still somehow had lights on when the lizards came. At night.

"People got paid to make this," Wayne said.

Diggy sniffed. "I love America."

"This is more like a Japanese *kaiju* film," Pop said.

Diggy gaped at Pop. "*Kaiju?* Where do you come up with this stuff?"

Pop tapped his temple. "Kidneys, man, kidneys."

Diggy thumped his head on the chair's back cushion.

"Is this a conversation?" Wayne asked. "It feels like dialogue from one of these movies."

Diggy snorted.

When the lady with big boobs got eaten, Diggy started yawning. Waking up at dawn sucked for having late-night plans. Though he felt it his duty as a teenager to stay up until all hours, he just didn't have the energy for it.

Waking up at dawn had its perks, though. He and Wayne felt safe enough in the barn to plan their April Fools' Day.

THE PRIME PRANK REQUIRED A CALL

TO GRAF. WAYNE SEEMED OKAY WITH IT—
even a little relieved. When Graf showed up in person to
report on his end of the deal, Wayne didn't say anything about
his having told his dad to stay away, and Graf didn't ask if it
was okay that he was there. Diggy shook his head at the it-
never-happened routine, but it had its perks. No drama, and
the boys got their prank. The whole thing depended on Graf
and his friend.

But prank planning took a backseat when he got to school
on Monday and Crystal asked him about the shaved steers. He
didn't have time to find out what she knew before the first bell
rang, and he didn't hear anything the teachers talked about
in his morning classes. He raced to the cafeteria, picking up
Wayne along the way, and would have skipped the lunch line
if his stomach wasn't already rumbling.

"What's going on?" Wayne asked.

"Crystal already heard something about the shaved steers."

Diggy got to the usual table first and bounced his leg while
he choked down his chicken sandwich. Wayne took the seat
next to him, but he didn't eat so much as swirl the "zesty Mex-
ican dip" with a carrot.

When Crystal and Jason finally sat down, Diggy asked, "So, what did you hear?"

"Wayne," Crystal said in that way that was kind of "Hi" and kind of "What the heck are you doing here?" She might have gotten used to him at their 4-H meetings, but it wasn't like they all hung out together during them.

"Just tell us," Diggy said. Supposedly, Wayne was Diggy's partner in crime—Wayne needed to hear whatever Crystal was about to say, too.

"I heard you two went out and shaved some steers." Crystal scowled.

"You heard it was *us*?" Diggy yelped. He knew Crystal had heard about the shaved steers, but it hadn't occurred to him that his and Wayne's names would have gotten out. He looked at Jason for confirmation, but Jason just hunched over his food and shook his head. Which was weird. Jason was always part of the conversation, even if he only listened, and this was big.

"Anyone who's friends with Diggy wouldn't believe it," Wayne said.

"I am his friend," Crystal snapped. "I'm saying, be careful. Someone's setting you up."

Jason choked on his chocolate milk, but Crystal quickly thumped his back.

"Do you think we can find out who?" Wayne asked before Diggy could.

Crystal studied Wayne as if she could read his brain waves. "Are you worried about being in trouble?"

Wayne frowned. "I don't like anyone thinking we'd do something like that when we've been working so hard. Diggy's been raising steers practically his whole life."

Diggy stared at Wayne. It was almost like the guy was defending him.

Jason grunted and nudged Crystal. She elbowed him back, distracting Diggy. "What's going on with you?" Diggy asked.

"Nothing," Crystal said, giving Wayne a weird look.

Diggy tried to pry more details out of her, but Crystal said she didn't know anything else. Wayne picked at the edges of his sandwich bun until Crystal huffed and told him to just eat already. Before Wayne could say something back, Jason asked about their presentations for 4-H, and lunch was pretty much back to normal, even with Wayne there.

Diggy worked on plotting a few private pranks for Pop and Wayne, but it was hard to concentrate with the accusation of steer shaving hanging over his head. Fortunately, he was able to keep busy, because March was the last sure month the calves could get out in the cold much. Regular people groaned about winter, but steer exhibitors loved it, because that was when their animal's hair grew best. Spring and summer were the tough times, because higher temperatures and sunlight discouraged hair growth. It was logical—steers didn't need thick hair to keep warm in summer—but inconvenient. Diggy often wished the State Fair was in April rather than the end of August, the hottest time of the year.

Diggy took Joker out every night and began to toughen up his nerves by walking him into the tree line. Though the steers didn't seem spooked anymore when they heard Kubat's dogs barking, Diggy wouldn't let them anywhere near the woods alone—even less so now, with someone out there shaving steers. He had rigged a bunch of cowbells on the barn door so he would hear if anyone tried to get in there.

Wayne didn't always lead Fang into the woods when Diggy took Joker, because some nights the steer just wouldn't go. But tonight Fang was following lead pretty well. The four of them walked close enough to the trees and bushes that branches rustled just over the steers' heads, and leaves brushed across their sides. The point was to get them accustomed to unusual sights and sounds, because the show ring would be full of them.

Diggy liked being out in the dark. Sounds were different. Smells were different, too, damper and more distinct. And, of course, things looked different at night. They had more meaning. In sunlight, a tree was a tree. In moonlight, a tree was a shadow that whispered strange secrets. Daylight was easy.

"Did you used to do this alone?" Wayne asked.

"I walk the steers," Diggy said, confused.

"I mean, without another person," Wayne explained. "It's creepy out here. It doesn't get this dark in town."

"You don't have trees in town."

Diggy practically heard Wayne roll his eyes. "*Town* doesn't mean *wasteland*."

"Where do you want to be when the zombie apocalypse hits? In a crowded town with lots of easy pickings for the living dead or in our wide-open countryside, where we can see them coming and defend ourselves?"

"That's your criteria? A zombie apocalypse?"

"You've got to plan for these things, Wayne."

Wayne laughed like he didn't want to.

When they headed out of the woods, they saw Graf's truck in the drive first, then Graf himself. He stood at the barn door, looking out into the darkness. He didn't spot them until they were close enough to hear; then he quickly walked out to meet them.

"You boys okay?"

Diggy glanced at Wayne.

"Yeah," Wayne said slowly. "Why wouldn't we be?"

Graf looked from side to side like a burglar in an old cartoon. "Let's get the steers back inside. Lawson know you're out here?"

"Of course," Diggy said, not liking Graf's shiftiness. "What's going on?"

"Shh," Graf said. "Wait until we're inside."

Diggy and Wayne rushed the steers in and tied them up but left off the brushing and washing routine. Diggy crossed his arms and waited for Graf to talk. He had a very bad feeling.

"There anything you two want to tell me?"

They exchanged looks. Wayne shook his head.

"Because you can trust me, you know. I'm the last one who gets to judge anybody."

"We *are* trusting you, remember?" Diggy pointed out. Then he frowned. "Is your friend backing out of our prank?"

"No, no, he's still good."

"What's going on?" Wayne said. "Just tell us already."

"Another steer got shaved."

"Did the cops call you, too?" Diggy shouted. The steers mooed, and he automatically patted a rump.

"Another one?" Wayne asked.

"Why do people keep thinking it's us?" Diggy said.

"Pop's truck was spotted leaving the scene," Graf explained.

"As if we could sneak it away. That's what makes the prank—"

"And a tall kid and one with orange hair."

"I'm tall!" Diggy protested.

"So if you two are in trouble and need some help, I'm your man. No questions asked."

Diggy didn't know what to say. It was crazy to think that someone was out there shaving steers in the first place— it was too weird a thing to do. Then to have people think he and Wayne had done it, something absolutely in no way possible . . . Now Graf was out here, offering his help. Diggy didn't know whether to be ticked that Graf believed they had done it or glad that he wanted to help them no matter what.

Wayne cleared his throat. "Thanks, Dad."

Graf looked taken aback, then cleared his throat, too. A couple of times. "Sure."

"We didn't do anything, though. It wasn't us," Wayne said.

"You sure?" Graf asked.

"Of course we're sure!" Diggy bellowed. "Where did this one happen? The last one was in Goodhue County. We couldn't get that far and back again without getting caught."

"We can barely drive around the block," Wayne pointed out reasonably.

"*You* can barely drive. *I* could get us there, no problem."

Wayne stared at him. "Are you trying to get us in trouble?"

Diggy huffed. "I'm just saying. Don't lump me in with you being a crappy driver."

Wayne threw up his hands, then grabbed a comb to brush Fang out.

"They're looking good," Graf said, nodding at the steers.

He hung around while the boys set up the steers for the night. They talked some about the prank they had planned, but Diggy was paranoid Pop would come into the barn and made them stop.

That night, he had trouble sleeping. Every noise sent him to the window to see if someone was trying to get into the barn to shave their steers. He only calmed down when it occurred to him that if someone was trying to set up him and Wayne, their steers would be the last ones shaved.

He hated that other 4-H'ers were getting tagged like that, though. It was early enough that the steers' hair could grow back and show fine. But that wasn't the point. It was a question of fairness. Those other kids had worked as hard as he had all winter and were getting ready to add even more hours to their days, practicing for the show ring, meticulously planning feed, and grooming their steers. They deserved a fair shot at Grand Champ. And Diggy wanted a clean win.

Diggy promised himself he would find out whose steers had been shaved and make a point of saying hi to them at the show and wishing them luck.

ON APRIL 1 DIGGY WOKE WELL
BEFORE DAWN, WRAPPED HIS BLANKET AROUND

his shoulders, and sat in his bedroom doorway. No way was he missing Wayne's first April Fools' Day.

Wayne took forever to wake up, though. Diggy was tempted to shout at the kid to get him moving. Finally, he heard the usual morning scufflings, and then Wayne walked through his doorway—and straight into a wall of Saran Wrap.

It half fell over him, so one arm was stuck at his side, and his face and hair were plastered down like he was prepping to rob a bank.

"What the . . ." he mumbled, the words muffled by plastic. "Diggy!"

Diggy held his stomach and tried not to pee laughing while Wayne struggled with the clinging wads of plastic wrap.

Pop came out and shook his head. "I'm sure the box says it's not a toy."

Diggy pointed at Wayne. "You should see your face."

Wayne glared at him, then slowly smiled. "You should see yours."

Pop peered at Diggy, then smiled, too. On his way to the bathroom, he ruffled Wayne's hair. "Good one."

"What?" Diggy protested, the laughter gone. He felt his head and body. "What did you do?"

Wayne shrugged and wadded up the last of the plastic wrap into a ball he threw at Diggy.

Diggy shouldered his way into the bathroom, where Pop was peeing. "Kid," he warned, but Diggy saw his face in the mirror. He was covered with red, blue, and green streaks on his face, in his hair, and all over his hands and clothes.

He groaned. "The Kool-Aid trick."

Wayne had sprinkled the colorful powder in Diggy's bed while he slept, and he had rolled around in it all night.

Pop flushed the toilet and gave Diggy a shove. "Out. Now."

"But I've got to shower!"

"Later." He shut the door and turned the water on for himself.

Diggy shushed Wayne, even though Wayne hadn't said anything, and pressed his ear to the door. "Wait for it," he whispered.

Wayne watched with a puzzled but interested expression. It seemed to take forever, but they finally heard Pop take his turn saying, "What the . . . Diggy! What did you do to the soap?"

Diggy guffawed. "Fingernail polish!" he shouted through the door. He thumped Wayne's shoulder and headed downstairs. He checked himself out in the mirror by the front door, shaking his head. "You did pretty good for an amateur."

"Thanks. Did you check outside yet?"

Diggy half fell trying to get to the kitchen window. "I was too busy watching for you," he muttered. "I didn't think to yet."

They looked out. Pop's truck was gone.

Diggy did a jumping kind of soundless dance, punching his fists into the air and smiling enough to break his face. It hurt trying to hold the laugh in his chest. "I can't believe they pulled it off!"

He made himself stand still and took several breaths. He ran his hands up and down his face. "Okay, okay. Poker face. We've got to be straight when Pop comes down, or he'll know something's up."

Wayne watched him, his expression less than confident. "I hope you don't actually play poker."

"Say anything you want today, Wayne," Diggy announced magnanimously. "Your idea is working." He rubbed his hands together. "This will be the best April Fools' ever."

He looked up at the ceiling. "How long does it take to shower?" he hollered at Pop. He couldn't wait to see Pop's face.

"What did you do with fingernail polish?" Wayne asked.

Diggy shrugged the question away. "Paint the soap with it, it won't lather. It was a secondary prank to throw him off track."

"Why didn't you tell me about it?"

They heard the water cut off, and Diggy pushed Wayne

toward the cabinets. "Get some cereal out. We have to look normal!"

"Poker face, remember?"

"Move!" Diggy clattered out bowls and spoons and nearly tore off the refrigerator door getting the milk out. The rush ended up being totally unnecessary. Their bowls were empty again by the time they heard Pop on the stairs. "Does he always take that long getting dressed?" Diggy pondered to himself.

Wayne squinted at him. "You think he's planning something?" he whispered.

"Definitely," Diggy said, then sat up straight in his chair. "Morning, Pop."

Pop frowned at him.

Wayne made a face at him, too. He mouthed silently, "Poker."

Diggy bit his lips and made his face as flat and normal as he could.

Wayne shook his head.

Pop turned on NPR while he made his coffee before joining them at the table. He looked out the window, but from where he sat, he couldn't see where his truck should have been. The truck that was gone. The truck Graf's friend had towed away last night, somehow doing it without waking up Pop.

Diggy couldn't believe the plan had actually worked. If Pop didn't get up and look outside soon, Diggy might burst.

He opened his mouth, not sure what he meant to say—

something to get Pop to the kitchen window—but got kicked under the table instead. "Ow!"

Wayne glared.

Pop eyeballed them. "What's going on?"

"Nothing," Diggy said, way too earnestly. Pop was clued in that something was up. Diggy wished he could kick himself under the table.

Fortunately, the phone rang before Pop could grill them.

"What are you doing?" Wayne whisper-shouted. "You're going to blow it!"

"I know!" Diggy said. "I'm sorry. I'll get it together, I promise."

Pop leaned in the doorway, still on the phone. He stared at them, not a drop of good-natured suspicion left on his face.

"What's wrong?" Diggy asked.

"Hang on a sec," Pop said to the person on the phone. He set it down, then walked to the kitchen window and looked out.

Finally! But something was wrong. Pop gritted his teeth, jaw perfectly tight. He returned to the phone.

"It's not here," he said. Though he spoke to whomever was on the other end, he stared at the boys. "Do you think that's necessary?" Diggy got a sick feeling in his stomach. This was serious. "I'm sure it's a mistake." Pop nodded. "Fine. Thanks for warning me." He hung up.

He stayed in the doorway, arms crossed. "So, where's the truck?"

This was supposed to be the moment. The funny. The prank unveiled.

Diggy's mouth tasted bad. "April Fools'?"

"Mr. Johnston thinks it's in a ditch near Kasson. Out by where another kid's steer got shaved."

Diggy leapt to his feet. "No way! We had it towed. It was your April Fools'!"

Wayne stood, too. "Really." He raised his hands, palms up. "We wouldn't take your truck."

"Yet it's gone," Pop pointed out. His tone was far too reasonable. Diggy knew he was seriously ticked.

"That was the prank."

"And how do two teenagers get a truck towed in the middle of the night without me hearing a thing?"

Diggy chewed his lip. He didn't mean to, but he glanced at Wayne.

"My dad," Wayne admitted. "He has a friend who tows cars."

Pop rubbed a hand down his face. "Harold."

"We made him," Diggy argued. It wouldn't be fair for Graf to get in trouble, too. "We begged him."

"The cops are on their way."

"What?" both boys gasped.

Red and blue lights flashed in the driveway.

DIGGY AND WAYNE RUSHED TO THE
WINDOW. A POLICE CRUISER SAT IN THE DRIVE.

"Holy crap," Diggy said. He blinked at Wayne. "Holy crap."

Wayne was white and wide-eyed.

"Pop," Diggy said, "I swear. We didn't take your truck or shave any steers. You've got to believe us."

Pop eyed them, not actually angry but not necessarily convinced, either. "I'm trying to," he admitted, "but they seem pretty sure."

The front doorbell rang. Diggy could have jumped out of his pajama bottoms. "Don't let him in!"

Pop grimaced. "This won't get resolved if we leave the officer on the doorstep. Then he'd *know* you're guilty."

While Pop answered the door, Diggy paced around the kitchen. "What do we do?"

Wayne somehow got even paler. "We can run for it." But the statement was ludicrous. The kid couldn't even blink. Running was out of the question.

"Boys," a new voice said.

Diggy and Wayne froze. When they made themselves turn to face the officer, they practically creaked.

"So, we're going to take a ride," the cop said. "Downtown."

Pop made some kind of sound, almost like a snort, but his distress was real. He finished clearing his throat. "Is that necessary, Brandon?"

The cop shook his head. "Sorry, Pop. Procedure is procedure."

Diggy frowned. "You know Pop?" Hope bloomed. "Then you know we'd never get away with something like this. He'd never let us!"

"Mr. Lawson," the officer said to Diggy. "Mr. Graf. If you'll come with me."

"I'll have to ride with you," Pop said.

"Yup. Minors have to have a legal guardian with them. Can't talk to them otherwise."

It was like one of those cop shows on TV. Diggy couldn't believe it was real, that this was happening to them. "Pop?"

Pop shook his head. "Just go with him, boys. We won't get this straightened out until we get to the station."

He headed for the front door. The officer waited until Diggy and Wayne passed before following them out.

Getting into the back of the police car was like a weird dream. The situation was so unreal, Diggy stopped being scared. He stopped feeling anything. He waited to wake up.

The closer they got to town, however, the more his thoughts crowded in on him.

They were riding in the back of a police car. They were going to the police station. The police thought they had crashed Pop's truck into a ditch and had been shaving show steers all over the state.

Diggy elbowed Wayne, leaning in so they wouldn't be overheard. "You don't have to be here."

"I am here," Wayne pointed out.

"Seriously. You thought shaving the steers would help them out, grow better hair. You don't know anything except what you've seen me do. You can say it's all me."

"You think I'd do that?" Wayne burst out, though quietly.

"I think you don't need to get in trouble if you don't have to. This is serious stuff, Wayne."

"Forget it. They said it was two guys. I'm the other one."

Diggy wanted to protest, but he was too grateful. He didn't particularly want to be in this alone. "We'll figure something out," he promised. "We didn't do what they said. There's got to be some way to prove it."

Wayne nodded, pretending he was confident. Diggy tried to do the same.

Both of them failed. By the time they hit the station, they were shaking.

The officer opened the door for them, not saying anything as he led them into the station. "The cells are in back."

"The cells?" Diggy and Wayne squeaked.

The officer kept going, and the boys followed, not knowing what else to do.

Diggy saw Graf, then July and a bunch of other Johnstons,

Crystal and Jason, and some other people. Had they all been arrested, too?

"April Fools'!" everyone shouted, laughing and pointing.

Diggy punched Wayne's arm. Hard.

"Why are you hitting me?" Wayne yelled.

"Were you in on this?" Diggy yelled back.

"No!"

Diggy turned on Pop. "This was you!"

Pop grinned, then didn't try to hold back the laugh. "If you had seen your faces."

Diggy looked at Pop, looked at Wayne, scanned the crowd of faces, smiled automatically at July, figured the guy next to Graf was the tow-truck friend, then looked back at Pop.

"This might be the best prank ever," Diggy said, awed.

"But what about the kids shaving steers?" Wayne asked.

Diggy thumped him again. "There weren't any shaved steers. It's all part of the joke."

Wayne blinked many, many times.

"What's all over your face?" Crystal asked Diggy.

Wayne and Diggy burst out laughing at the same time.

APRIL 1 WAS A BIG DAY FOR TWO

REASONS. AFTER THE APRIL FOOLS' SHENANIGANS,

it was time to start the steers on finishing rations. Playtime was over. It was day one of the countdown to the State Fair.

All winter, the steers were kept on alfalfa-grass hay, gaining a little more than a pound a day. With finishing rations, they gained about three pounds a day, going from eight hundred to twelve hundred and fifty in five months.

Joker would, anyway. Fang had continued to lag behind and was almost a whole fifty pounds lighter than ideal. Wayne wanted to get him on full feed right away and was stubborn and snotty enough about it that Diggy would have let the kid do what he wanted, if it wouldn't have hurt the calf. But too much grain too fast meant stomach problems, sometimes even permanent damage. Diggy wouldn't let Fang suffer for the rest of his short life because his owner was a meathead.

The month of April was spent in weeklong intervals. The first week, they substituted a quarter of the usual hay, about five pounds, with the finishing ration, a grain mix with a protein and mineral supplement. The next week they bumped it up to half. By the third week, the steers got about fifteen pounds of finishing rations and five pounds of hay. The last week, they added another five pounds of finishing rations, the hay remaining at three to five pounds—whatever their steers ate to clean up their feed bunks between meals. Fang tended to eat only three pounds, while Joker chewed through five, which was a lot better.

By the end of the month, the steers looked like they had been puffed up with air and were as awkward as when they had first come home.

"It's like they forgot how to walk," Wayne complained.

The way he jerked on Fang's lead, it wasn't any surprise the calf didn't follow. "You know they're sensitive to moods. You're being impatient, so he's getting stubborn."

"I'm not impatient." He jerked again. Fang leaned away from him.

Diggy wasn't willing to leave Fang stuck dealing with Wayne's crap. "What's wrong with you?"

"He looks scrawny next to Joker!"

"Big deal. For one, he's going to bulk up fast now. And two, not that it matters for you, because your chances of placing at the fair are as good as you winning the Indy 500"—Diggy snickered, Wayne shot him a glare, and Diggy finished—"a lot of times the Reserve Champ is the lightweight crossbred. If Fang ends up in that category, and I'm not saying he will, he's still got a shot at winning a purple." He emphasized, "A light purple." The dark purple was for Grand Champ. He meant that one to go to Joker.

Wayne rolled his eyes at Diggy, then sighed. "I don't want

him to look stupid, that's all. He's been a good calf."

"He'll look fine." Diggy pointed to where the dog had gotten Fang. "The hair's grown back good over the dog bite, too."

"In the wrong direction."

Diggy shrugged. "That's what spray adhesive is for."

The longer days meant that they had to wait longer to walk the steers in the dark. At not-quite sundown, though, Graf drove up. He sat in the truck awhile before getting out.

Diggy wasn't sure why, but he got that twisting feeling in his stomach. He had a vivid memory of when Wayne was dumped at their house and Graf drove back later that night and sat in their driveway, his truck lights on, smoking, until Pop went out to meet him. Diggy looked toward the house, but either Pop hadn't heard Graf pull up, or he wasn't worried about Graf's being there.

Diggy wasn't sure why *he* was worried about Graf's being there. It didn't make sense to be. Graf got out of the truck and asked them stuff about the steers. He was sober. He said all the right stuff. But he was different about it. Like he had to concentrate on being sober and saying the right stuff.

Diggy glanced over at Wayne and felt a little more sick. Wayne had that look like something wasn't right, too. The steers' behavior was an exclamation point on the unnamed worry. They shied away from Graf, and Joker managed to get a hoof on Diggy's foot. The steel-toed boots protected his toes, but it had been forever since he had needed them to.

"That April Fools' was some good time, huh?" But Graf sounded as if it had been a bad time.

Wayne didn't say anything, so Diggy said, "You had a good time, too."

"Oh, yeah," Graf agreed sarcastically. "I like seeing my son all settled in with Lawson. Just warms my heart right up."

"You were part of it," Diggy protested. "If you hadn't double-crossed us, it wouldn't have worked!"

"I'm the double-crosser?" Graf shouted. He glared at Wayne. "You ever even think of coming home?"

Fang had put himself between Graf and Wayne. Wayne opened his mouth, but nothing came out. He petted the calf.

"I stay sober, you come home!" Graf yelled. "That was the deal." He flashed a green coin he must have gotten from Alcoholics Anonymous. "I got three months straight. Now I'm getting letters from school about your eighth-grade graduation. You've been here a whole year!"

It wouldn't be a year until after the State Fair, but Diggy caught himself in time to chew the words back in. Wayne had been here most of a school year, and his dad wanted him home.

Diggy felt that same distortion of space/time like when Wayne first moved in. The unreality of Wayne's being there. The *why* of his being there. They had looped back to the beginning, but not really. It wouldn't be back to normal, because even though it would be Wayne *not* there, it would be Wayne not there after having been there. That was a very different thing. Diggy could practically see the parallel universes split before him, and he wasn't sure if he felt sick because of the double vision or because he didn't know which branch he was supposed to want.

Graf was right about their deal. But Wayne lived with *them* now. When had Diggy gotten so used to Wayne's being around that it was weird to think of him *not* being around?

Wayne said, "I have to take care of Fang."

Graf clomped a few feet away, as if that would keep the boys from hearing the curse words he muttered before he came back to them.

"You like Lawson better now? Is that it?"

Wayne looked over at Diggy, and Graf got even louder.

"Don't look at him!" Graf stormed up right next to Fang, squeezing the steer between him and Wayne. "I'm your dad. Me! I'm the one you're supposed to stay with."

Wayne blinked in slow motion. "I need to go take care of Fang."

Diggy was afraid. Until that moment, he had never met anyone who might truly do anything. No one was entirely unpredictable, not really. Except Graf. In this moment, he could do any of a thousand things—to regret, to fear, to hate, to mourn. Waiting was like teetering at the edge of a cliff, and it was made worse because it was clear that Graf didn't know what he would do, either, and meshed within his rage was simple dread. In that moment, Diggy realized the most terrifying person was someone afraid of himself.

Only two or three seconds warped like forever; then Graf stomped off. With all his might, he reared back and threw his AA chip far, far away. The coin didn't know any better and glinted like a wish in the sunlight.

Graf's tires spat gravel as he revved down the driveway.

Diggy's hands shook. A part of his brain calculated that probably not more than five minutes had passed in Graf's presence. His hands shook more.

That was Graf *sober.*

"Don't tell Pop," Wayne said.

Diggy nodded. Pop would be *ticked.*

Except the next morning, Graf came out to make amends, so Pop found out anyway. Pop had a lot more patience for Graf than he did for the boys, which was so backward, but neither of them could explain why they hadn't told him what had happened. Everything was such a twisted mess, they couldn't wait to get to school, and if that wasn't the sign of the end of normalcy, Diggy didn't know what was.

Fortunately, the routine of school was a powerful force, and Diggy actually took comfort when a math problem about two tractors traveling at different speeds inspired some kid to say, "That one's for Diggy." Getting teased about his mom's escape on the tractor was just so ordinary. By the time he and Wayne got off the bus and headed out to the calves, it was like Graf's rage had never happened.

MINNESOTA HAD ITS QUIRKS.
SNOW HAD FALLEN IN LATE APRIL BEFORE.

No one really trusted spring until May.

Spring was crazy time. Birds sang their guts out. Kubat's dogs barked at every speck of dust, or so Diggy figured. He heard them going nonstop whenever he got to the tree line during his walks with Joker. Joker didn't get worked up hearing the dogs anymore, but he didn't like their springtime frenzy, either, so Diggy cut short that part of the loop for a while. Joker needed to be used to distraction by the time he got to the fair and the show ring, but that didn't mean he had to put up with dogs too dumb to know what was worth barking at.

Diggy wasn't really surprised when he got Joker back to the barn and found Wayne fighting with Fang about standing still for his wash and blow-dry.

"Stupid cow!" Wayne hollered. "You *like* this part!"

"Whoa. You know, you only make it worse when you get mad."

"What do you know about anything?" Wayne twisted the hose faucet to high, stomping back to Fang like he would blast the steer.

"I know Kubat's dogs aren't the only ones who have lost

their minds." Diggy nodded meaningfully at the spray nozzle in Wayne's hand.

Wayne threw it to the ground, then shoved his hands into his hair and, like, *growled*.

"What is up with you?" Diggy asked, tying Joker's lead so he'd be out of the way of Wayne's mood. Diggy tried to maintain his calm for the animals' sake, but he had no patience for a kid who'd take his frustration out on a steer. He had thought Wayne really cared about Fang.

"Pop keeps getting calls," Wayne grumbled.

"Uh . . ." That was not at all what Diggy had expected. "So?"

"About going out! About meeting at Otto's and having some drinks and playing pool," Wayne mimicked nastily.

"Pop has friends," Diggy argued. "Jeez. He's hardly gone anywhere but Ole Jib's and the grocery store since you got here."

"I haven't given him the messages."

"What?" Pop would be ticked when he found out. Wayne would get the bawling-out of his life. He had certainly had a license to walk all over Diggy for months. Maybe Pop would finally understand what it felt like.

"I don't care," Wayne said, brushing Fang against his will. The steer's hooves caught Wayne's steel-toed boots a couple of times, but Wayne never flinched or moved. He mumbled, "They won't talk to me."

"Pop's friends?"

"Her parents! I kept calling, but they didn't return my messages until today. I got her mom, and she—" He clutched the Scotch comb so tightly, he had to be breaking skin. "She told me off and said not to call anymore."

Wayne had called Diggy's mom's parents.

Wayne had called Diggy's mom's parents more than once, even though Diggy had told him not to call at all.

And they hadn't said anything.

Diggy wasn't sure what to think about that information, but he sure as heck knew what he wanted to do about Wayne.

He hauled Wayne away from Fang so quickly, Wayne tripped over his own feet and fell down. Diggy was thinking Fang had the right idea about walking all over the guy, but Wayne was up too fast and lunging at Diggy. Diggy got out of the way just in time to avoid a collision but turned fast enough to shove Wayne down again. Diggy was pretty sure he couldn't get into a real fight with Wayne right now, because if Diggy started hitting Wayne, he was afraid he might never stop.

Wayne rolled over, and maybe he saw something in Diggy's face, because he didn't get up. "You should be glad. I'm actually doing something to find her."

"Haven't you noticed, *Wayne*," Diggy sneered, "you only care about finding *my* mom when *your* dad screws up."

Diggy blinked at his own words. He hadn't noticed that before. He hadn't known those were the words that would come out of his mouth when he opened it, but they were true. "Just go home already." Diggy sighed. "It's what you want."

"It's what *you* want. You never cared about me. My mom is *dead*!"

"That's not—"

"Pop is my real father!" Wayne yelled.

"Your dad is your real father!" Diggy yelled back. "And my mom is my mom. Just . . ." It was Diggy's turn to growl before adding, "Just stay away from her, and stay away from me."

The next day, Crystal needed all of one look and three seconds to figure out something had happened. No questions were asked, though. She looped her arm through Diggy's, grabbed Jason, and walked into school, never once looking back at Wayne.

SUMMER

THE SCHOOL YEAR ENDED. FINALLY.

DIGGY MET UP WITH CRYSTAL AND JASON

as often as he could, usually at Jason's, since Crystal had to go there anyway to take care of her sheep. But her mom's hours had changed at work, so it was hard for Crystal to get rides when she wanted them. The long days meant she could ride her bike, but it was a haul from town. Diggy and Jason ended up on their own as often as not, catching sunfish in the oxbow river that made a nice, deep curve near Jason's farm.

Diggy's grandparents were supposed to come up to visit for the month of June, as usual, but Grandpa caught bronchitis. Grandma told them he'd be fine, but Diggy knew Pop worried. Last summer, he and Pop would have flown to Texas for a week instead, but now there was Wayne.

Diggy spent a ton of time with Joker. Wayne avoided him by jumbling up the routine, rinsing and blowing Fang while Diggy walked Joker, then heading out when Diggy came in. Wayne spent even more time tramping through the woods or up in his room.

Diggy was thoroughly, completely, absolutely fine with Wayne staying out of his way. He had zero interest in having anything to do with the kid. He had too many other things to think about. First and foremost, the county fair. He had to do well at county to earn a trip to State. He needed to focus, and Wayne complicated Diggy's thoughts.

It was kind of a relief when Graf came out with his bright blue six-month chip. With the way things were, Diggy fully expected Wayne to go home with his dad this time, and Diggy was glad, thrilled, ecstatic. He wanted normal again. Whatever that looked like.

But Graf screwed it up. He didn't ask Wayne to go home with him.

Instead, Graf spent almost an hour talking with Pop alone. Then he took Wayne somewhere for the rest of the day.

After Wayne got dropped back at the house, he kept giving Diggy weird looks until Diggy finally snapped, "What?"

Wayne seemed surprised at being caught out but quickly reverted to his hard-jawed snottiness. "You don't need to know everything I'm thinking all the time."

"You were the one looking at me," Diggy grumbled. "And no one knows what you're thinking. Including you."

Wayne stomped upstairs, and Diggy threw himself onto the living room couch. He flipped through some channels but turned off the TV in frustration. Nothing was ever on when he needed it to be.

Pop sat down next to him. He squeezed Diggy's neck, then thumped his knee.

"Not this time, Pop," Diggy protested.

"The first anniversary is coming up, and Fang will go to the packer on top of it. I'm just asking you to be patient."

"So will Joker!" Diggy said. "Are you telling Wayne to be patient, too?"

"I'm telling you."

"That's not fair!"

"Lots of things aren't fair, Diggy. We do what we have to."

That phrase again, from back when Wayne first moved in. The one that used to claw at Diggy's heart like a yeti on the hunt. Not anymore.

Diggy finished his level-three model rocket and devised a plan for getting his hands on the eighteen-and-older-only engines.

Fair preparations ramped up. Mid-July was the county fair.

But first came July Johnston's birthday.

Not that Diggy felt much like a party. When he wasn't ticked about Wayne, he worried about Joker and showing him well and whether he'd win a trip to the State Fair, even though it was 99 percent sure he would. That 1 percent chance of not making it would be on him.

And July's party made him sad. It was her birthday party, but it was also her graduation party. She would start at UMN in the fall. She'd be gone.

When Pop offered to take them into town to buy her a

present, Wayne announced that he had already gotten her one.

Diggy stared, his stomach hollow. Wayne glanced at him, then looked away. He shrugged his shoulder like it was no big deal, but Diggy went from feeling hollow to hot. Warm air breezed over his cheeks like a breath on a spark and lit him up even more.

Wayne hadn't said a word about July, her birthday coming up, or getting her a gift. If Pop hadn't said something, would Wayne have let July's birthday come and given her a present while Diggy stood around like a jerk with his hands in empty pockets?

"It's no big deal," Wayne said to the house. "Just something I found." His face was red.

Good, Diggy thought. Let him be embarrassed. Diggy would give July the most perfect gift, and Wayne could blush all day.

Of course, there was the figuring out of the "perfect gift." Diggy groomed and walked Joker and thought so hard, his brain steamed.

The moon was up early and bright in a clear sky, but Diggy felt a few raindrops, then a few more. There was one gray cloud smudging the night overhead. One cloud and it was raining. On him. Which felt about right, considering the last few months.

Diggy hunched his shoulders against the fat, scattered plops and headed for the barn. A raindrop popped hard into a dry spot of dirt, a ring of dust puffing up in a tiny explosion like the exhaust when he ignited a model-rocket engine.

Diggy tilted his face into the rain, mouth open and smiling. He knew what he would do for July's birthday.

Saturday morning, Diggy packed up the level-three, two-stage model rocket and carefully stored the engines and other supplies to take to July's birthday party. Pop and Wayne looked at his duffel bag, but neither asked him about it, just like Diggy didn't ask Wayne about what looked like a shoe box wrapped in red paper and a blue bow.

Diggy thought they would be early, but the party was well under way when they arrived. There were people everywhere, and more than half of them were Johnstons. July was the youngest of six, and four of her sisters were married with kids. Both sets of grandparents were not only alive and present, they were herding grandkids like it was a challenge to see who could collect the most and seat them with a plate of food the longest. Since the kids were more interested in their cousins than potato salad, the grandkid-feeding contest was always on.

Stereo speakers had been positioned at a window—which would only have been weirdly old-fashioned if Pop didn't still have his dad's old system in the house, too—and someone had put on a polka record, of all things. The polka should have been ridiculous, but Mrs. Johnston made it seem the only logical musical choice as she circled in and out of the house and around picnic tables, first with a pitcher of lemonade, then a bowl of sliced cucumbers, then a plate of thumbprint cookies, and on and on, the tables already loaded with fresh rolls and cut fruit and sliced meat and grilled bratwurst and homemade pickles and chocolate-covered peanut-butter balls and a dozen other good things.

The other guests were high school kids and everyone from 4-H. Diggy barely had a chance to talk to Crystal and Jason, though, because people started catching him to talk about his steer and the State Fair.

He knew a lot of them from the hardware store, or as 4-H parents, or farmers Pop met with sometimes—they weren't people Diggy normally talked much with. But this was July's crowd, and everyone knew that July was grooming him to take over as the next Grand Champion.

It was pretty cool at first. The men asked him questions about Joker, his routine and feed schedule, and really listened to his answers. Someone made sure he got a bowl of "the green stuff"—a combination of pistachio pudding, whipped cream, and fruit cocktail—his favorite and always the first dessert to disappear. And it seemed like everyone at the party made a point of stopping by to say hi, announce he didn't have to worry about county, and wish him luck at State.

Diggy rode the wave of attention, enjoying it that little bit more when he saw Wayne watching him with a sour look on his face.

Diggy felt like a winner.

Except that he hadn't won anything yet.

Pretty soon, all the people and the party got to feeling *loud*, even though no one was doing anything different than they were before.

Everybody seemed to know everybody else, and everybody talked at the same time. The kids, the music, the laughter, a baby crying, someone hollering, "Give that back," and every other person having that distinct Johnston look that announced, *Family*.

Wayne wasn't left out, though. In fact, he fit right in. The Vogls were there, along with most of their kids and grandkids—the Vogl and Johnston girls all knew one another from forever ago. But Wayne's grandma was all about him, bringing him plates of food and talking nonstop and asking questions he didn't get a chance to answer while she went on about how his hair was too long and he looked thin and he should come for a visit soon and stay as long as he wanted.

Diggy grabbed a bratwurst and found a spot under a tree where he could see July.

She wore a white sundress, her hair pulled back in a low ponytail, and she just about glowed in the sunlight. She talked and smiled with everyone around her, people drawn to her in waves. She hardly got to move from her spot, so it didn't take long to notice that one guy didn't move, either. He stood next to her and touched her arm every now and then or looped an arm across her shoulders as he leaned over to shake someone's hand. He did *not* look like a Johnston. And July frequently smiled up at him in particular. A lot.

Diggy didn't like the look of him. Then he recognized him. It was the guy who took Reserve last year at the fair. The one July beat and who didn't live around here.

The memory should have made Diggy feel better, but the guy continued to stand way too close to July.

"Who is that?" Wayne asked.

Diggy hadn't heard Wayne come up, but knew he didn't want to deal with Wayne, and he turned away.

Crystal stormed up to them, arms crossed. "What are you doing, Wayne?"

"Standing here."

She looked ready to launch into the kid, but Diggy asked about her sheep, hoping she'd take the hint. He was not in the mood for yet another argument centered around Wayne.

Jason found them, then a couple more kids from 4-H joined in, and they talked livestock for a while. Then someone started singing "Happy Birthday." Mrs. Johnston and all five of July's sisters walked out, each carrying a homemade cake lit up with candles. Wayne gave a low whistle.

Diggy nodded, wide-eyed. "Mrs. Johnston doesn't mess around."

"I bet there won't be any left, either," Wayne replied.

That was all the encouragement Diggy needed to join the

throng and snag at least one piece of cake—hopefully, two. It was during the cake-eating lull that Diggy realized he should give July her birthday present. He had spied a good spot in the pasture where July had raised her purple-ribbon steers. He got his stuff out of the truck and found July. With that guy.

"Hi, Diggy," she said, giving him a sideways hug. "I saw you and Wayne hiding out under that tree and was a little jealous."

She had looked for him! Diggy blushed and grinned and couldn't actually look at her. He pushed the birthday card into her hands. "I've got to set up some stuff, but be sure you watch, okay?"

He took off before she could say anything else, his head reeling from her cut-grass smell that he loved.

When he went out into the field, the younger Johnston cousins gathered around, asking questions and generally making him nervous. This was his first level three; he needed to concentrate.

In a rare act of actual helpfulness, Wayne talked the little kids into going back by the group so they could see better. After weeks of mutual avoidance, Diggy wasn't sure why Wayne was hanging around him, especially considering the look on Wayne's face when everyone was congratulating Diggy for something he hadn't even done yet. But then Diggy remembered how happy Mrs. Vogl was, talking nonstop and fussing over Wayne like he was a little kid. Diggy decided he was okay with calling a temporary truce—he was afraid the well-meaning crowd might have jinxed his and Joker's chances, so letting Wayne stick around was penance or something. Besides, Diggy needed the extra hands.

The field was still mucky from the rain a couple of days earlier, and Diggy didn't want to set anything on the ground he didn't have to. He made Wayne hold the rocket while Diggy set up the launch pad. He pushed it deep into the soft earth. A lot of pressure would be deflected off the pad when he ignited the motors, so it had to be firm. The launch rod went even deeper into the ground, but Diggy had thought to get a two-piece rod so it would be tall enough. He slid the blast deflector on and turned to work on the rocket itself.

Ever so gently, he opened the pouch where he'd stored the motors and pulled them out. They were a big deal—a D12-0 and E9-4. They would boost his rocket to an altitude of 2,100 feet or more—a show guaranteed to make July's birthday the most memorable ever.

"What's with those?" Wayne asked.

"Jeez, Wayne!" Diggy yelped. He had nearly forgotten the guy was there.

"You're holding them like glass eggs."

"These are D- and E-class engines."

Wayne cocked an eyebrow.

"You have to be eighteen to buy them."

"And how did you get them?" Wayne frowned.

"I let Ole Jib's wife sell them to me." Diggy pretended it

was no big deal, but he had sweated it when he carried those rocket engines to the counter. Ole Jib's wife didn't know anything about motors, though, and rang him up like it was nothing. Diggy, however, had wasted no time getting out of the hardware store, just in case.

"In other words," Wayne said, "something is about to go terribly wrong."

"Funny," Diggy said. "I've built rockets since I was nine. I know what I'm doing."

"I'm just saying, with all these people around."

"Exactly. I would never do anything I thought might hurt someone. Jeez." Diggy was confident in the rocket's design; he had basically made an exact replica of a level three he had found online. He knew better than to fool around with his first two-stage rocket, especially if he wanted to prove to Pop that he could do it. And especially because he wanted to give July a present no one else could.

He carefully fitted the motors into the body tubes, then butted the two pieces together so the ejection charge from the first could ignite the second, and aligned the two sets of fins so they looked like one. Finally, the rocket was assembled for flight, mounted on the launch rod, and clips attached to the igniter leads. He tossed the bag away and handed Wayne the altitude measurer.

"I don't know what this is."

"Hold it close to your eye and sight along the top. When

the rocket reaches its peak, press the slide down so we can get the angle. I want to be able to tell July how high it went."

Wayne didn't look particularly confident about his role, but Diggy couldn't worry about that. He had the launch controller in hand.

"Mom would have liked this," Wayne said.

Diggy caught himself holding his breath. Wayne hardly ever talked about his mom. Diggy wasn't sure what he was supposed to say.

"She was always looking for stuff she could teach that would be fun, too."

Wayne stared at the rocket.

Diggy raised the launch controller in the air. "A tribute," he said softly. "To Mrs. Graf. A great teacher and a nice lady."

Wayne glanced at him but didn't speak and didn't smile, and Diggy started to feel stupid and maybe a little like a jerk until Wayne nodded. He looked at the rocket again and raised the inclinometer. "To Mom."

Diggy waited until Wayne nodded again, then checked to be sure no kids had roamed back into the launch area. Then he looked for July. When she waved at him, he began his countdown.

Diggy began his countdown at ten instead of the usual five, counting louder as voices joined with him until he had to shout and still wasn't heard above the crowd. "Three! Two! One!"

Everybody started hollering. Diggy pressed the button and shouted, "Happy Birthday, July!" as the first motor lit with the usual *pffft* sound. But instead of lifting off, it knocked around on the launch rod, like it was caught somehow. The motor's thrust pushed against the pad. The soft ground gave and tilted the rod until the rocket finally broke away, moving at an angle more than ten, maybe a whole fifteen, degrees off vertical.

"Was it supposed to do that?" Wayne asked.

Diggy moved in the direction of the rocket, which took him closer to the crowd that still shouted like everything was okay. The launch had seemed slow, but it happened in maybe three seconds. The motor still had another nine seconds of thrust, and that was only the *first* one.

Six or seven seconds later, Diggy could no longer see the rocket itself but watched the pale gray corkscrew of smoke heading up at the wrong angle. The first twelve seconds ended in a poof of darker gray as the ejection charge went off, and the second motor ignited the even-more-powerful E-class engine.

The extra burst ripped two fins free, and the rocket's nose suddenly dipped, nearly reversing itself. The smoke tail now streaked *down*, something explicitly forbidden in the NAR Model Rocket Safety Code. The rocket would go a long way in nine seconds. Diggy only needed two to register that it was heading straight toward July's house.

EVERYONE'S SHOUTS WENT FROM
HAPPY HURRAHS TO SCARED GASPS. PEOPLE

grabbed little kids and each other and ran away from the house, toward Diggy, getting in his way while he and Wayne tried to race *to* the house, though Diggy had no idea what he'd do when he got there.

"The ejection charge will go off first," Diggy panted to reassure himself. He had to hope the first engine had taken the rocket high enough to make up for the second engine's downward thrust. Once the ejection charge went off, the parachute would pop out and slow the rocket down. But the engine had a four-second delay before the ejection charge went off.

Suddenly, someone had him by the shirt and jerked him back. "Where are you going?" Pop shouted. "You can't do anything now but stay out of the way."

Diggy hated that Pop was right. He stared at the smoke tail, still headed toward July's house but also still high enough that it might not hit anything. It didn't matter that it was more likely the rocket would break apart than do any real damage to July's house—Diggy had already ruined her party. If the rocket broke something on her home, too, it would make everything that much worse.

The smoke cut off—the engine had burned out its nine seconds. But there were still four to go before the parachute deployed.

Diggy tried to guess—was the rocket a hundred feet up? Seventy-five? He counted the four seconds at least eight times, watching the rocket drop closer and closer, like a tiny missile of birthday-party doom.

The rocket couldn't have been more than twenty feet from the house when the ejection charge finally went off, the chute opened, and the confetti he had tucked inside *poofed* like a mushroom cloud. The rocket swung back and forth as it floated down, then landed almost on the sidewalk leading to July's front door, confetti billowing prettily in the air.

Diggy figured it was irony or something.

"That was your level three, wasn't it," Pop said. It wasn't a question, and his hand was heavy on Diggy's shoulder. "If I had thought for even one second that you would be reckless enough to fly an untested design with a crowd like this around . . ."

He let Diggy go, paced away, and took a couple of deep breaths. Pop was beyond ticked. He looked like an ejection charge ready to go off, but Diggy knew he wasn't getting a parachute to soften the landing.

Pop paced back, and Diggy pleaded his case. "It should have worked. I'd never hurt anyone."

Pop turned away, shaking his head like he was too mad to

even look at Diggy. Which was horrible. Pop had been mad at Diggy plenty, but this was like he was disappointed, too, and that made it ten times worse.

"Well, that was exciting," July said, coming up to them.

"I'm so sorry!" Diggy burst out, grabbing her hand. "I didn't mean to ruin your party."

"It's okay, Diggy," she said, squeezing his hand in hers. "No one was hurt." She laughed. "And it was certainly memorable."

Which was what he had been going for, but not like that. July's being nice to him about it only made him feel worse.

Then Wayne's grandma arrived.

"You are a madman!" Her German accent was thick, and she visibly trembled.

Diggy might not have particularly liked her—she had never acted very grandmotherly in front of him—but he would never want to scare an old lady, and he could tell she had been really scared, which made him feel like the worm in an ear of corn.

"My grandson should not be around such a person who would frighten little children and make them cry." She put an arm around Wayne to lead him away, but he resisted.

"Rose—" Pop said.

"Mrs. Vogl—" July began at the same time.

"Wayne, you come with me now." Mrs. Vogl sounded near tears, though the shaking wasn't quite as bad now. "You should never have been without family for so long."

Something in Diggy's gut dropped. He had felt bad before,

but now he felt almost sick. He had wanted Wayne to go home for a long time, but hearing Mrs. Vogl talk about Wayne's being without family . . . Diggy felt like she was wrong, even though she wasn't, really. Was she?

Wayne pulled far enough away from Mrs. Vogl to turn around and hug her tightly. "I'm sorry you were scared, Grandma. Everything's all right now."

She started crying, and July patted her back while Pop looked around and spotted Mrs. Osborn, waving her over.

"Mom?"

"She was frightened by the rocket," Pop explained.

Mrs. Osborn took over caring for her mom, and Mrs. Vogl let herself be led away, seeming embarrassed, though Diggy was the one who felt like a complete and total jerk. He had made an old lady *cry*. It didn't matter that all around him most people were starting to laugh about what had happened, and a bunch of little kids were already crowded around the rocket, though Jason and Crystal kept any of them from touching it.

Pop held his shoulder. "She was in Germany during the war," he explained. He glanced over at the fallen rocket. "I'd better get that before the little guys figure out they outnumber Jason and Crystal three to one. Why don't you get the rest of your gear from the field?"

Pop headed over to the circle of kids, who quickly started in with, "How'd he do that?" and "Do it again!"

"I'm really sorry," Diggy said again to July.

"It's really okay, Diggy. Accidents happen." She smiled. "It made me wish even more that some of my sisters had been brothers." She looked over at two of them and waved.

They laughed with the guy July had been hanging out with earlier. Diggy's faint relief waned. "Who's that?"

"Trevor? He's back from his first year at SD State."

"I think he likes you."

July giggled. "I think so, too." She glanced at Trevor and blushed.

It was mind-boggling. July didn't *giggle*. She didn't *blush*. She was *normal*, not like one of those makeup girls. Before he could stop himself, Diggy burst out with an accusatory, "Do you want him to like you?"

His tone clearly jolted her. Suddenly, Diggy was 100 percent her total focus. And, just as suddenly, he no longer wanted to be. He tried to leave to get his rocket stuff like Pop had said, but July held his shoulders and studied his turned-away face. It was as hot as sunburn.

She seemed to stare forever, but it was only a few seconds before she hugged him close. A full-on hug, not the sideways hug he usually got. The kind of hug she gave Wayne and that Diggy had been wanting. But not now. Not like this.

He pulled away, but July was used to twelve-hundred-pound steers. He wouldn't get loose until she let him go.

She rested her chin on top of his head. "I'm sorry, Diggy. I didn't realize."

That made it worse. He mumbled, "It doesn't matter."

She leaned back. "Yes, it does."

He saw Pop carrying the rocket to the truck. Jason must have distracted the kids by offering "rides"—he had a kid tucked under each arm while Crystal organized who got to go next. "I've got to get the rest of my gear," Diggy said.

"I care about you a lot," July said.

And next she'd say, "Like a little brother." He couldn't let her and jerked away, slouching off in what ended up being the wrong direction, but he didn't want to turn around and look more stupid than he already did, so he kept going.

Wayne followed him. Diggy wasn't sure what to make of that. Back at home, the guy spent most of his time avoiding Diggy.

After a while, Wayne said, "I got her the same card."

Diggy squinted back at Wayne.

"I saw it this morning while you were looking for a pen or something. I had already filled out the same card for her." He shrugged. "Funny."

Diggy thought about July opening his and Wayne's cards and shook his head. She would think they were crazy. "What did you get her?"

"I found a snakeskin." He shrugged again. "It was whole and pretty big. Kind of rainbowy. I didn't know we had snakes out here until I found the skin."

"Mostly garter snakes," Diggy said. "They won't bother you." Wayne was outside so much these days, Diggy forgot that he'd grown up in town. He wondered if sometimes Wayne looked around, especially when he was shoveling cow poop or something, and felt like he was on a different planet.

Diggy caught a glimpse of July but didn't look away fast enough. She didn't smile and glow quite as brightly as she had when he first got there. He hated to think it was because of him. "Hang on a sec," he told Wayne, then jogged over to the crowd that had again congregated around July.

He pushed his way in, then stopped, not sure what he had thought to do. "Uh. Happy birthday?"

She smiled one of those smiles that looked more sad than happy, and then she hugged him again. He let her.

"Thank you," she said.

He nodded and pulled away. When she brushed his hair off his forehead, he let her do that, too. Then he grinned and messed it up again. This time her smile was real. Before he could say something stupid, Diggy dashed away, this time in the right direction to collect his gear, and he was kind of glad that Wayne trailed him again so he could say, "I'm sorry about your grandma."

"She'll be okay," Wayne said. "She gets worked up sometimes, but my aunts always know what to do."

A few people slapped Diggy on the back, laughing and shaking their heads at the same time. No one seemed mad at him, though a few moms definitely gave him the stink-eye.

"That wasn't so bad, actually," Wayne said.

"Did you *want it* to crash into her house?" Diggy asked incredulously.

"I meant Pop. I thought he'd be madder."

Diggy winced. Pop was mad, all right. Diggy hadn't gotten away with anything. "You know he doesn't yell much." There would definitely be grounding, though. Diggy had no idea what other form of torture Pop would inflict, but there'd be something.

When they got to the launch pad, slipped sideways now in the rain-softened ground, Diggy remembered their tribute to Mrs. Graf. "Maybe your mom's spirit will protect us."

Wayne had grabbed Diggy's duffel but froze for several long seconds before slowly standing up again, his back to Diggy, and shaking off the drying mud from the bag, making Diggy pause, too.

Mrs. Graf's funeral was the first one Diggy had ever gone to. The coffin was made of pale golden wood polished to such a high gloss, it glowed. It had hovered over a sunbaked hole whose sides looked more like chiseled rock than dirt. Dark-clothed people topped with gray faces had circled the coffin. Wayne had been his palest ever. That had been at the beginning of the school year, and now school was over.

"It's not really that long ago, is it?" Diggy said.

Wayne stared at the duffel bag.

Diggy felt like he should say something else, but he couldn't think of anything. After a while, he came up with, "Think she still would have liked this?"

"The Fourth was her favorite holiday." He slanted a weird look at Diggy. "Your mom would have liked it, too."

It was Diggy's turn to freeze. Wayne had that tone, like he knew something. "What do you mean?"

"She listed fireworks as one of her favorite things."

Diggy spoke very slowly and clearly. "You've still got those yearbooks?"

"Of course," Wayne bit out, defensive but trying to act like he wasn't. "I've been studying them. That's my business."

"She's *my* mom!"

"You don't want her."

"She doesn't want *me*!"

"You don't know that. That's why we should find her." Wayne almost sounded like he was begging. "She might be trying to find you."

"I'm *exactly* where she left me!" Diggy shouted. "It's called logic, Wayne!"

"Maybe Pop kept her from you," Wayne said back. "Did you ever think of that? Maybe she wanted to come home, but Pop wouldn't let her."

The idea stopped Diggy. He blinked. A lot. "He wouldn't do that."

"Are you sure?"

All it took was three seconds. "Yes," Diggy said firmly. "I'm sure. Pop wouldn't do that." Diggy knew it absolutely. Pop might make him crazy sometimes, even furious, but he had always tried to be straight with Diggy. If Diggy stopped believing that, he couldn't believe anything about the world.

"We should find her anyway," Wayne said. "To ask why she left, if nothing else."

Now Diggy felt like an E-class motor on the verge of igni-tion. He jerked at the launch rod, breaking the two pieces apart before he'd gotten it all the way out of the ground.

"'Why' matters," Wayne argued.

Diggy pulled at the bottom half of the launch rod, feeling too tired to get a good grip on it. He knew "why" mattered—he didn't need Wayne to tell him that. Diggy had wondered "why" his entire life. Which was also how he knew that get-ting the answer to "why" wouldn't really matter at all.

Why did he have to tell Wayne the same thing over and over? Diggy knew Wayne was sad about his own mom, but could he really not see that keeping at Diggy about *his* mom was like peeling off a giant scab every time? After everything that had just happened with the rocket, Mrs. Vogl, and July, Diggy didn't have the energy to fight about it anymore. He sighed. "Just let it go, Wayne. Please."

JULY'S BIRTHDAY WAS THE LAST

DIGGY SAW OF THE GIRL HE LIKED. WITH THE

county fair two weeks away, a new July Johnston appeared, one who started in with telling Diggy and Wayne what to wear and how to wear it. She told them to get haircuts, *when* to get haircuts so they wouldn't look too fresh, and what kind of haircuts to get. The girl was just plain bossy.

Diggy was surprised he got annoyed with her. He knew she wanted to help him do well. And he wanted to win. But this was his fourth year. She knew that he knew what to do. He could pretend most of her directions were for Wayne, but it didn't seem that way.

Still, the times he got testy with her, he felt like a jerk. Especially when he admitted that, though this was his fourth year, it was the first one that really mattered. He wasn't simply competing his calf. He was meant to fill July's boots.

Not that he had a lot of time to worry about it. Days after July's party and the rocket fiasco, Pop still hadn't announced Diggy's punishment. Which was a bad sign. Pop never did anything until his temper had cooled. If Pop waited much longer, Diggy was afraid he'd be relegated to cleaning out the septic tank, which wasn't actually possible for him to do, but Diggy figured Pop could rig up something if it suited his mood.

So it was almost a relief when Diggy came in from the barn one night and heard John Fogerty's *Blue Moon Swamp* CD playing. Pop's getting ready to go out meant he could blow off some steam, which was good news, as far as Diggy was concerned.

He found Pop in the living room, wet hair combed flat, trying to button his shirt and tuck it in at the same time.

"We're going out?" Wayne asked.

"*I'm* going out," Pop corrected, with a pointed look at Diggy. "There's a double-stuffed meat pizza in the freezer. Defrost some broccoli, and we'll call it a balanced meal."

He went back into the hallway.

"Going out *where?*" Wayne gritted out.

Diggy didn't bother answering. Wayne knew Pop was going to meet friends at Otto's. Wayne had thrown away Pop's phone messages about doing so whenever he got the chance.

"We should stop him," Wayne said.

"Why?" Diggy followed.

"So he doesn't do to someone else what he did to our moms."

Diggy recoiled from the first thought that came to mind. "Uh, he's probably just meeting friends, and he doesn't always stay out that late anyway."

Wayne glared at him. "What if there are more of us out there?"

Pop trotted down the stairs and got his leather jacket out of the hall closet.

"I don't feel good," Wayne said. But he said it through his teeth and didn't act sick at all.

Pop squinted at him. "You don't look sick."

He had that tone—that how-stupid-do-you-think-I-am tone—that Diggy heard every time he made up some lame excuse for skipping homework or chores or for why he'd gotten into a fight with Wayne again. He would have warned Wayne to scrap his plan, whatever it was, but Wayne was ahead of him.

"I think the tuna we had for lunch was bad."

Diggy closed his eyes. Wayne was so bad at this. Both Pop and Diggy had had the tuna, too, and neither of them was sick.

Pop shrugged the leather jacket into place across his shoulders. Wayne was big compared to Diggy, but Pop was that much bigger. He studied Wayne.

Wayne fidgeted, his jaw tight, those giveaway red circles on his cheeks. Diggy knew Wayne's feeble attempt had already failed, but Wayne seemed to think he still had a shot.

Pop's eyes narrowed. "I get to have some fun every now and then, too."

"Like you did with our moms?" Wayne accused.

Now Pop's jaw tightened. He opened his mouth, then bit back whatever he had thought to say. Instead, he said, "I like to go out by myself and be with other adults sometimes." He spoke in a calm, reasonable tone. "Your mother liked to do the same occasionally."

Wayne froze. "She went out with her girlfriends."

Pop was gentle. "Where do you think she went?"

"She didn't go out with you!" Wayne's hands were clenched at his sides.

"No," Pop said, his voice still low. "She didn't. I'm only trying to explain that every now and then grown-ups need to have time on their own to have fun with friends their age. There's nothing wrong with that."

"Except when you say 'fun,' you mean 'sex.'"

"No. I don't. But that part of my life is personal. It's not anything you get to comment on."

"Why not? I'm the result of it, aren't I? Did you lie to her? Did you tell her you cared?" Wayne's voice got higher and more shrill with every syllable.

Pop's face was like stone. "I cared about your mother."

Wayne snorted. "And Diggy's mom, and some other kid out there waiting to be left on our doorstep?"

"I learn from my mistakes," Pop bit out. Then he chewed his lip. "I should have been more careful with your moms. That was my mistake." Pop looked away, his eyes seeing some time long ago, before the boys. "I cared about them both." He zeroed back in on Diggy and Wayne. "But that doesn't mean I wasn't as stupid as any other twenty-something college kid."

Wayne breathed heavily—Diggy could see his back expand

with each fast breath—but apparently he was out of words.

The boys watched Pop zip up his coat. At the kitchen door, he slipped into his good boots. "You could try to be in bed before I get home."

Diggy nodded. He didn't think Pop would have much fun tonight.

Wayne stared.

Pop left.

They stood in the kitchen, listening to the pickup's engine turn over and its tires crunch gravel. The sound of the motor faded.

"We're *mistakes*."

Wayne's teeth were clenched so tightly, Diggy was surprised he was able to get any words out at all.

"He didn't mean it like that." But Diggy's stomach turned over again, remembering Pop's words. Thinking about him all those months ago when Wayne arrived, saying, *We have to*.

Wayne lurched out the kitchen door.

Diggy followed. "What are you doing?"

"I'm going to see what he does." He opened the barn doors. "I'm going to stop him if he goes off with a girl."

"This is stupid. Pop's a good person."

"Why?" Wayne stared at him. "Because he took you in when he had no other choice?"

The words hit Diggy like a fist, but he refused to go down. "Because he took *you* in."

Wayne shook his head.

Diggy followed Wayne into the barn just to follow him, but then his brain caught up. "How do you think you're getting into town?"

Wayne grabbed keys off the hook and walked to the tractor.

"No," Diggy groaned. Then he shouted, "You are not taking the tractor!"

The engine cranked on Wayne's first try.

Wayne messed around with gears and levers until the tractor bucked forward a few feet, and Diggy had to take several large steps to get out of the way. He *knew* it had been a bad idea for Pop to show the guy how to drive it. Diggy waved his arms. "Wayne! Stop! You won't make it into town."

Wayne looked down. "Do you think he ever tried to find your mom? Do you wonder if he tried to give you back? Why aren't you as mad as me?"

"I am!" Diggy shouted back.

He blinked fast, but the words stayed said. He *was* mad. He had been mad at Pop all year, but he thought it was for taking Wayne's side all the time, for being so worried about *Wayne's* feelings. Diggy knew the whole thing he'd done with the rocket was because he was mad at Pop. But he had never let himself think that part of the reason he was mad was about his mom. But it was there. He could feel it, a tangle of barbed wire wrapped around his chest.

Wayne got the tractor moving more smoothly and headed down the drive.

Diggy jogged beside him. "What will you do when you get there? You can't do anything!"

Wayne got to the end of the drive and slowed to make the turn onto the gravel road. He looked both ways.

Diggy hopped onto the tractor's steps and got ahold of the door handle. The door swung open, and Diggy swung wide, a foot slipping off a step. The toe of his sneaker caught on one of the treads of the slowly turning giant tire and pulled him down. His one-handed grip loosened. He kicked his toe free and pulled as hard as could, swinging himself back around. He hung from the open door with feet braced against a step as the tractor jostled and stopped.

"You coming?" Wayne asked.

"It's not worth it, Wayne. Turn around."

"Get in, or get off." Wayne shifted back into gear.

Diggy climbed into the cab. It wasn't designed for two people. He leaned against the back glass, bracing his hip on the seat and a hand on the roof. He spread his feet wide but still wobbled when Wayne got the tractor going again.

Diggy watched the dark road ahead. The tractor had lights, but Wayne hadn't turned them on. Diggy waited until he got the rhythm of the ride, then quickly leaned forward and flicked the switch. The headlights shone out across the gravel.

Diggy thought of his mom. It had been light out when

she left town. Middle of the day. Maybe she had wanted to get caught. But Pop had walked through the woods to Kubat's to talk about some new agri-engineering design idea and never even knew she was there. People who saw her on the road waved her by, smiling, even, to see such a small lady on such a big tractor. That's how people always told the story. But maybe she had wanted to be stopped, until suddenly a line was crossed, invisible but real, and she knew she could never go back and kept riding.

Wayne had asked if Pop had looked for her.

Diggy had never once in his life wondered that until Wayne had started asking. There were too many things to wonder about it, and he wanted it all to stop. *Had* Pop ever thought about trying to make Diggy's mom a part of their lives? If he hadn't, why not? Was leaving him on Pop's doorstep such a terrible thing to do, she couldn't be forgiven? That was what Diggy had always told himself, but ever since Wayne got dumped at his house, Diggy wasn't sure about anything anymore. Pop had always been the good guy, the one who'd kept Diggy. But if Pop didn't have a choice . . .

Diggy told himself it was the bumpy ride that made him want to puke.

At the next turn, they finally hit asphalt. Wayne hugged the road's shoulder so the tractor rode unevenly, lower on the right, making it a little easier for Diggy to keep his balance upright against the seat back.

A car passed them going in the opposite direction. It was a blur of light, there and gone in moments.

"It will be hours before we get to town," Diggy said. Even at top speed, the tractor was a lot slower than Pop's truck.

Wayne breathed loudly through his nose. He didn't care how long it took.

"We don't even know for sure where Pop went."

Wayne ignored him.

Diggy sighed. They both knew Pop was at Otto's.

They rode in silence. A few more cars passed them.

The engine coughed.

Diggy frowned at the gauges.

Wayne worked the gears. The engine grumbled.

The ride got bumpier.

Diggy saw that the gas gauge was on Empty just as the engine gave out. The tractor rolled a few feet, then ran out of momentum and stilled.

Diggy crossed his arms. Closed his eyes. They were stuck miles from home with a tractor. They would be found. His mom's story would come up. Like mother, like son.

He fumbled the door open and went too fast down the steps. He stumbled and cracked a knee against the road. He let himself feel the pain for a few seconds, then righted himself and started walking.

"Hey," Wayne called out. "What are you doing?"

Diggy turned around and marched back to the tractor. He

looked up at Wayne, still seated in the cab. "You did this!" Diggy shouted. "You got me out here in a *tractor*."

"You didn't have to come," Wayne said loudly in return, climbing down to the road.

"And why?" Diggy went on. "To keep Pop away from your mom? It's too late for that!"

"This isn't about my mom!"

"Yes, it is," Diggy said, his voice breaking on a high note. "It's about both our moms. You want it to be about Pop, but it's not." Diggy shook his head. He was tired of yelling. "It's about how our moms didn't say no."

Thinking that, it dawned on Diggy what else Wayne's mom hadn't said. "And she didn't tell you."

"Go home," Wayne snarled. "You don't know anything."

He turned to climb back onto the tractor, but Diggy grabbed his arm. "She let you think Mr. Graf was your dad. She let *him* think it, too. She *lied*."

Wayne pushed Diggy so hard, Diggy tripped backward, couldn't get his feet under him, and fell. His palms slid across asphalt. Seconds later, the pain registered. He struggled back to his feet, trying not to use his hands.

"You know what's so stupid about you being mad?" Diggy asked. He blinked to clear the wetness out of his eyes. "You had her. You had her for fourteen years, and she was great. I know she was, because I knew her, too."

"You don't know anything."

"I know how lucky you are."

Wayne grabbed the front of Diggy's shirt. "My mom's dead!"

Diggy let himself be shaken. Tears flew off his face. "You had a great mom, and now you have two dads, and both of them want you to stay with them."

"But not for the right reasons."

"That's crap! Your dad loves you. He wants you to come home. And that's big, because technically you're not even his kid. Why else would he want you back unless he loved you?"

Wayne pushed Diggy away from him.

"You're all interested in finding my mom, but you don't know why. You don't get it. *You've* got someone who wants you back. *I've* got someone who doesn't want to be found."

Wayne turned his back, looking out over the fields.

Diggy wiped a forearm across his eyes. He looked at his injured hands, remembering the night of the dog attack, but he was too far away to get any use out of the tractor's head-lights.

"My mom was not a liar."

Diggy looked up and saw Wayne staring at him, face blank, eyes cold. He scared Diggy a little. He looked like his dad. Like he might do anything.

"I don't think she was," Diggy said. "She was a nice lady, and she loved you."

Wayne nodded. "She *kept* me."

It was like a punch to the chest. Diggy breathed it in and couldn't get it out again. Wayne stared at him with that same hard face.

Diggy began the walk home.

Wayne shouted after him, "I'm winning that competition, and then I'm leaving."

Diggy walked on.

Eventually, flashing red and blue lights drew up across the road. Brandon, the cop who had "arrested" them, told him to get in. Diggy was tired enough that he did. Wayne sat at the other side, staring out the window.

Brandon then drove them home. He talked along the way, but Diggy didn't pay attention. His head was a cotton ball, full but empty.

POP HAD A LOT TO SAY ABOUT THE
TRACTOR INCIDENT, BUT NEITHER BOY DID.

All Diggy wanted to do was focus on the fair.

All Wayne wanted to do was move out.

He called his grandma to come get him, but when she arrived, Pop convinced her to drive off somewhere with him.

Wayne had packed all his stuff, and he fumed, waiting in the living room, switching channels too fast to tell what was even on.

Pop and Mrs. Vogl were gone a long, long time.

Every now and then, Diggy caught himself at the living room door, staring at the back of Wayne's head for he didn't know how long, and made himself move on, only to find some other excuse had taken him back there again without his even realizing it. He hardly felt like he was in his body at all, let alone controlling it. He wondered if this was what people felt when they described out-of-body experiences, surprised they had ended up where they had.

When Pop and Mrs. Vogl finally came back, they had Graf with them, which made the out-of-body feeling ten times stronger. Mrs. Vogl and Graf together? On purpose?

When Pop asked Diggy to go up to his room, Diggy didn't

even think to argue. He just went, then wondered how he'd gotten there.

The hum of voices below rose and fell. Every now and then a phrase floated up: "... can't run every time life gets ..." "... matters how you leave things ..." "... deserve better than being left behind ..." Diggy didn't try to think any of it through, to piece together whatever the whole thoughts might have been.

All he could think about was Wayne's overstuffed suitcase. And backpack. And two trash bags. And a cardboard box. All his stuff packed up and piled next to him as he sat on the sofa, ready to go.

Like it was easy.

WAYNE'S STUFF WAS MOVED BACK
TO HIS ROOM.

Diggy was more than surprised—with both Graf and Mrs. Vogl there and Wayne *wanting* to go . . . Though he didn't particularly want to talk to Wayne, Diggy was curious enough that he had to ask what had happened.

"My *dad* convinced Grandma I should stay, because I can't keep running away from problems, when *he* was the one who dumped me here in the first place." Wayne glared at Diggy. "They don't know anything, do they?"

But Diggy didn't have the energy to answer or to think about who was the problem. He decided it must be because he just didn't care.

He didn't have anything to say when Pop tried to talk to him about the tractor incident. At first. But before Pop could leave the room, Diggy blurted, "You said we're mistakes."

Diggy had told himself that Pop hadn't meant the words the way they sounded, but they rattled in his head whether he believed them or not.

"I'm sorry," Pop said. "It came out wrong. I love you and am so grateful that you were born." Pop took a shaky breath, then made a point of looking him in the eye. "As glad as I am to have you in my life, I also wish I had been more careful with Sarah, for her sake."

"But she was pregnant for nine months." That was the thing Diggy had figured out, the sticking point. His mom would have been pregnant for nine months just like any pregnant woman. And Pop *had* to have heard about it. So what had Pop done in that time in between, before Diggy's mom left him on Pop's doorstep?

Pop ran a hand down his face, then sat next to Diggy on his bed. "Diggy, there are some things a parent doesn't discuss with his child—"

"I'm almost fourteen!" Diggy interrupted. "I don't know anything about her, and she's my *mom*! I deserve to know everything you know."

"She was a good person, Diggy," Pop said. "But she was angry. Her parents have never tried to be in your life, so that tells you a little about what her life was like."

"Which makes it worse," Diggy argued. "She was pregnant and alone."

Pop paused long enough that Diggy thought he wouldn't say any more, but then he admitted, "She wasn't alone."

Diggy frowned, confused. "You—"

"Not me, Diggy."

It took a few seconds for the meaning to sink in, but then it was like a whirlpool drilling into his brain.

When she had broken up with Pop, she started dating someone else. She had been with someone else when she was pregnant with Diggy. Pop had left her alone, even after he heard she was pregnant, because she *let* him. She didn't think the baby was his.

Not until she saw Diggy's orange hair.

Diggy put his head between his knees.

"Your mom was a good person," Pop repeated. "She was young and angry and looking for . . ." He shook his head. "I was too young to understand what she was looking for or how to give it to her. But I wish I could have, Diggy," Pop said. "I really wish I could have."

Diggy hardly knew what to think, but Wayne's question floated up in his brain. "Did you look for her? After?"

Pop nodded.

"And?" Diggy asked.

"I found her." Pop sighed.

It felt like Diggy's head exploded. Pop had gone looking for Diggy's mom, and he had *found* her?

"She was angry. And I was too angry to see that the *reason* she was angry was because she was upset and scared. We were both just *so young,*" Pop said.

"Why were you angry?" Diggy whispered.

Pop gently squeezed the back of Diggy's neck. "Having you in my life changed mine for the better. But I was scared to death those first few months, and I hadn't had any warning."

Diggy could kind of understand that. And he had nearly fourteen years with Pop to know that Pop had gotten over it, whatever he had felt back then.

"What did she say?" Diggy asked. "How did she— What did she—" How did she explain that she could *leave him*, before she'd gotten to know him at all? How did she explain that she was leaving and wouldn't ever come back?

"At the time, I thought she said what she wanted to hear in order to make herself feel better, but looking back I get that she was right and she *knew* it. She knew you and I would make it." He smiled sadly. "I wish I had had her conviction, but I truly believe that she thought leaving you with me was the most loving thing she could do for you."

Diggy started crying then. Some reflex in his brain wanted to make him embarrassed about it, but he didn't care. His mom had left him on a *doorstep* and run away on a *tractor*, but maybe she had loved him a little bit, too.

After Pop left, Diggy went into Wayne's room and found the yearbooks. He looked at pictures of his mom and just felt so sorry for her. In the pictures, she looked like she had a future, a bright one. But something had fizzled.

When Wayne first moved in, Diggy remembered figuring out that Wayne was trying to save himself. Maybe Diggy's mom had been trying to save herself, too. A drowning person couldn't keep another person afloat.

He was looking at the yearbooks, hardly aware that he had

sat on Wayne's bed to do so, when Wayne came in and asked what Diggy was doing in his room, messing with his stuff. Diggy didn't have it in him to argue, and knew he didn't need the pictures anymore anyway.

After their talk, Diggy felt older, but he was still Pop's kid. It wasn't long before Pop got around to assigning them their punishment for the tractor incident.

Diggy and Wayne got stuck with finally painting the kitchen with gallons of light yellow paint. Diggy figured the work was supposed to make him and Wayne friendly again.

They managed to paint the entire room twice without ever saying one word to each other.

Diggy was too busy thinking about everything he had learned about his mom to care. He knew he kind of had to tuck it away for now—he needed to focus on the fair—but it wasn't easy.

He spent hours and hours with Joker, grooming him, practicing setups, grooming him some more. Even when Wayne came into the barn to work with Fang, Diggy didn't care. Being around Joker was the important thing. Being with Joker was always the best part of Diggy's day, making him feel like the person he wanted to be all the time.

Then a week before the county fair, July talked the local paper into a front-page story about the 4-H students competing for a trip to State. One of the horses and Diggy and Wayne's two steers were the biggest part of the story and got full-color photos. People wished him luck but said it like he didn't really need it. Since he'd been coached by a two-time winner, everyone expected him to make a good showing. Nobody really said so, and definitely not in front of Wayne, but Diggy knew the town expected another win, and they expected it from him.

The daze he'd been in since the tractor incident and his talk with Pop vanished.

Overnight, he became a full-fledged fidgeter.

Diggy told himself over and over it was ridiculous to get so worked up about a county fair. He would earn a trip to State— he always had before, and Joker was his best steer yet. Plus, his worry was starting to affect Joker.

Joker acted out, digging in his hooves, setting up at four corners when Diggy was going for staggered, trying to drop his head and sidling away every chance he got.

Bad. Made worse by Fang, who acted like the most perfect show steer ever. The hair had grown around the scar in the wrong direction, but the spray adhesive held it in place fine, and the calf did exactly what he was supposed to with Wayne hardly doing anything. An outsider looking in would think Wayne was the one with three shows under his belt and Diggy the beginner.

Bad, bad. Telling himself to get a grip only made it worse. He didn't sleep the night before the fair. It was hot, even at dawn, so Diggy went ahead and shampooed and blow-dried Joker one last time, even though it was pointless, since after the ride to the fairgrounds he'd have to do it all over again.

"I thought we weren't doing this until we got to the fair," Wayne said.

Diggy glared at him.

Wayne shrugged and took Fang through the usual routine, both seemingly unworried, until Lenz pulled in with the trailer. The screech of the ramp sliding out might as well have been an electric prod. Wayne jumped three feet, then froze. He stared and stared at the truck, glanced at Fang, stared more at the truck. If he blinked at all, Diggy never saw it.

As simply as that, Diggy's nerves fell away. He was the experienced one. He'd let the last couple of weeks make him wacko, but that had to be put behind him now. He had a job to do, for himself and for Joker.

First, he made lavish, heartfelt apologies to Joker, who took them in stride and soon became his usual, straight-man self. Then, even though he felt like it was almost the last thing he wanted to do, Diggy took a stab at calming down Wayne. Diggy was still mad at him and ... whatever else, and Wayne was still stupid, but Wayne had worked hard all year, and Fang was a good steer who deserved to be shown well.

Diggy's efforts had the opposite effect. By the time they pulled into the fairgrounds, Wayne was a fidgety mess, and Diggy wondered how Wayne and Pop had put up with *him* when *he* was the one acting loony. Fortunately, Fang took his cues from Joker rather than his handler.

Diggy liked the county fairs. It was important to take them seriously, but they were more informal than the State Fair, with more time to greet friends from all the other 4-H clubs throughout the county, catch up on the past year, and talk livestock with no one's eyes glazing over. His fair friendships were as real to him as his friendship with Crystal and Jason. Seeing one another only once a year didn't matter, because they all had the shared experiences of 4-H and the fun, work, and intense emotions of raising, competing, and selling animals they loved. It was always a little weird to see how much older everyone looked, especially the girls, but the strangeness lasted about five minutes, and then it was like no time had passed at all.

Crystal and Jason came by the stall to help set up all the gear Diggy had brought along, which was especially great, since Diggy got stuck introducing Wayne around. But if the guy remembered even one name, Diggy would have fallen over. No one minded, and everyone tried to help in different ways, some by leaving Wayne alone, others by passing on tips, and a few by talking about random stuff to distract him. July kept brushing his hair back from his forehead, then hugging him, then brushing his hair back again. Diggy thought she was making things worse, but it seemed to help Wayne after all. By weigh-in, he didn't look quite so shocked anymore.

Then Graf and pretty much every single Vogl in the county showed up.

Diggy should have figured they would come, but he was so caught up in his own worries, he hadn't really thought about it. Seeing Graf reminded Diggy of why Wayne had entered the Junior Market Steer competition in the first place. So he could leave town. Even though it was ridiculous for a fourteen-year-old kid to think he could win some money and take off—and it would never happen, because he would be tracked down faster than Ole Jib's wife could dig up gossip—the wanting to leave was what mattered.

Diggy watched Wayne with his dad, and it was almost like watching any kid with his dad. If Wayne still thought about why he'd entered the fair, he didn't show it.

The Vogls acted like every second was a photo op. They took pictures of Wayne and his dad, Wayne and his steer, Wayne shoveling poop—which made everyone laugh like crazy people. They even made Wayne and Diggy stand together forever while every female in the family took her own personal photo ten times over. Diggy had never had ghost spots as bad as he did after all those flashes went off in his face.

Pop stood around talking with everybody and answered questions about the fair—letting Graf explain some of the rules about showing steers—and generally trying to keep the mayhem down to a minimum.

Diggy barely trusted his flash-spotted eyes. It wasn't long ago that Mrs. Vogl had acted like both Pop and Wayne's dad were devils on earth and Diggy a madman. Wayne didn't seem as surprised by everyone's apparent friendliness. The fact that Harold Graf had somehow convinced Mrs. Vogl that Wayne should stay with Pop and Diggy was hard enough to believe, but to actually make her like them? Not only had Wayne *not* gone home with anybody who had wanted him to *for months*, but also they had all decided to be friends?

It had really, finally happened. Diggy had traveled to a parallel universe.

Then things got that little bit weirder.

Crystal announced that Jason had asked her out. And she'd said no.

Which apparently meant she had to drag Diggy into the girls' bathroom so she could cry on his shoulder. Not only did it totally spook him that Crystal was crying, but he had no idea why she thought *he* could help her, when there were a ton of other girls around. He didn't know what to do, actively wanted to get away, and could only think to pat her the way he would Joker.

She pulled away and grabbed a paper towel from the dispenser to wipe her eyes. "I'm not a steer, Diggy."

"I'm not a girl, Crystal," he said pointedly. "Why didn't you say yes anyway? You got what you wanted. That's supposed to be a good thing."

"He only asked because he found out I wanted him to."

"So?"

"We've talked about this before," Crystal grouched. "I

want him to want to ask me out because he wants to, not because I want him to."

He squinted at her. "You know you're crazy, right?"

"I am not!" she said, and started crying again.

Diggy patted her again. "This isn't hard. You like Jason. He likes you. You guys hang out together all the time with the sheep and stuff."

"But—"

"Nope," Diggy interrupted. "Jason might have gone out with Darla just to go along and see. But he *asked* you. He didn't have to, but he did. And now you get to be happy. The end."

Diggy would love to ask July out and have her say yes and be happy, the end, but that would never happen. Crystal was getting her chance and throwing it away. She had always seemed so normal, but sometime during the school year she had lost her mind.

She studied him in that way that creeped him out, like she was reading his thoughts, and he really didn't want her to see how he felt about July—*had* felt about her; he knew it was time to move on. But still. He walked to the door, but Crystal stopped him.

"Love isn't that simple, Diggy."

"Yes, it is."

Jason waited outside. Diggy said, "Your turn," and held the door for him. It was maybe the first time Diggy had seen Jason *not* mellow but more like a wide-eyed lamb at its first shearing.

Diggy gave his friend credit for going in even though he had no idea what he was about to face.

But the conversation bothered Diggy all the way back to Joker's stall. Was that what he really thought about love, that it was simple? Ever since Wayne had moved in, absolutely nothing had felt simple. But Diggy also knew deep down that he was right about Crystal and Jason. All she had to do was say yes.

Apparently she did, because they walked out of the bathroom holding hands. Diggy wanted to be glad, but something in his chest heaved. If they were a couple, where did that leave Diggy? All he could think was, *Out.*

They came over to talk to him, and it was almost like normal except that Crystal was *bubbly*, and the only time Diggy had ever seen Jason smile the way he did was at the State Fair when he won every single sheep shearing contest there was to win. They talked a little about 4-H stuff before the two of them left to tend their sheep, still holding hands. Diggy didn't want to be nervous about how their friendship would change, so he decided to just be grateful he wouldn't get dragged into the girls' bathroom anymore.

Besides, he had to get his head back in the barn and *focus*. Joker was counting on him.

Weigh-in got Diggy's hopes up. He had been only nine pounds off in judging Joker's weight, which meant that all of his feed mixes and calculations were right on target for where he wanted Joker by the time the State Fair came around. His bubble deflated a bit after he saw Fang's weigh-in numbers. Diggy couldn't help doing the math to figure out that, even though Fang was still a little underweight, he had the better rate of gain since his first official weigh-in in January.

With weigh-in out of the way, the boys didn't have anything they *had* to do until the next morning, when they'd prep for the afternoon show. Not that it mattered. July had plenty of stuff for them to do, recruiting them to help with some of the younger 4-H'ers and ordering them to support the kids whose shows were that afternoon, which they would have done anyway.

The arena wasn't big enough and there weren't enough competitors to truly hide from July, but soon everyone was trying to stay out of her way. Maybe it was because this was the first year she wasn't competing. Diggy had never seen her this nervous. Ever. Everyone breathed a sigh of relief when Mr. Johnston finally saw what was going on and pulled his daughter aside. Diggy watched them and for a second got scared— July looked like she might *cry*. But then she took a big, long breath and hugged her dad. He said something that made her laugh, and suddenly she was normal again. The mood in the arena shifted back to serious but fun, and kids started laughing about stuff that wasn't even that funny. Relief and nerves. Everyone felt it and pretended they didn't.

Diggy never did much of the fair stuff—no rides or games

or concerts—no one much did. All the kids hung out with one another in the 4-H building and the show arena. There were only five steers this time but a ton of sheep and swine entries. As long as they didn't totally crap out at showing, Diggy knew he and Wayne would make it to the State Fair. It was Jason, Crystal, and the others with sheep and swine that would have a tougher go, and he talked with all of them, feeling guilty that he not only didn't have much to worry about but also that he'd be able to get his show over pretty fast, while they had to wait until the day after.

The one fair thing Diggy always did was food—as much fair food as he could stand. Name any single thing, and someone had put it on a stick and fried it.

Mrs. Vogl tried to talk them into eating the packed lunch she'd brought, but Pop knew how Diggy felt about fair food. Graf grabbed Wayne, and they all were on the hunt. Diggy insisted they make a first pass to check out the offerings before deciding what to get. The giant turkey drumsticks were easy to ignore, since that's what he got for Thanksgiving.

Wayne made a face at the chicken-fried bacon. "That should have a warning sign."

"Huh. Didn't think a county fair would go all out like this," Graf said. "That bacon won Best Taste at the Texas State Fair."

Everyone stopped to look at him.

"I think that year the Most Creative was a fried banana

split," he added, turning redder the longer they stared at him. "What?"

"Why do you even know that?" Diggy burst out.

"I started looking up stuff when Wayne got his steer," Graf admitted.

He seemed embarrassed, but Pop clapped him on the shoulder. "Knowledge is a wonderful thing."

Graf rolled his eyes but hung around.

Diggy pointed at the fried spaghetti-and-meatball on a stick. "What about that one?"

"Homegrown," Graf announced. "Minnesota State Fair original."

They wandered around, with Graf piling on the tidbits of info about whatever new thing they found to eat—"How do you fry *Coke*?"—and the boys giving him crap about why he knew so much about stuff like that and Pop buying samples of every other thing, because how could they *not* try a Scotch egg? A hard-boiled egg, wrapped in seasoned sausage, rolled in bread crumbs, fried, and served with ranch dressing had to be heaven on a stick, and it was.

The endless noise and diesel fumes from the rides eventually drove everyone back to the barns, and they sat around awhile to visit and digest. It was that weird kind of normal again.

July came around and insisted on taking more pictures. Thinking of those photos in the camera, of the four of them together, made Diggy's stomach twist, but he told himself it was the fair food. He was only mildly nauseated by the time they headed home for the night. County fairs wouldn't let competitors stay with their animals all night like at State.

But everyone who had a show the next day was back at first light.

Wayne and Diggy lined up for the hoses and scrubbers and used the backs of their Scotch combs like squeegees to get excess water off before leading the calves to their stalls to blow-dry them. July coached Wayne on his clipping and blocking touch-ups, though he'd actually developed a pretty good eye for what looked best. Diggy ducked next to Joker's legs and dry-rubbed soap on the hair. Then he pulled up the hair with the Scotch comb, checked the results, rubbed on more soap, and combed again until it was right. He teased the tail and sprayed a cloud of lacquer onto it.

Graf got there and thumped Wayne's shoulder, saying how good Fang looked, and asked if he was nervous and didn't let him answer, telling Wayne about the first time he had raced barrels and how he'd puked. Wayne paled at the story, but Graf didn't seem to notice and kept talking until Diggy realized that *Graf* was nervous and every too-loud word he spoke ratcheted up Wayne's nerves until Fang decided to lie down, presumably to sleep.

Diggy saw it coming, but the shock and horror froze him. It was July, from all the way across the barn, who tried to stave off disaster and yelled, "Stop!"

Every single person in the place stopped. Except Fang. He went all the way down to his side.

July dashed around wheelbarrows, cow patties, 4-H'ers, and parents and grabbed Wayne's shoulders. "It's okay. We can fix it."

Her words released everyone to get back to whatever they were doing, though they did it while trying to watch the events at Wayne's stall. His bewilderment was clear, so Diggy quickly tied up Joker and rushed to get Fang back to his feet. When Pop came over, he grabbed some of Fang's grooming stuff.

"What?" Wayne and Graf asked at the same time.

July pointed. "Once they're groomed, you can't let them lie down."

The hair on the one side had pressed flat and stayed flat because of the lacquer, and wood chips clung to Fang's legs.

"Oh, no," Wayne groaned.

"It's okay," July said again. "We can fix it."

Fortunately, everyone prepped for the show early, because they couldn't handle the nerves of waiting and not doing anything. July thought for about two seconds and decided they had time to shampoo and blow-dry Fang's lower half again, being careful about not messing up the top half too much. The other three steer showers all pitched in, holding Fang steady and carefully scrubbing the water only where it was needed, lending blowers so that three were going at the same time. Fair rules meant only Wayne, Diggy, Pop, and Graf could do the actual grooming. Pop and Graf didn't quite know what needed doing, but every little bit helped. The urgency seemed to have calmed Wayne down. He was focused, and they got Fang ready to go with enough minutes to spare to fix themselves up again, too.

And for Wayne to puke.

Diggy didn't witness it. Wayne had walked away, but when he came back, he had that distinctive greenish face that everyone recognized.

"Did you puke?"

"I feel better."

He started to look better, too. He even smiled a little. No reason why, and it was kind of creepy-looking, but a smile was better than more puke, so Diggy was all for it. July started in with a few last-minute tips, then stopped herself midsentence. She gave them both big hugs and wished them luck, then made her way to the bleachers and the crowd of Vogls there to cheer on Wayne.

Diggy felt that kind of shaky calm he got every year. Inside, he was wobbly, but it was like it was someone else's insides. On the outside, he was calm and doing exactly what needed doing. That person wasn't him, either, just someone playing him, and that was fine.

The judge called them in, and the five of them lined up head to toe; walked a loop; stopped when asked to, automatically setting up staggered; walked some more; lined up side by side, four square setups this time. The judge patted the steers and asked lots of questions, having competitors turn their animals and watching how they set them up again.

Wayne was the only first-timer, and though he didn't remember to smile at the judge and turned Fang toward him rather than away, his setups were good, and he answered the questions like he knew what he was talking about. Plus, Fang looked perfect, especially considering that it was second-time-around perfect. He ended up winning the rate-of-gain ribbon. Both boys got blues, and Diggy got a showmanship. Then, as the judge lined them up, with Diggy at the head, he knew—he just knew! He got the purple ribbon. Joker was the county Grand Champion!

Everyone congratulated one another, relieved to have this part over, even if they were disappointed with their results. Of course, Diggy was thrilled with his. And Wayne was happy, too. Both of them had won their trips to State. July, Pop, Graf, and every Vogl on the planet surrounded them, hugging and thumping shoulders and taking enough photos to paper the entire fairgrounds.

Winning didn't mean there wasn't work to do, however. Besides the packing up and cleaning, there were the other shows to support, especially Crystal's and Jason's. The paperwork for accepting their trips to the State Fair. The ribbon auction that raised money for their 4-H clubs. Writing thank-you notes to the auction donors.

By the time they got home and back to some kind of routine, Diggy felt like he had been on another planet that was all steers and all fair all the time. It was a relief to turn on a sci-fi movie about people actually *on* another planet.

But Diggy's brain couldn't quit the county fair that easily. He kept thinking about the rule about grooming, how only the exhibitor or members of the immediate family could groom a show steer, and how that had included Wayne, Diggy, Pop, and Graf.

THE TRUCE UNOFFICIALLY CALLED
DURING THE COUNTY FAIR HELD WHEN THEY

got home. Though they weren't making a point of hanging out together, Wayne wasn't avoiding Diggy, either. But Diggy couldn't stop thinking about Pop and Graf and all the Vogls together like it was no big deal.

After a few days, he couldn't stand it anymore and cornered Wayne in the barn. "So what really happened that everyone's okay with you still being here?" It was about more than Wayne's not running from problems.

Wayne's expression reminded Diggy of the yeti from that movie, digging out hearts and tearing off legs. For fun.

"You know what I mean," Diggy huffed. "You were all packed to leave, remember?" He had no trouble recalling the pile of Wayne's stuff, ready to go.

"And you wished I had."

"Whatever, Wayne." Diggy was sorry he'd asked. He pulled over a blower to start Joker's grooming routine. The noise might not hide his burning cheeks, but at least it would cover up the loud silence.

"They acted like they were more worried about you,"

Wayne grumbled. "They said our 'relationship' was too important, and we needed time to work out our problems."

"I'm not the one with a problem," Diggy argued.

Wayne scowled. "And they said I need to follow through on my commitments."

"Duh. Fang deserves that."

Wayne's face got all hard. "I know what commitments I need to keep."

There wasn't anything to the sentence that was a threat, but it made Diggy nervous, nonetheless. He turned on the blower and told himself he had plenty to worry about without making up new stuff to add to the list.

On August 3 Diggy turned fourteen. Though it wouldn't last long, he was finally the same age as Wayne.

The morning arrived earlier than usual with a bullhorn Pop had borrowed off his cop friend Brandon, and Pop thinking it was funny as heck to wake up Diggy with a test of the emergency broadcast system. Breakfast included cake, as always, though this year it had a file baked into it—"for breaking out of jail"—and a T-shirt that read *Alcatraz Triathlon: Dig, Dash, and Dive.*

July, Crystal, Jason, their parents, and Graf came over. While Pop got the grill going, Diggy got out July's birthday rocket to much dismay. Pop played along, acting like he didn't want Diggy to launch the rocket but was too distracted by his job as grill master to stop him. Crystal and Jason caught on to the prank pretty quickly, but July and all the parents tried to talk Diggy out of the launch without actually disciplining him, since that was for Pop to do. Pop had already helped Diggy figure out that he'd used the wrong glue—the more powerful engines created much more drag, and so the glue had to be a lot stronger than the kind he usually used. Diggy had a blast drawing out the tension while the others worried, and the moment was capped off with a flawless launch.

Later, Diggy had finished brushing his teeth, ready for bed after a good long day, when Wayne gave him a card. The card was funny, but Wayne hadn't signed it or anything. The only words written in it were *The Flamingo*.

Diggy looked up.

"It's in Vegas," Wayne said.

Diggy's skin tingled. A noise made him look down and see that he had bent the card in his fist. "Why do I care what's in Vegas?"

Wayne gritted his teeth. "Your mom worked there. Maybe still does."

Diggy became hyperaware of being in his room, standing in the middle. The walls dusty blue. The navy quilt hanging off the end of the bed. Dresser drawers pushed in unevenly, one squeezing off the toe of a sock. A pile of somewhat-folded laundry on his chair. A rocket lying across the desk. The hall table shoved in a corner, overflowing with rocket supplies.

The supplies he had moved so Wayne could have the other bedroom.

"How do you know where she worked?"

"The yearbooks. I called a couple of people who looked like her friends, and one of them said the last time she'd heard from Sarah Douglas, she was in Las Vegas."

Diggy closed his eyes. He had to. The world was too big to look at now, and it was only his old room. Wayne had called all over town.

"You're crazy," Wayne fumed. "I barely had to do anything to find her, and you still want to wait?"

"I'm not waiting," Diggy retaliated. "I'm *not looking.*"

"Are you that much of a scaredy-cat?" Wayne sneered.

"Wayne," Diggy said, sighing. "My mom won't replace your mom."

Wayne went wide-eyed white, then slammed out of the room.

Diggy hated feeling so . . . so . . . angry, betrayed, scared. He couldn't even think what he was feeling. There was too much. How many times had he told Wayne to let it go?

What did it help Diggy to know his mom might be in Vegas? He couldn't go there. Didn't want to go. And Wayne had said she'd worked there, only *maybe* still did. If she wasn't at the hotel or club or whatever it was anymore, maybe she wasn't even in Las Vegas.

But what if she *was* at The Flamingo? What was he supposed to do with that information? Especially with the little more he knew about her now?

Diggy fell back onto the bed, wishing with all his fried-hot heart that it was January so he could throw himself into a bank of snow.

Pop walked through a field of flamingos grown tall in pink, cornlike rows. Every now and then he lifted a wing or pried open a beak to check for pests and ensure the birds were growing on schedule. The flamingos all had their eyes closed, but only until Pop passed. Then they opened an eye, followed his progress, let the other eye open, leaned toward his back. Leg stalks pulled out of the ground, and flamingos gathered in a swelling wave behind Pop, Pop never once looking back. From above, Diggy could see the mass begin to engulf Pop, who still methodically checked the crop, and Diggy shouted, but he was a cloud, and only faint hisses and air emerged.

Diggy woke up like that—mouth open in a soundless shout from the memory of his dream.

He pulled on shorts and climbed out the window.

Easily making the short leap to the tree, Diggy climbed up and up until he could see over the house.

A ton of birds congregated in one of the bigger trees on the far side of the field. They were black dots in the dawn-green shadows. Diggy never would have seen them except that none of them could stay still. They landed on a branch, considered the location for a few seconds, then flew maybe a foot away to another branch and tried that spot out. Over and over and over. All of them did it, like it was a dance and if someone missed a step, there would be trouble.

Diggy breathed deeply, feeling the bark press into his bare back and the soles of his feet. He imagined the oxygen the tree breathed out, feeling it in his lungs before he blew it out again, transformed into the carbon dioxide the tree needed to live. The breath circled through him like the branches circled around him.

He wouldn't let Wayne do it anymore. He wouldn't let Wayne get into his head.

Pop called out Diggy's name from the back door. Joker echoed with a moo.

Diggy climbed back to his window.

He had nothing to say to Wayne while they ate breakfast or tended the steers. The kid acted like *he* was mad, when Diggy was the one with the right to it.

Diggy ended up not having anything much to say to Wayne for weeks.

He focused all his attention on Joker and getting ready for the State Fair.

THE MINNESOTA STATE FAIR

IT WAS A RELIEF TO BE AROUND

PEOPLE HE COULD BE HIMSELF WITH, AFTER SO

many weeks of weirdness with Wayne. Diggy dumped his stuff in the fairgrounds dorm, generally known as the 4-H Hilton, and took forever getting down to the cattle barn, because every other person he saw coming and going was someone he knew and had to catch up with. He was such a smiling loon, his cheeks got sore.

His happy buzz dimmed when he neared the barn and saw Wayne at the washing area of the cattle annex, using all his weight trying to check Fang's forward momentum.

Apparently the steer had faked his placidity since the dog attack. He did not like the people, the noise, or the other steers. Wayne finally got him stopped and used his show stick to scratch Fang's belly. The steer shuddered, but he stood still.

Normally, the other kids would have helped to calm the calf or talk with Wayne, but Wayne had a look—all closed up and a little mean. Diggy wondered if smacking him upside the head would help. The fair was hard even with everyone's support—the tension, all the things to remember, the various deadlines, and ultimately selling the steer. Wayne was making it a hundred times worse by isolating himself from the other competitors. Sure, they were competition, but they were friends, too.

Diggy reminded himself that he didn't care about Wayne's problems. That Wayne didn't care about Diggy's feelings when it came to his mom. But that reminded Diggy that Wayne's mom had died this time last year. And that the guy had no idea what it would be like when it came time to give up Fang. Diggy wanted to be angry—he *was* angry—but he couldn't help being sad, too.

Diggy went into the barn and headed for the Dodge County stalls.

He gave Joker's rump a good scratch, pleased to see the steer excited but well behaved. Several kids stopped by to say how good the steer looked, a couple with that twinge of disappointment for their own prospects. Last year, Diggy would have been beside himself about the praise, but this year was too tangled up with Wayne.

He busied himself with tidying up their county's section. The stalls weren't actually boarded out. They were basically sections of tall wooden fences marked off into rows labeled with letters such as *Q/R* or *S/T*, then further delineated by county—Carlton, Kanabec, Goodhue—so that competitors could find their assigned spots. On either side of the fence, hay was stacked in flat, deep rows, building a floor for the animals on top of the concrete. Except at the far ends of the rows, there wasn't anything to keep the hay in place. Using a flat board mounted on a push-broom stick, Diggy pressed animal-loosened hay back into squared-off edges to keep the stalls neat and the aisles clear.

There were dozens of aisles and a couple hundred heifers, steers, dairy cattle, and calves—and the barn wasn't even large enough. The fairgrounds had an annex next door with four more long rows filled with cattle.

Having so many people and animals crowded inside was noisy, but it wasn't smelly like the swine barn. Sure, there was poop and pee, but mostly the barn smelled like sawdust, straw, and only slightly of animal. The 4-H'ers were strict about scooping up cow patties and depositing them in the wheelbarrows at the end of every other aisle. And every animal itself was scrupulously clean.

The noise was soothing. Fans topped stalls at even intervals for air circulation. Blowers were in constant use. Clippers buzzed. Cattle grunted and mooed. Exhibitors discussed checklists and tips. The public shuffled through, mostly too shy to ask questions, only pointing at the animals or smiling at the exhibitors. Little kids made up for their grownups by asking anybody everything. Periodically the overhead speakers squawked a jumble of electronic syllables.

"Are we supposed to understand that?" Wayne asked, clutching Fang's halter.

Diggy hadn't noticed him coming back but easily could

have picked him out of a crowd if he'd tried—the kid was green, and his eyes were huge.

"You get an ear for it," Diggy said.

"You understood that?" Wayne squeaked.

Diggy shrugged.

"I'll miss it! I won't hear my name called. They're crazy if they think we can hear that. That's the worst speaker system I've ever heard!"

Diggy gaped. The kid was losing it. "Wayne, you've got to breathe."

"Breathe?" Wayne said it without using any air, like breathing was a forgotten function.

"We don't show until tomorrow," Diggy pointed out.

"Moo!"

Wayne jumped a foot. Diggy was startled, too.

They turned to see a toddler standing at their stall, staring at Joker and mooing his guts out. He mooed with such force, his entire body tensed up, and he almost tipped himself over.

"What's he doing?" Wayne wailed.

"I think he's trying to get Joker to moo at him," Diggy said, confused. Like everyone else's cows, Joker's head was tied at the fence. The kid mooed at Joker's butt, even though Fang was only a few feet away in the aisle, face front. But the kid looked so excited and happy, like he was proud as heck he knew the sound a cow made.

A flash went off, and Diggy saw the mom taking pictures before hugging the little boy and leading him away. The public was crazy. Taking pictures of kids mooing at cows' butts. Joker should have dropped a load. That would have been a picture worth taking.

He turned to tell Wayne the joke but stopped himself.

Wayne stared into the faces of the passing crowd as if they held the meaning of life and he wasn't sure he wanted the answer. He glanced back at the signs with his and Diggy's names, then returned his attention to the people in the aisles.

Diggy frowned. "You won't miss Pop or your dad. They're too tall." The Vogls would come tomorrow for the competition.

Wayne blinked at him. Once. Twice. Then his face got all red and hard again. He tied Fang to his spot, then walked away.

Diggy threw up his hands. The guy was crazy.

July rounded up their 4-H chapter for dinner, checking that all of them had their meal vouchers. As much as Diggy loved fair food, he and the others didn't have time to dawdle about the fairgrounds taking in the sights. No one particularly wanted to, either. Everyone spent every possible second with their steers, which meant that he didn't recognize half the people he saw in line for food. Those were the swine, sheep, poultry, and horse kids, not to mention the ones who were there for the non-livestock stuff like gardening and baking and all the other thousand things 4-H'ers did.

Naturally, with so many, many opportunities to not sit alone, Wayne found a spot off by himself.

Diggy refused to think about him and sat with some kids from Goodhue County. They usually had the largest group at State. Several of them were from family farms dating back to the 1800s, and some of those with show steers had invested in cool rooms, the air-conditioned stalls designed to help steers grow great hair. In previous years, Diggy couldn't help being a little jealous, but this year it reassured him to hear talk about Peace Pellets and Roto Fluffer brushes and the national shows the kids had already attended. These kids knew steers like he knew steers. And they loved their animals just as much.

He was finally beginning to relax when he saw Crystal and Jason walk over to Wayne. They sat with him awhile, and *Jason* did most of the talking, which never happened. Diggy lost track of the conversation at his own table. When Wayne dumped his tray and headed back to the cattle barn, Diggy headed over to where Crystal and Jason still sat.

"What was that about?" he asked.

"Hello, Diggy," Crystal said, like she was correcting his rudeness.

"You're *my* friends," Diggy reminded them. He had worried when they started dating that things might change, but he hadn't expected them to go to the other side.

"We know that," Crystal said. "We wanted to—"

"This 'we' business isn't helping," Diggy snapped.

"I told him about the time when Grandpa was really sick," Jason said. "It was when I was in Mrs. Graf's class."

Third grade was before the three of them became friends. Jason's grandpa was in pretty good shape for an old guy; Diggy didn't know he'd been sick.

"I think everyone was scared he was going to die, but I didn't understand all that. I was mad that Mom was gone all the time."

The idea of Jason mad was hard to imagine. Sheep fell asleep in the guy's arms, at the *fair*.

"Mrs. Graf talked to me some, but mostly what I remember is how she explained that Grandpa is Mom's dad."

Diggy blinked. He knew what it was like when the seemingly obvious suddenly hit you—like when he had realized it wasn't only Wayne's mom who had died but Mrs. Osborn's *sister*, as well—the same person, but different.

"Mrs. Graf helped me see that I wasn't mad at my mom," Jason said, "but scared she was going away. And that that was what my mom was scared about, for her dad." Crystal put her arm around Jason's shoulders. "Mrs. Graf was a really good teacher," Jason finished.

She was. "But why tell him that now?" Diggy asked. It seemed like reminding Wayne about how great his mom had been would only make things worse for the guy.

"Because I don't think Wayne is actually mad at anyone," Jason explained. "Especially you."

Diggy looked across the table at Crystal and Jason, looking back at him with the true friendship of people who cared enough to worry about him, and think about his problems, and find real ways to help.

He cleared his throat. "You two teamed up are like the Wonder Twins."

"The girl was the one who could take the form of an animal, right?" Crystal asked. "I'm cool with that."

Jason just shook his head, while Diggy and Crystal laughed.

Diggy joined up with a couple of other kids and ducked back into the dorms to get some things before heading back to their steers for the night. Not everyone slept in the barn overnight, but those with the best steers always did, and some of the others did because it was fun to hang out.

It wasn't party time. A few grouped in twos or threes to talk quietly before trying for impossible sleep while stretched awkwardly in portable chairs. Others slept propped in the hay, leaning against their cows.

Wayne messed with the hair at Fang's scar, making Fang more anxious than restful. The steer frequently looked over at Joker and mooed, as if to say, "He's making me crazy." Joker looked back, crunching feed, as if replying, "They're humans. Who knows what they're thinking?" Diggy chuckled at the dialogue he made up.

"What's so funny?" Wayne said, jaw squared tightly.

Diggy sighed. "Nothing, Wayne."

Wayne snorted. "I should have known you'd blow it in the end. You've spent more time socializing than working."

"You can't pre-poop the cow," Diggy said.

While Wayne blinked at him, Diggy set up his canvas chair, pulled his baseball cap over his eyes, and pretended he might sleep.

AT DAWN, JULY WOKE HIM WITH A

BOOT TO THE BUTT. SHE LISTED THE THOUSAND

things he already knew he had to do, then repeated the same list to Wayne, who had heard it the first time but paid wide-eyed attention, seemingly afraid to forget anything. Diggy stretched and took a couple of minutes to wake up. He loved the barn first thing on show day.

There were a lot of cows, but there were even more 4-H'ers. They ranged in ages from eight to nineteen, almost as many girls as boys, and all of them were very busy already at dawn. Two cows were in the tiled shower at the far corner of the barn. It looked like a drive-in car wash, with the wand hoses hanging from the ceiling. It was too small, though, for the volume required this morning. Outside, one entire side of the cattle annex was outfitted with plumbing and hoses. Cows were shampooed and rinsed by kids dressed in rain gear, while more competitors and their cows hung around out of water-spray range waiting their turn. A few feet beyond the indoor shower, a girl held a steer near a floor drain while another girl squeegeed excess water off the freshly washed animal. Two older boys walked by wheeling barrels full of manure to deposit in the manure pit out by the loading dock.

More cows were already in the aluminum grooming chutes. A boy stood on a stool next to his steer and rubbed gloss into its hair. A few chutes over, three boys worked a cow with electronic clippers, going over and over and over the same spot, like they cut only one hair at a time. Across the aisle, a girl wiped fresh paper towels over her steer's hair, checked them, then did it again in a new spot.

Many of the cows were black crossbreds, with deep-lagoon eyes that made Diggy feel very young and small when he looked back too long. Some cows were red like autumn leaves, others white like vanilla ice cream. All of them were beautiful.

Diggy spotted a kid sprawled half off a lawn chair, sleeping with his head twisted back under a baseball cap. The kid was too little to show so probably had been up half the night in order to get there early enough to help his brother or sister get the steer ready. Diggy grinned. The kid was so young, it probably helped his family most that he was asleep.

Pop, Graf, and Mr. Johnston passed the kid, nodding hellos to the equally drowsy parents.

"You two managing?" Pop asked, but he was looking at Wayne.

Diggy glanced over and saw that Fang was not cooperating with Wayne's attempts to halter him. Plus, except for the black hollows of his sleep-deprived eyes, Wayne was as white as Fang was black. The kid was not holding up well.

July shouted, "Diggy Lawson!"

She was at the other end of the barn; he shouldn't have been able to hear her from that far away. But he and everyone else turned and watched her gesture sharply toward the showers.

"She's got some lungs on her," Mr. Johnston muttered.

"Guess you're not moving fast enough," Graf snickered.

"Takes after her mother. Troops got to fall into line," Mr. Johnston added.

Pop patted Diggy's shoulder, wishing him a quiet good luck, then went to soothe Fang and talk to Wayne.

Diggy watched Pop hold Wayne's shoulder, talking to him quietly and seriously, and knew that a few months ago, the picture they made would have ticked him off. Those feelings weren't there anymore. Mostly, Diggy was grateful there was someone who knew how to calm Wayne down.

Diggy led Joker to the wash rack, getting in and out fairly quickly. After the blow-dry, he worked adhesive onto the head, tail, and legs, making the tailhead look square and deep and the head have a nice point. He worked mousse into the hair to make it pop and combed the leg hair to stand up so the legs looked nice and sturdy.

He kept thinking about his dream a while ago, when Pop was out checking the flamingo crop that swarmed behind him after he passed, close to overwhelming him. It didn't make any sense that Diggy should remember it so vividly when he needed to focus on Joker, but he hardly had any room left in his brain to think about *why* he was thinking about it, because all he could think about were those pink birds with their black-tipped, hooked beaks.

It was a relief when staff started calling groups of competitors out to the staging area.

The steers were first judged by breed. The purebreds—Black Angus, Hereford, Shorthorn and Shorthorn Plus, Charolais, Limousin, Maine-Anjou, Simmental—were divided only by breed, not by weight, and went first. Then finally the crossbred divisions were called.

The excitement was for the crossbreds, because that's where the Grand Champion of all Junior Market Steer usually came from. This year a total of about seventy crossbreds were entered in the three categories of lightweight, middleweight, and heavyweight.

There was only ever one judge for all the steers, so he moved and spoke quickly. Once he got to the crossbreds, he couldn't see all the steers of any weight category all at once—there were just too many. Instead, the steers were brought out eight at a time. The judge made the exhibitors line them up side by side so he could examine their shape for a straight back and well-structured legs. He'd sometimes run his hands across the back, over the ribs and the haunch, but not for every cow, dashing the hopes of that competitor in an instant. Then he'd instruct the kids to lead their steers in a large circle around the pen and studied how the steers moved, looking for agility. They stopped, lined up head to tail, and the judge pointed, organizing the steers from least to best.

Those pointed at first led their steers back to the curtained rail blank-faced, automatically positioning hooves at four square for their final side-by-side lineup. Their months-long efforts ended there. When they exited the ring, a "beef princess" met them, one of the girls each county selected based on her knowledge of the beef industry and involvement in the Cattlemen's Association. She did other stuff during the year—teaching kids about where food comes from and parades and things—but at the fair she handed out ribbons as competitors left the ring, first reds, then blues. The ribbons were quickly stuffed into pockets or handed off to nearby parents, while losing showers managed their steers and their disappointment.

The boys or girls in the top two spots waited to the side and put some effort into appearing calm, but their nervous energy showed itself in a sudden need to comb the steer's hair one last time or reposition the steer's legs into a more attractive stance. When the top two of each batch of the weight class were culled, the judge had those chosen few do it all over again, line up and parade in a circle.

All this happened in only one half of the coliseum. In the

other half, divided by a waist-high temporary barricade, the dairy-cattle exhibitors went through the same routine.

The process seemed to take an unbearably long time but in reality was performed at a surprisingly fast pace. The judge was careful and respectful of each of the exhibitors and his or her time invested, but he was also efficient. There were a lot of steers to judge and rank, and it had to be done in one long morning. The championship event happened the same day, late in the afternoon.

The exhibitors knew that their opportunity to catch the judge's eye was short. The girls often wore sparkles—belts, necklaces, barrettes. The boys stuck to neatness—shirts fitted and tucked. No one took their eyes off the judge, watching for any signal or word, ready to react instantly and hoping for the chance to.

As the judge ranked steers, he talked the crowd through what he liked and why he placed certain steers over others. The speaker system was better than inside the cattle barn, but the cavernous ceiling of the coliseum bounced his words back and forth so much, it required some concentration to understand what he said.

Diggy had Joker mostly ready to go hours before he needed to. To blow off some tension, he snuck away—from July, since no one else would have minded. The bleachers that circled the show ring were less than half-filled with spectators, though a bunch of Vogls had staked out prime territory front and center and had saved spots for . . . Diggy's grandparents!

Diggy threaded through the seats as fast as he could, throwing his arms around his grandma first. "What are you guys doing here?" he laughed.

Grandpa mussed Diggy's hair. "We missed you, kid. Mark said this was shaping up to be a big year for you. We wanted to be here."

It was always weird to hear someone call Pop "Mark," but Diggy couldn't keep himself from laughing again. He knew it was nervous energy, but he was just so glad to see them. He hugged his grandfather tightly. "Thanks."

When he stepped back, he looked at their audience. "And you guys know the Vogls?"

"Of course we do," his grandma said as she adjusted his shirt.

Mrs. Vogl took a turn and fixed his hair. "You are a good boy. A good friend to our Wayne."

Diggy was so shocked by that, he let them fuss over him without protest. Grandpa was the one who stopped them. "You've got work to do, Douglas. We'll see you after."

"I was going down to the ring," Diggy said.

"Go, go!" Grandma and Mrs. Vogl both said.

Diggy let himself be shooed away in a cloud of good-luck wishes from everyone there. It was strange walking down to join the crowd on the coliseum floor, mostly parents and other competitors, knowing so many people were watching him, but he figured it was better to get used to it now. Once he brought out Joker, he couldn't let his attention be divided.

He stood near the ropes that separated the competition and viewing areas, letting bits of conversation float around him. "I told him to smile. We're not here for a red." "I was shocked. Heifers got five reds." "Ooh, he's going to show well." "They're giving whites at State!" Diggy paid more attention to that one until he realized the kid had come from the swine barn. One woman was on the phone the entire time, keeping a list of the placements by class and relaying the info back to whomever she was talking to. Diggy figured she had a kid showing in the crossbreds.

It didn't take long for the familiar commotion to calm him.

He decided to head back, made a small wave to his grandparents and the Vogls, then spotted Wayne examining faces in the seats that ringed the coliseum, slowly turning in a circle. Diggy almost walked by him; he couldn't miss the large mass of his family, and chances were high the kid would shake the calm Diggy had found. But Wayne looked so . . . lost. Passing by him without saying anything seemed cruel.

"It's going to be all right," Diggy said.

Wayne didn't look at him. "When you left, I thought you'd seen her."

"Who?"

Wayne completed his circle, then pressed his palms to

his eye sockets. When he dropped his hands, he seemed like a blind person, eyes open but not seeing anything. "Maybe she's waiting, to see how we do. Maybe she doesn't want to distract us."

Diggy closed his eyes, wishing he had kept walking. He didn't want to, but he asked again, "Who?"

"I never got her. I had to leave messages. But I told her about the steers and the fair and that we'd look for her here."

Diggy couldn't ask again. He was too sure he knew the answer.

Wayne's eyes refocused, on Diggy. They looked bruised and hopeful and despairing and too bright. "She was still at The Flamingo."

Diggy punched Wayne in the face.

THE ARENA FLOOR WAS COVERED
WITH LOOSE DIRT. WAYNE FELL BACK FLAT IN

a poof of dark brown particles.

Diggy started walking away before anyone noticed. The hardest thing he ever did was not peer up at the stadium seats. He kept his eyes exactly straight ahead at the staging area he could see through the entrance.

Until someone caught his arm and twirled him around. His eyes streamed over the audience, too fast to see anything but a blur, but he closed them anyway. He would not look up there.

People said stuff—he didn't try to pay attention—and pulled him away.

Wayne was somewhere too close.

Diggy concentrated on keeping his eyes closed, even though that meant he was almost literally dragged out of the coliseum. Once he sensed the change in the air and knew he was out of there, he permitted himself to open his eyes to the barest slits. He watched his boots stumble over sawdust, dirt, concrete, more sawdust.

4-H administrators were there, saying things. Pop, Graf, and July were there, saying other things. German words popped in as Mrs. Vogl asked Diggy's grandparents what was going on. Diggy couldn't hear over the buzzing in his head.

Until Wayne spoke. Wayne, Diggy heard perfectly. "It was me. I did it."

"Punched yourself in the mouth?" a stranger in a green 4-H shirt said. "This is not the kind of behavior we permit among our exhibitors."

He said some more stuff, and both Pop and July argued. Diggy began to realize they were talking about whether or not to let him compete.

A year. A whole year! He glared at Wayne, but as quickly as the rage built, one good look at Wayne poked holes all through it.

"It was me," Wayne said again. "I did it." No one listened to him. He looked like a ghost. Maybe no one could hear him. "I'm sorry," he said. "I'm sorry."

Diggy felt like a flock of flamingos was pecking him all over with their black-tipped beaks.

The 4-H administrator suggested that Diggy could compete but not be eligible for a ribbon.

Wayne made a sound like a groan and a yell combined, like he was physically in pain. Everybody quieted, then Wayne shouted, "We're brothers! Brothers fight. I did something really, really . . ." He choked, then shouted again. "If you don't let him compete, it'll be like I cheated. It will be a cheat! He only hit me because I . . ." He swallowed. "It wouldn't be fair.

You'll have let me steal the show from him. I should be the one who can't compete. That's the only thing that would be fair."

The 4-H administrator frowned at Diggy. "Is that true? Did he intentionally provoke you?"

Diggy opened his mouth, but he couldn't say that. He had hit Wayne. He could have not.

"He won't say so," Wayne said. "We're brothers, remember? But it's still true."

The administrator, Pop, and July talked together while Graf led Wayne aside. Someone had popped one of those ice packs from a first-aid kit. Wayne dabbed it at his mouth but not with any real attention.

Graf held Wayne's shoulders and asked him something. Wayne ducked his head and looked sideways at Diggy. He answered. Graf took a turn at being a ghost; then he jerked Wayne to him in a too-tight hug. Graf's shoulders shook for a few seconds. Wayne hugged him back, then they pulled apart, turning their backs away from everyone while they scrubbed their arms over their faces.

Graf turned back first and spoke too loudly. "You've got to let Diggy show."

Wayne came up to Diggy. "I'm sorry. I'm really, really sorry."

Diggy didn't have room to hear him. All he could think about was that his mom wasn't there. She couldn't be. If she were, she would have seen what had happened and come to check on him. Wouldn't she? Isn't that what moms did? So she wasn't there. Wayne had called her, and she hadn't come.

It didn't matter that Diggy hadn't asked her to come, hadn't wanted her to come, hadn't even considered that a possibility. She hadn't come.

If all the show steers walked over him on their way into the ring, he might feel better than he did right now.

The 4-H administrator conceded that there may have been extenuating circumstances but noted that solutions required thought, not physical violence. 4-H required more from its youth and would seem to condone Diggy's behavior if they didn't penalize him. Actions had consequences. Diggy and Wayne would be permitted to show, but they would not be eligible for a purple or even a blue ribbon.

July started crying.

Pop shook the administrator's hand, thanked him, then grabbed both boys and dragged them toward the barn. "They're starting to call the lightweights."

"What's the point?" Wayne moaned. "I've ruined it. I've ruined it for everyone."

Pop stopped them, his face fierce. "You will compete. You will compete to win, even if you can't. Your steers deserve it. That's what commitment is. Following through no matter what."

"You don't know what I did," Wayne mumbled.

"I don't care what you did," Pop said. "What matters is what you do now." He took Diggy's shoulders. "You've never been one to hold a grudge. Now's not the time to start. It'll wear at you all year if you don't do what you need to. You can hash out everything else later. For Joker's sake, focus on what you came here to do."

Diggy knew Pop was trying to tell him something important. He even tried to listen.

July came up to them with a fake but determined smile on her face. "We've got to get moving. They'll be looking for you in the staging area soon. If you're not lined up, you're out."

"What do you want to do, Diggy?" Wayne asked. "Whatever you want to do, that's what I'll do."

Wayne's mom used to say that people fight instead of think. Wayne had told him that, too, and Diggy had asked what was so great about thinking. That seemed truer than ever.

When Pop nudged them, Diggy moved on.

Diggy was called with the first set of middleweights. He led Joker out to the staging area while July used the blower on Wayne, getting the dirt off his back and jeans from his fall.

The staging area was a strange mix of loud and quiet. As in the show ring, one side of the staging area was for steers, the other for dairy. A herd of people walked through in steady numbers, many of them general public talking to be heard over the rumble of crowd, animals, and fair business as they made their way to the exhibits in the cattle barn. The kids waiting to enter the coliseum, however, were quiet.

In front of the entrance, a family of five worked up a steer one last time. While the exhibitor held his steer's head, the dad sprayed it, using one of the various styling products stuffed in his pockets. A sister made repeated paper-towel swipes. A brother had his Scotch comb out at all times. The mom held the steer's tail away from its rump, protecting the perfectly teased end from bodily functions.

Other kids stood quietly, waiting. Maybe a few whispered to their steers. Every once in a while, they would brush or spray something. Diggy watched a boy spray shine at a steer, only to have the wind catch it and cover the girl showing the steer instead. She gave him such a dirty look, the boy intentionally squirted her again.

Diggy leaned against the temporary steel barricade. The swirlies in his stomach confused him. He didn't have any reason to fuss or worry.

His group was called into the coliseum, but getting inside only meant more waiting, this time in a line roped off next to the wall beneath the seats.

The seats were still only half-filled with people, but those people made plenty of noise, calling out greetings and good lucks to kids they recognized. Joker stepped sideways a few steps at the first onslaught, and Diggy gave him a good belly scratch with the show stick.

Then Diggy looked up into the stands.

He was so close, he made accidental eye contact with people who automatically smiled at him and wished him luck. A part of his brain tried to order his eyes to Joker, the show ring, the dirt—anything else. Instead, Diggy scanned the crowd, face by face. With each new face that wasn't hers, his heart flipped a little harder.

He hardly noticed when his group was called again, this time for the real thing. Joker followed the line into the show ring, seeming to lead Diggy, but when the steer saw open space, he broke from the line and rodeoed.

How many times had Diggy reminded Wayne to keep calm, that Fang only acted out because Wayne's nerves drove him to it? Joker was such a mellow steer. This display was all Diggy.

The other exhibitors kept their cool and their steers' leads tightly gripped. The danger of one steer rodeoing was that others might be spooked and do the same.

Diggy knew he should get out there and get a grip on Joker, but he couldn't stop scanning the crowd. He probably looked the way Wayne had earlier, turning in a slow circle, searching and hoping, though he wouldn't name what he hoped for.

He saw his grandparents. The throng of Vogls.

Turning more, he saw Crystal and Jason.

Then, at the entrance to the arena, Diggy's gaze landed on Pop.

Pop held himself like something in his chest ached, and Diggy knew it was for his sake. Pop loved him and wanted to make everything okay but couldn't. Diggy was beginning to appreciate how hard it was to live with that.

But then Pop quirked his eyebrows and nodded toward Joker, clearly saying, "Focus, kid."

Behind him, Diggy saw July and Graf leading Fang in from the staging area.

He turned and saw Wayne heading in to make a grab at Joker.

Diggy let go of all the other faces around him. He had found the ones that mattered.

He rushed into the ring, then couldn't keep himself from stopping again. Joker rodeoed his heart out and had a blast doing it. He looked like a fresh calf only just weaned from his mama, bouncing around like he had springs for hooves.

Diggy burst out laughing.

Wayne must have heard him. He stopped trying to flag Joker down.

Joker, for his part, was courteous about his display. He kept to the open ground, away from where the other steers lined up at the curtained rail.

Wayne walked over, chewing his cheek. "You know, he's just doing what you're feeling."

Diggy peered at him. "I'm mad at you."

Wayne nodded.

Diggy shouted, "Joker!"

The steer trotted over to him, set up in a perfect staggered position, and raised its head to show height. The purple-ribbon steer wouldn't look half so good in its prize photo.

DIGGY AND WAYNE TOOK THEIR
RIBBONS IN STRIDE, EVEN DISPLAYED THEM

prominently back at Joker and Fang's stalls.

The boys combed, scratched, and otherwise lavished attention on the steers, both of whom stood with the air of expecting no less.

Wayne cleared his throat. "I'm not sure it was her number," he said softly. "The message was one of those computerized voices that just says the phone number you've reached."

Diggy's body tingled. He waited until the sparks had passed through his fingers. "Once I find her, she can't ever come back."

Wayne frowned. "She can move back anytime."

"No. I mean, if I find her first, she can't ever decide on her own that she wants to come back for me. I'll have made her come back, by finding her."

Wayne paused long enough that Fang mooed at him. Finally, he said, "You're fourteen."

Diggy flinched. That was the sticking point. Fourteen years meant she likely wasn't ever coming back. But that wasn't the point. After his talk with Pop, Diggy had decided he was okay with the decision his mom had made for him. He was happy with Pop and hoped his mom was happy somewhere, too. He said as carefully as he could, "Finding my mom won't bring your mom back."

Wayne breathed deeply. When he looked at Diggy, he had tears on his cheeks. "I wish it could."

Diggy sighed. "I know."

They scratched the steers' rumps a good, long time. Wayne looked up at their red ribbons tucked into the signs with their names on them. "Purple's a girly color anyway."

Diggy laughed. Right up until one of the fair people found him to confirm details about the next day's auction.

———

The packer's truck was parked at the cattle barn, ramp in place and several steers already loaded.

Diggy and Wayne had made a spot for themselves off to the side so Joker and Fang could stand right next to each other.

Diggy whispered to Joker all the thanks and praise he could think of for being such a fine, good-natured steer and for having worked so hard and done such a good job. He tried not to cry in front of the steer, but the more he worked at not showing how sad he was, the calmer Joker got, as if he knew Diggy needed soothing. By the time Diggy pulled off Joker's halter, he couldn't help the tears.

To Joker, the halter coming off meant time to go home.

He easily walked the ramp into the truck, Fang right behind, neither of them with the least hint of anxiety.

Diggy went ahead and found a corner of the barn to bawl in.

After a while, he wiped his face with his sleeve. His breathing was still choppy, and if he let himself think of Joker too much, the tears welled again, but he wiped his face and told himself the worst was past.

Wayne sat next to him. He didn't look any better than Diggy.

"This is bad," Wayne said.

Diggy squinted at him. "Hard. Not bad." He hesitated, then added quietly, "Everything dies."

"You think I don't know that?" Wayne burst out. "I know that!" he sobbed.

Diggy wasn't sure what to do, but after a while he couldn't stand how alone and lonely Wayne looked, sitting hunched up right beside him, shoulders shaking. Diggy rested an arm across his back.

Wayne calmed some and wiped his face on his knees. "Just because everything dies doesn't mean it's right or good."

Diggy squeezed his shoulder. "It doesn't mean it's wrong or bad, either."

He felt like they were talking about more than the steers, probably because they *were* talking about more than the steers. But he didn't know what else to say.

Wayne stared over at the packer's truck, where other kids

hugged their steers, crying but letting them go. No steer balked at crossing the ramp into the trailer.

"Is there a difference?" Wayne choked up again. "Fang and Joker think they're going home, don't they?"

Diggy hated that part, too, the feeling that he had tricked his best friend. "You remember that science report you did on the feed lots?"

Wayne glanced at him but otherwise didn't respond.

Of course Wayne remembered the feed lots. The crowded, filthy, manure-laden pens were the kind of thing a person couldn't forget once he had any kind of experience with them.

"I think about Joker in a place like that." Diggy had to pause to swallow. He could hardly bear to think of it. Joker, the perfect straight man, part of that soulless mass of meat on the hoof? "We gave them a better life."

"For what?" Wayne didn't bother to brush at the tears. "They'll still be steak."

"But we had a year to love them. And they had a year of being loved."

Wayne put his head on his knees, not caring about the noises he made. Diggy found he had more tears in him, too. He leaned back and let them roll down his face.

At these moments, at the end, a year never felt long enough. For Wayne, a hundred years with his mom wouldn't have been enough. Only fourteen was just unfair. But that didn't change anything. Mrs. Graf was gone. And it was time for the steers to go, too.

After a while, Diggy noticed the sounds of the barn again. The periodic but steady drum of hooves on the aluminum ramp. The unsteady shuffle of boots passing by, always accompanied by sniffles and suppressed sobs. An older boy he knew held his sister's hand. She was too young to have competed herself, but she cried like the steer was her own. Loading day was a low day for everyone involved.

Wayne wiped his face again and pulled in deep breaths. He watched the muted activity for a while. "You're going to do it again."

Diggy nodded. "They're steers. It's part of the cycle."

"I don't know if I can," Wayne admitted.

Diggy thought for a bit. "Some kids buy their next calves here."

"You don't."

Diggy shook his head. "But it's usually only a couple of weeks before it feels too weird not having to wake up early and do the morning routine."

"I used to think it was weird that you liked the work."

"I want to feel like I've put something good out there." Two girls from Goodhue County walked by, holding on to each other. They tried to smile at him, and he nodded back. "And I like to come here."

Diggy and Wayne sat quietly for a few minutes; then Diggy gave his face a good, final wipe with his shirtsleeve. He sniffed deeply to clear his nose and figured he looked almost normal again, even if he wouldn't feel it for a long while yet. He opened his mouth to suggest they go find everyone, when Wayne murmured, "Dad wants me to move back in with him."

Diggy felt like his heart stopped. He cleared his throat. Had to do it a second time. "Are you going to?"

Wayne shrugged. He dribbled wood chips between his fingers, then sighed. "I think so. With school starting again, it's like . . ." He trailed off.

"Yeah. That makes sense," Diggy agreed, though he wasn't sure he really did.

Wayne looked at him. "But Pop said I could keep my next calf with you guys. If I get one."

Diggy's heart restarted. He grinned, pushed himself to his feet, and reached down to help Wayne up. Diggy chuckled and shook his head.

"What?" Wayne frowned at him.

"You'll be getting up even earlier than me," Diggy pointed out.

Wayne winced but didn't hold it long. He halfheartedly grinned, too.

They stood there, and though Diggy felt weird, he felt he had to do something. He would never have picked Wayne if given a choice, but the guy *was* his brother.

He hugged Wayne. A couple of quick pats on the back and it was over, both of them pushing away and examining the wood chips at their feet.

"So," Diggy said.

"Yeah," Wayne replied.

Diggy snorted and thumped Wayne on the shoulder. "Don't get all mushy."

"Me?" Wayne protested. "You're the one getting all huggy."

Diggy laughed. "You'll never prove it."

They headed back to the stalls, where everyone was cleaning and packing up. Diggy spotted July giving orders, Pop running his hand down his face, and Graf huffing as he did what July said. Diggy almost could have laughed, but the scene choked him up. Joker's stall was empty.

Wayne grabbed Diggy's arm. "I'm sorry about what I said. At the tractor."

Diggy blinked, then caught up to Wayne's thought process. "Me, too."

Wayne stared ahead at the group waiting for them. "My mom would have loved this." He wiped his eyes quickly. "She would have cried her eyes out, but she'd have loved it."

Diggy thought so, too.

"I *was* lucky to have my mom for as long as I did. To get to love her." Wayne swiped at his eyes again but gave a shaky smile. "But you're lucky, too."

Diggy looked over at him.

"You've had Pop all this time. You've still got Pop."

Diggy smiled at Wayne. "We both do."

Already at four hundred pounds, this Hereford calf is only six and a half months old and has not been weaned. But he'll be ready for the show ring in no time!

IN CASE YOU WERE WONDERING

4-H

Officially, 4-H was founded in 1902, though its roots stretch back to the late 1800s. Today, the organization has six and a half million members and more than *sixty million* alumni. In other words, there are a *lot* of 4-H'ers out there doing lots of interesting stuff. Among the categories are environmentalism, filmmaking, robotics, veterinary science, photography, sewing, video game design, theater, butterfly research, animal care ranging from dogs and bunnies to larger livestock and horses . . . and much more.

The four *h*s are Head, Heart, Hands, and Health, which is reflected in the four-leafed logo and the 4-H pledge:

> I PLEDGE MY HEAD TO CLEARER THINKING,
>
> MY HEART TO GREATER LOYALTY,
>
> MY HANDS TO LARGER SERVICE,
>
> AND MY HEALTH TO BETTER LIVING,
>
> FOR MY CLUB, MY COMMUNITY,
>
> MY COUNTRY, AND MY WORLD.

You can visit 4-h.org for tons of helpful information about 4-H and how to find (or form!) a chapter in your area.

RIBBONS

Ribbons are awarded by class, division, and show.

A class is simple categorization by breed—such as Maine-Anjou, Charolais, and Hereford.

A division is when a class is too big to be judged all at once and is subdivided by weight: lightweight, middleweight, and heavyweight. (Usually, this is needed only for the crossbred class.) In each class and division, a Champion and Reserve Champion are selected.

Show is awarded by competing all the class and division Champion and Reserve Champion winners together to choose a Grand Champion and Reserve Grand Champion. So, the Grand and Reserve Grand Champions will win two purple ribbons by the end of the fair—one for winning their class or division, and another bigger and flashier ribbon for winning the entire show.

Purple—Champion and Grand Champion

Light purple—Reserve and Reserve Grand Champion

Blue—"Meets most standards" of the category*

Red—"Meets some standards" of the category*

White—"Meets few standards and lacks the quality of other exhibits"*

(By the time competitors get to State, they have all earned at least a blue and usually a purple at a county fair, so you can see why receiving a white at State would be extremely disappointing!)

*Definition per the Minnesota State Fair's *4-H Rules & Premiums* book

LIVESTOCK TERMS AND TOOLS

There is so much to know about livestock and related items, I could write a dictionary! Instead, I've listed only some of the terms from *Steering Toward Normal*, those that are part of Diggy and Wayne's regular routines.

bedding: Straw, sawdust, or sand where a steer may lie down. Clean bedding keeps the temperature down (because urine and manure generate heat) and prevents stains on the hair coat. Good hair care is key to raising a competitive show steer!

bull: A male that may sire calves.

bunks: Feed boxes.

clipping and blocking: The trimming of a steer's hair to minimize flaws and enhance strong points.

cow: Mature female; has birthed at least one calf.

crossbred: An animal with parents of different breeds.

halter breaking: A lot like training a puppy how to behave when you take it on a walk. A student uses the halter to manage a steer's movements in the show ring, so it's important to break

A 4-H competitor with his steer at the Goodhue County Fair. He will use the show stick to pull forward the left front leg for a nicely staggered setup in this head-to-tail lineup.

an animal to halter quickly. Steers grow faster than you do, and are a lot heavier, so teaching a steer important signals like "stop" and "go" as soon as possible will make the steer much easier to manage.

heifer: Immature female; has yet to birth her first calf.

rate of gain: In competition, rate of gain is judged from an initial weigh-in to show day. But heaviest is not necessarily best! Good rate of gain demonstrates a well-managed steer and feed schedule likely to produce a high-quality meat with efficient use of feed.

rice root brush: One of the most important grooming tools for training the hair of a competitive steer. The densely packed bristles help to clear out dust and dead hair as well as train the hair to stand up straight.

roughages: Hays or grasses that round out a steer's rations and help keep the digestive tract healthy.

saddle soap: A glycerin soap used to make a steer's hair stand up when grooming to show.

Scotch comb: A long, narrow comb with sharp points used to groom a steer's hair.

setup: The proper positioning of a steer's feet.

show stick: A four-and-a-half-foot stick with a pointed hook on the end, sharp enough to get a response but not cut. Used to position a steer's feet for the show ring.

steer: Castrated male; not able to sire calves.

There are many great handbooks produced by university extension offices across America. Much more comprehensive material is available online via these schools, 4-H, or state fair websites.

A 4-H competitor walks his steer out of the show ring at the Goodhue County Fair, blue ribbon in hand!

PRANK-STEER GUIDE

Most of the pranks described in *Steering Toward Normal* have a long history of success.

Do not play these pranks on people you don't know well or who don't have a good sense of humor. Do not attempt a prank that will make a mess without an adult's permission. Prank at your own risk!

The Egg Carton Prank

This prank is easier to set up with a Styrofoam or recycled-paper egg carton. Open the carton and cut out a hole in the center, so you have a space in which to place the mousetrap.

Set the mousetrap, then wrap a rubber band around the platform and hammer so you can disengage the hold-down bar without springing the trap. Thread a length of fine string or fishing line through the catch, and secure the end with a knot. Replace the hold-down bar and remove the rubber band.

Carefully place the mousetrap in the egg carton, and thread the other end of the string through one of the holes in the carton's cover. Set your projectile on the trap—a bite of fruit, a bottle cap filled with flour, a miniature action figure. (You may need a *tiny* bit of adhesive to hold it in place.) Then close the cover more than halfway; pull the thread taut, being careful not to spring the trap; and tie off the end of the thread around the cover. When someone opens the egg carton, the trap will spring and launch your surprise!

The Orange Juice Water Bomb Prank

Using a large juice carton, the kind with a screw cap, cut a large hole in the bottom of the carton. Insert a balloon through the top hole of the carton and fill the balloon with water. Fold the end of the balloon over the side of the top hole and twist the cap back on. Use a utility knife to trim the exposed balloon end under the cap, so that it is not visible—the cap will hold the water balloon in place. When someone twists the cap off to take a drink, the water balloon will fall out!

Variation: Cut the hole in the carton as above, but this time stretch the empty balloon end around the top hole of the carton. Then, once the balloon is filled with water, twist it from underneath to prevent water from shooting out as you replace the cap. When the cap is secure, untwist the balloon. If the balloon end shows under the cap, trim. When someone opens the container of "juice," the water will shoot out of the spout!

The Leaky Bottle Prank

Select a full, plastic bottle of soda, juice, or water. Use a pushpin to make six or seven holes in a ring around the bottle an inch or two down from the top. It will squirt as you make the holes but won't leak when you pull the pin out. When someone tries to twist open the cap, liquid will squirt out of the holes!

Variation: Use a plastic ketchup bottle, or another plastic, squeezable condiment with a flip-top dispenser. Unscrew the cap and block the hole on the cap *from underneath* with something like hot glue. Use a lot of glue to make sure the hole is entirely blocked, but not so much that the glue squeezes through the opening or you can't screw the cap back on the bottle. Once the glue is firmly dried, put the cap back on the bottle. Use a utility knife to slice a short slit into the neck of the bottle about an inch from the top. When your friends try to squeeze ketchup on their fries, it won't come out! When they squeeze harder, it will ooze out of the hole you cut in the side!

ACKNOWLEDGMENTS

I HAVE BEEN CHARMED AND GREATLY INSPIRED BY THE MANY AMAZING student competitors and 4-H members I interviewed and trailed at shows over the years.

Ryan Claycomb was fourteen when we met, competing Blister at the Pennsylvania Farm Show with such calm authority and skill, he taught me something I hadn't understood about Diggy's character. To top off the experience, Ryan took Grand Champion! It's entirely possible I cheered louder than his family.

Drew and Mark Bray, Daniel Brown, Abi Earle, Casie and Mikaela Ingram, and Jeremy Wyche graciously let me poke around and ask questions at the North Carolina State Fair. Several were even brave enough to read early pages of the manuscript, and helped me take the story to the next level in honoring the full experience of what competitors do each year.

Trevor Holm and Kendrah and Maddie Schafer, competitors at the Minnesota State Fair, were brave and generous in answering personal questions about the emotional side of raising and selling steers. Maddie and Bryce Seljan were also very helpful in answering questions about their involvement with 4-H and their chapters.

Thank you all. Though I have left out many elements for the sake of fiction, this novel would not have been written without your help. You are all Grand Champions in my book!

4-H parents and fair staff are just as committed as the students. Thanks go to Bill Henning, Dorinda Bray, Carol Turner, Monica Schafer, and Kelly Wilkins for their help with introductions and answering questions, as well as all the family and staff who make these shows happen with such positive energy year after year. A particular thank-you must go to Steve Pooch, former deputy general manager of the Minnesota State Fair, who has been an invaluable resource since we first met in 2009. And Laura Seljan, who saved the day with her wonderful photographs.

Thank you to Shawn Fayle, who, among other things, introduced me to Jimmy Holliday. Jimmy showed me around his farm, introduced me to several weaning calves, and encouraged me to put my fingers in their mouths! He also gave me one of the book's pivotal scenes when he mentioned having to watch out for dog attacks.

Steering Toward Normal was supported by a travel and research grant from UNC Wilmington. Thank you also to SCBWI Carolinas for creating opportunities to meet so many wonderful people. And to the ladies at Alpha, who have supported me in more ways than they know.

I have been incredibly lucky in my friendships with other

writers, and thank everyone who has read pages, or listened to me ramble about steers, 4-H, revision, titles, and more revision. I would be nowhere without my reading buddies and critique partners.

Renée Dixon has been my longest friend and champion, and at just the right time reminded me that it was okay for Diggy to be mad at Pop. Maria Nolletti Ross read at least four drafts, and each time her sharp eyes spotted those inconsistencies and details that can make or break a story's realism and accuracy. Kathleen Fox and Debra Rook have added true middle school spirit and experience to these pages. And Sara Beitia and Carrie Harris came through with speedy and insightful reads as I was panicking over deadlines.

I was also fortunate to have middle school students Anna Sattler and Julia Ross read drafts, giving me both their time and insight. Thank you!

Special thanks to my agent, Kate Testerman, and editor, Howard Reeves, for believing in *Steering Toward Normal*, and to everyone at Amulet Books for their enthusiasm and talent.

And thank you to my family and friends, many of whom unknowingly lent their names to characters in the book. Thank you to my sister, Jesika, and my parents, Teri and Duane, who never faltered in their support as I pursued this writing thing.

ABOUT THE AUTHOR

REBECCA PETRUCK is a Minnesota girl, though she has also lived in Louisiana, Mississippi, New York, England, Connecticut, and, currently, North Carolina. A former member of 4-H, she was also a Girl Scout and a cheerleader, and competed in MATHCOUNTS. She reads *National Geographic* cover to cover. She *may* have pulled a few pranks in her life, though no one can *prove* she wrapped that entire car in cellophane. You may visit her online at rebeccapetruck.com.

ML   7-14